The Necklace

The Dusky Club June 1962

Linda S. Rice

ISBN: 1500671894
ISBN 13: 9781500671891

FOR Marsha Lynn Thompson-Nolan-Law, my best friend since childhood.

Acknowledgments

Many thanks to friends, acquaintances, co-workers and relatives who helped edit and critique this writing, and who encouraged me to move forward with publishing it. Special thanks to my sister-in-law, Nancy Flood, for her encouragement and the time she spent editing and re-editing, to Siobhan Deason, who gave me the push to publish and greatly assisted in the cover design, to my cover models, Viki Navardauskaite and Daniel Reyes, and to Shelley Bridgman-Baker, Mari Richards, Pam Brown, Annette Warren, Sheron Rice, Karen Lages, Colleen Buysse, John Hunter, and especially Marsha Lynn Thompson Nolan Law, all of whom provided suggestions and inspiration for the story. Lastly, I'd like to thank my husband, Michael, for his patience while I wrote, re-wrote, revised and edited over the many months it took me to complete this book and the sequel, *"The Necklace II."*

To contact the author, e-mail Linda at: LindainMtLaguna@aol.com.

Yeah, she was only seventeen; you can guess what that means...

Prologue

The Sleeping Beauty Castle

The year was 1968 and Susan was sixteen years old. She'd come to Disneyland with her family, but as soon as they'd entered the gates, she waved goodbye to her mother, brother and grandparents, saying she'd meet up with them later at the ice cream parlor on Main Street. She scurried down the street and across the bridge to the Sleeping Beauty Castle before her mother had a chance to protest. She knew she'd later be in trouble for running off, but she didn't care; she wanted to be alone and away from her family for at least part of the day.

The entrance to the Sleeping Beauty attraction was an obscure doorway that wasn't well-marked and the attraction itself was infrequently visited. Inside the doorway, narrow stone steps led upward past the story scenes hidden behind glass windows. Various tunes from the movie played as the stairway ascended, but it was at the very top of the stairs where Susan wanted to be, where she felt was the very best place in all of Disneyland. The small, shadowy room contained a window to the largest and best scene of all, the forest scene where Briar Rose (Princess Aurora) meets her dream prince, Prince Phillip.

For four years now, Susan had been infatuated with a certain someone in a band, in fact, the most famous band of all time, who she'd seen in concert three times. James, one of the band members, had become her dream prince, saving her from her unstable mother's verbal and physical abuse, and an uncle's inappropriate and repulsive fondling.

ix

James had become her safe haven, wrapping his arms around her in her dreams and telling her he loved her, that everything was going to be okay, that someday he would come and take her away to be with him forever.

Yes, it was just a dream, but it had become very real to her. When things got bad, she'd run to James, and he was always there for her, the one person she could always count on.

When she reached the top of the stairs in the castle, she sighed as she looked upon the idyllic scene laid out behind the glass, imagining that she was the princess and James was the prince. As had been the case every other time she'd been here, she was completely alone. She began singing along with the music to her favorite Sleeping Beauty song, *"Once Upon A Dream."*

"I love you…you danced with me once upon a dream…When I saw you… the sparks in your eyes were so familiar to me…"

She closed her eyes for a moment, thinking of James and savoring the pleasurable and happy feelings coursing through her body, and turned in small circles around the room as she sang. She didn't notice that someone else had come into the castle and was standing in the shadows at the top of the stairs watching her as she continued to sing and spin, her long, blonde hair flying around behind her.

"So I'm sure it's true…that first love is rarely what it seems…but now I'm with you… I know what is true… You'll hold me again…just as you did then… upon a dream…"

"Lovely," said a voice out of the shadows. It sounded so familiar, it made her come to a sudden halt and freeze in place. "Will you sing it again for me?"

When she spun her head around and saw who was standing there, her eyes grew as big as the tea cup saucers in the *Alice In Wonderland* attraction. She was speechless and her knees felt as if they might buckle under her.

It was James. The real, live and in person, James.

How or why he was here, she didn't know. Had she conjured him up from her imagination?

All she did know was that the sight of him took her breath away and made her heart feel as if it would pound out of her chest. She licked her lips thinking she would choke if she tried to say something. She blinked and closed her eyes for a moment, thinking he was just a vision, but when she opened them again, he was still there.

James moved forward out of the shadows, into the small room and smiled at her, the corners of his eyes crinkling in amusement, and she could see the amber highlights in them glinting in the half light.

"Cat got your tongue?" he asked teasingly.

All she could do was shake her head, but she finally managed to say, "No…you…you just startled me is all…" Her words were merely a whisper.

"So, will you sing me the song again?" he prodded.

"Oh, no! I can't sing very well…I…I thought I was alone…and…" she stuttered.

"I thought you sang quite nicely. Please, will you sing it again?"

Susan was glad the room was so dark, as she was blushing crimson all the way from the roots of her golden blonde hair down to her toenails. She could feel the heat in her face.

"Really…no…"

He stepped closer until he was only a couple of feet away. "Please?" he said, raising his eyebrows.

She'd been holding her breath and let out a great exhale. For almost a full minute, she couldn't think or speak as he continued to look at her imploringly.

"Well…I guess…" she finally managed.

She walked up to the glass and looked in at the scene, turning her back to him. She felt him come up behind her and was shaking at the thought that he might actually touch her. She knew that if he did, she would pass out on the floor right then and there. She took a deep breath and began to sing again.

As her trembling and unsteady voice faded on the last notes, he said, "That was very nice, thank you."

She turned around to face him. "I'm sure you could sing it better…"

"Do you think so?"

"Well, of course I do!"

"So you know who I am?"

She gulped. "Uh...yeah...how could I not know?"

He laughed. "Well, if I'd left my disguise on, maybe you wouldn't. That's why I came here. That mustache and beard thing were getting all itchy. I was told that no one comes here very much."

She laughed back. "You're right; not many people know this is even here. That's one reason I like it."

"So, are you here alone then?"

"No. I came to Disneyland with my family, but this is my favorite place. I always come here first when we come to Disneyland. I told my mom I'd meet up with everyone later."

"Do you come to Disneyland often?"

"Once or twice a year...We don't live very far away."

"And why is this your favorite place?"

She bit her lip and turned to look at the scene behind the window again. "I've just always loved the Sleeping Beauty story, I guess."

"What do you like most about it?"

"Um...well...the falling in love part when he doesn't know who she really is and she doesn't know who he really is...and...and the end where he wakes her up with love's first kiss...and when they're dancing at the very end and two of the fairies keep changing her dress from pink to blue..."

"Ah...and what color does it end up being? Pink or blue?"

"Why, pink, of course!'

"I see...your favorite color maybe?"

"Maybe." She leaned back into the glass window to brace herself because her legs were shaking so bad.

When he reached forward and took a lock of her hair between his fingers, she was sure she would faint. She inhaled sharply, her eyes flying to his and their eyes locked.

"Perhaps you'd be interested in taking a ride on the Monorail with me?" he asked.

"The Monorail?"

"Yes, it goes all around the park, as you probably know, and it even makes a stop at the Disneyland Hotel. We could have a cup of coffee."

She sucked in her breath. "You mean...leave the park?!"

"Just for a bit. Perhaps I could even sing to you…"

A weak "Oh" was all she could manage.

He let go of her hair, sensing he was making her nervous.

And, he knew full well he was making her nervous; he knew the effect he had on girls. They constantly chased him and just about threw themselves at his feet. Being in a band that was now world famous had its drawbacks, but having beautiful girls pining to be with him, was one of the bonuses.

He assessed the girl standing in front of him, knowing that his closeness was affecting her. Although it was rather dim in the room, he could still see she was one of the loveliest girls he'd ever encountered. She was just a few inches shorter than him, with a very trim yet shapely body. She wore a pink, sleeveless sun dress with a modest neckline, yet there was still a hint of cleavage peeking out at him from the top. Her tanned skin was flawless and her face and hair looked almost like the Sleeping Beauty character behind the glass window. He wanted to touch her skin as he had her soft and silky hair.

It was her eyes, however, that he found captivating. They were a deep emerald green with flecks of blue and gray floating in their depths. His thoughts shocked him for a moment. He was normally not so quickly captivated by a pretty face. Most of the time they all seemed the same to him.

But, he wanted to find out more about this girl for some reason… her name…her age…what she looked like outside the dimness of the room. It was as if the Sleeping Beauty castle had cast some kind of spell over him.

As if she could read his mind, Susan flinched and moved towards the other set of stairs leading down through the rest of the attraction to a second door that led out of the castle. She was more than nervous; she suddenly and unexpectedly felt panicked. Here was her dream prince right in front of her, asking her to leave Disneyland with him, and she was so unnerved and flustered that she could barely breathe.

The thought of spending more time with him, having him touch more than just her hair, sent terrified shivers down her spine.

She had to leave. She had to get out of the castle and away from him. She didn't know why she was so frightened, but she began to shake uncontrollably before turning on her heel and racing from the room and down the stairs, hair flying behind her, as fast as her unstable legs could carry her.

Right before she reached the bottom, she glanced over through one of the windows and saw the scene with Prince Phillip waking up Princess Aurora with love's first kiss. She choked on a sob and tears began to pour down her face.

As she passed the final window with the dancing scene and the flashing blue and pink lights changing Sleeping Beauty's dress color, she heard footsteps behind her and knew it was James.

"Wait!" she heard him yell. "Where are you going?! What's your name?"

But, by the time he reached the bottom of the stairs and stepped out into the bright sunlight, Susan was gone.

Chapter 1

46 Years Later

"Thanks for taking me to the airport, John," Susan said, hefting one of several suitcases into the back of her Honda Civic. "I really appreciate it! Donald had an important court case this morning and had to be there, otherwise he would have dropped me off."

"No problem," said John, putting the last suitcase in the car and closing the trunk. "You said you're only going on a seven day cruise? Looks like you must have packed enough for a month or more!"

"Yeah, well," said Susan, "I like to have choices, you know. Girls like options."

"Uh huh," he responded, opening the door on the passenger side for her.

Susan slid into the seat and fastened her seatbelt while John went around to the driver's side, got in and started up the car.

"So," said John, "What made you and Lynn decide to go on a cruise together without Ernest and Donald? Couldn't they get time off?"

"No. Donald is involved in one of his big court cases and Ernest is working on some kind of super conductor or secret government project. Plus, we just decided we wanted to take a girl's cruise. No husbands. Plus, I'm still unsettled after going to that concert last year in Texas. I just felt like I needed a distraction."

"Oh, the concert where you went to see James you mean?"

"Yeah. Seeing him was like a dormant volcano came alive again. I shouldn't have gone."

"Susan, it's been fifty years, you know..."

"Oh, I know, I know, but you remember how it was with me in junior high and high school...Everybody knew about me and my 'James thing,' especially poor Brian. I still pity the guy having to put up with me and my obsession or whatever you'd call it."

"Oh yeah, I remember your 'James thing.' Everybody in school knew about it. Brian and I are still close friends you know; we play Frisbee together a couple of times a week."

"Really? I didn't know that. I knew you were still friends, but I didn't realize you see him that often. Sometimes I think about him and wonder if he remembers the horrible thing he did to me."

"What horrible thing? I always wondered what broke the two of you up. Even though he was my best friend at the time, he never really said what happened. You guys went steady for how long? Four years? A lot of people were sure you'd end up getting married after we graduated, and then all of a sudden, you were with Donald and ended up marrying him."

"Well, the 'horrible thing,' as I call it, had to do with James. Brian was picking me up from an after school class I was taking at the university, and when I got in the car, he had this big, giant grin on his face. When I asked him what that was all about, he just turned up the radio and started to laugh. The news was on and they were saying how James had just gotten married. I was beside myself...I started screaming and crying. And he just kept laughing and laughing."

"Wow...I didn't know that..."

"And then, he rubbed it in that James had married someone named Susan, and that it wasn't me. I remember him saying it was the happiest day of his life. It was the most miserable day of mine. I never forgave him for laughing at me. I never will... My bubble was burst and I was devastated. But for Brian to laugh at me and rub it in... Sorry, I know he's still your friend, but..."

"Hey, Susan, he was probably happy just because he was tired of having to compete with James, and he likely thought that would be the end of your infatuation with him. Face it, it wasn't as if you would ever have had a chance to be with James anyway; he was so out of reach for you."

"Maybe, but I still harbored some crazy idea that I really would be with James someday, and I knew there would never be an end to my feelings for him. Obviously, I was right, huh? He's so deeply embedded in my heart that I don't think I'll ever get him pried out of it."

"So, what does Donald think about your 'James thing?' He can't be real excited about it. Especially being married to you for forty four years now."

"He's man enough not to be threatened by it. He knows he's number one with me, despite my musings over James from time to time. It's not like James has seriously affected my life or the raising of our children or anything. Besides, and this is something I've never told anyone but Lynn..."

John looked over at Susan and raised his eyebrows.

"A couple of months after James got married, I was standing in front of my easel in art class, looking outside at the rain and feeling pretty dismal. As I looked out, I prayed to God, the Universe, or whatever power might be hanging out there. I asked that if I couldn't have James, which I knew deep down inside was an unobtainable dream anyway, then please, could I have someone just like him. Right then, the clouds parted for just a moment and a ray of sun came down and lit up the window next to me. And, you'll think this is really weird, but Donald passed me a note in the next class asking me for my phone number. I didn't think much of it at the time, but later..."

"That's pretty incredible, Susan. A prayer answered! So, do you think Donald is a lot like James?"

"I have no way of knowing. I've just always had James up on this pedestal, making him near perfect in my mind. He helped me get through my miserable and abusive childhood. When things get bad in my life, he's just someone to run to in my mind...in my dreams..."

"Well, I think Donald is one fantastic guy. Maybe going on this cruise with Lynn will take your mind off James. And, maybe you're right that you shouldn't have gone to that concert last year to see him. I still can't even believe how popular he still is, going all over the place at his age and putting on those mega concerts. Sounds like seeing him stirred the pot of memories for you."

"You could certainly say that! Hey, here we are at the airport already. I really do appreciate this. You're a great friend, John!"

"Happy to help you out, and I hope you and Lynn have a great time."

"Oh, I know we will! I just love cruises!"

John pulled the car up to the curb at the American Airlines terminal and both he and Susan got out. John helped Susan get her luggage to the curb-side check-in, then gave her a hug goodbye.

Susan smiled in anticipation of being with her best friend, Lynn, again and cheerfully walked into the airport to the security line. An hour later, her plane lifted off the ground and she was winging her way to Texas where Lynn would pick her up before driving them both to Galveston and the ship.

The flight to Dallas/Fort Worth was three hours. Susan had packed her Kindle in her carry-on bag, but became annoyed at herself when she realized the battery was near dead and the charger cord was in one of her checked bags.

"Oh well," she thought to herself, "I'll just have to entertain myself in some other way."

She looked at the movie guide as soon as the "fasten seatbelt" sign went off, but nothing appealed to her. Grateful to have a window seat, she looked out as the plane gained altitude over the ocean then made a turn to head east from San Diego to Texas. She looked down, trying to recognize something, but as usual, from the air, nothing looked familiar. She leaned back in her seat and closed her eyes.

She really was looking forward to being with Lynn, her best friend from elementary school. They shared so many good times and memories, and she especially remembered the ones where she and Lynn had gone to see the most famous band of all time.

The band had consisted of four boys from Brighton, England, named Derek, James, Ian and Blue. "Blue" was actually a nickname for Bernard, their drummer, because he wore the color blue all the time. Lynn became infatuated with Ian and Susan with James, attending three of their concerts in 1964, '65 and '66.

Susan thought back to the first concert in 1964 when she was twelve years old and watched James through a pair of binoculars. Everyone was screaming, and she remembered wishing they would shut up so she could hear better. She, Lynn and another friend, Joy, had tickets in what she called the "nose bleed" section, being so far from the stage. The only good thing about being so far back at the Hollywood Bowl, was that they were right below the speakers, so she could at least hear some of what one of the boys in the band would say when they announced a song.

The most memorable moment at that first concert had been when James stepped up to the microphone as Susan pressed the binoculars into her eye sockets, holding her breath, waiting to hear what he was going to say and wondering what song would be next. Shivers went down her spine as she heard his voice, and then he started singing what had become her favorite song, *"All My Kisses."* Tears poured down her face as her young, pre-teen heart wrenched for the want of something that she couldn't identify. All she remembered was that she was certain she had fallen in love, and she imagined James was singing to no one but her.

That particular stage in her life had been an unhappy one. Her father had passed away five years previously and her mother, unable to cope with his loss, became so mentally unstable that Susan, her brother and mother moved in with her grandparents.

Susan's mother had no patience for her and constantly berated her, often screaming and throwing things at her or even pulling her hair or slapping her. To add to her misery, her uncle, who lived across the street, began molesting her when she was ten years old. She was too young to fully understand what his touches and fondling were all about, and he made her keep it a secret between them, but for some reason, it didn't seem right to her. It made her feel dirty and ashamed.

The one joy in Susan's life was her ballet classes, and she put all of her energy into working as hard as she could to become a good dancer. It was her dream to be a famous ballerina one day, and until

James entered her life, she spent many hours in a fantasy world where she was the most talented ballerina in the world. The only drawback to ballet was the fact that her mother didn't drive, so her sole transportation to and from classes was her uncle. Every time he came to pick her up, she cringed, knowing what he'd want from her before they got home.

Then James and his band came to the U.S. in February, 1964. Susan joined in with Lynn and her other friends to become fans of the group, seeing them first on the Ted Flannagan Show, buying their records and looking at their pictures in magazines. But, it wasn't until the Hollywood Bowl concert that Susan went over the cliff with James and made him her dream prince, just like Sleeping Beauty had a dream prince.

James became her escape from the harsh reality of her life, and once he'd embedded himself in her heart, there was no turning back. He became everything to her, and whenever things became unbearable, she ran off to be with him in the fantasy world she had created for them both, especially during the times she had to spend with her uncle on the drive home from ballet class. She blocked what he did to her from her mind, thinking instead of James holding her in his arms and telling her everything was going to be okay.

And then the chance meeting in Disneyland…She chased thoughts of those moments out of her head. She still couldn't believe it had actually happened.

Susan opened her eyes as the plane hit a pocket of turbulence, rousing her out of her thoughts of the far past. She reached up to her chest and tugged on the silver necklace she wore around her neck. A pair of silver ballet shoes hung on the end. She flicked her finger at them.

Here she was at sixty-two years old and still thinking of James like a silly twelve year old. What was wrong with her anyway? Hopefully, spending time with Lynn and going on the cruise would wipe the cobwebs out of her mind along with her renewed feelings for James.

At least she hoped it would.

Susan's plane was ten minutes early arriving at DFW, and when she called Lynn to let her know, Lynn hadn't even left her house yet. Lynn's house was almost an hour away, south of Dallas. Susan began to fidget, annoyed at having to wait another hour.

She managed to get all of her luggage claimed and hauled out to the curb in the parking garage, then went back into the airport, asking one of the security people to keep an eye on her bags for a minute or two. She shortly returned with a foodie magazine, thanked the security guard and sat down on a bench to wait for Lynn.

She perused the magazine and started to feel hungry looking at all the pictures. A delicious-looking photo of Crème Brulee was on the cover, and she thought if they weren't driving straight from the airport to the ship in Galveston, she'd make some for Lynn and Ernest at their home. It was one of her specialties, and she always had fun with the blow torch when caramelizing the sugar on top.

She smiled. Lynn was no cook. Ernest always loved it when Susan came to visit because she always prepared fabulous meals and did her best to teach Lynn to cook. Cooking was one of Susan's favorite pastimes.

Susan read the magazine cover to cover before Lynn finally arrived.

"I forgot when your plane was due in," Lynn said sheepishly. "I thought you said 11:00, not 10:00."

"Lynn! How could you have forgotten? It's a five hour drive from here to our ship, and the ship sails at 5:30! We're going to be cutting it really close!"

"I know…I know…sorry, honey…"

"You forgot what time I was due in last time too, remember? When I came for the concert?"

"Oh, Susan, don't remind me of that!"

"Why not?"

"You turned into a basket case, that's why. I thought you were going to leap off the balcony when James started to sing *All My Kisses.*" I really did!"

"How ridiculous! I was *not* about to leap off the balcony! Why would I do that? I'm not that crazy!"

"Well, I'm not so sure about that when it comes to *him*...Plus, you told me going to see James made you start thinking about him again. You shouldn't be thinking of him at all, you know."

"Yeah, I know...But with Donald all wrapped up in his court cases and everything... Sometimes I don't even see him for a whole week, other than sleeping in the same bed for a couple of hours a night. And, sometimes he even stays at his office all night so I don't see him at all. He doesn't even make time to call me."

"Susan, he treats you like a princess, and you know it! He adores you. Once this court case is over, you know he'll sweep you off on a romantic vacation somewhere, just like he always does."

"Yeah, maybe, but in the meantime, I've got James stuck in my head again. I keep thinking of the time I met him in Disneyland... remember when I told you about that?"

"Oh yes! And you were just sixteen! What could he have been thinking wanting to go off with you like that? You would have been underage jail bait! And, what was he doing there anyway? Are you sure you just didn't imagine it?

"I'm very, very sure! It was definitely him. I keep wishing I hadn't run away. What do you think would have happened if I hadn't run away?"

"Something that you would have regretted, I'm sure. You probably wouldn't have been a virgin when you met Donald for one thing."

"He just said he wanted to take a ride on the Monorail and go for a cup of coffee."

"Uh huh...and I'm the Queen of Sheeba. I don't think so...It creeps me out just thinking about it."

"Whatever...I'm still going to always wonder. I'm always going to wonder what he's really like. He seemed so nice up in the Sleeping Beauty Castle... I'd give anything to go back and re-live that time... maybe even decide to go have that cup of coffee with him..."

"You and your thinking he's so darn perfect. He's just a made-up dream and you know it. Your real dream is what you already have. You should appreciate Donald more."

"I do! But it still doesn't keep me from thinking what it would be like to go back in the past and be with James again in the castle. Or... even better yet...What if I could go back in the past and meet him before the band became famous? Maybe he'd fall in love with me and then..."

"You're crazy, Susan. You would have been, what, about ten years old right before they became famous? I don't think James would have been interested in a ten-year-old. You should do more thinking about Donald, and then maybe you'd forget about James. I forgot about Ian a zillion years ago and you remember the crush I had on him!"

"I'll never forget about James..."

"Oh, Susan! What am I going to do with you anyway? You and your stupid James thing!"

"You're my best friend in the whole world, Lynn...just indulge me, okay?"

"I love you, Susan!"

"I love you too, Lynn! And, we're going to have a fabulous time on this cruise...I just know it!!!"

Chapter 2

On the Ship

Lynn and Susan arrived at the Port of Galveston an hour before the ship was due to set sail. They checked in, handed their luggage to the porters and headed up to their cabin where two bottles of champagne awaited them, one from Donald and one from Ernest. By the time the horn blew, announcing their departure, they'd managed to down both bottles.

The ship pulled out of Galveston harbor at sunset into calm ocean waters and a warm breeze. Susan hadn't had time to contact the Maître'd before dinner, so their table companions were going to be a surprise, but no matter. Along with the champagne, they'd imbibed enough wine by the time the dinner hour arrived, that meeting some new people would be amusing, and if they weren't compatible, they could always change tables the next night.

Lynn was the first to slide into her chair in the brilliantly lit dining room, Susan following, but there was no sign of their assigned dinner companions yet. Susan beckoned the waiter to bring a wine list, and as the girls were perusing the vast amount of choices, two other ladies slid into the chairs across the table.

Lynn looked up from the wine list, a somewhat startled expression in her eyes, and muttered a small, "Oh, hello there."

Susan glanced up, and said, "Oh my...hello," also in a surprised tone of voice.

Their two dinner companions were dark skinned, and the younger of the two displayed a broad smile and twinkling eyes. She appeared to be middle-aged, while the other lady looked quite ancient. Both were dressed in flowing garments of the most brilliant colors with matching turbans on their heads. The older woman nodded her head in acknowledgment to the girls.

"Your dresses are beautiful!" exclaimed Lynn.

The younger woman smiled again and extended her hand. "Thank you," she said. "My name is Marta, and this is my grandmother, Mika. We are most pleased to meet you." She had a slight French accent.

"Same here," said Susan. "I'm Susan, and I'm here from California visiting my friend, Lynn, who lives in Texas. We're taking a girl's cruise. We've been best friends since elementary school."

"We're from Haiti," responded Marta. "My grandmother has never been on a cruise before. I wanted her to have the experience before she got much older."

"It would be hard to get much older from the looks of her," Susan thought to herself.

Dinner progressed in usual cruise-style, with fabulous appetizers, soups, salads, entree's, and more wine. Both of the girls were feeling quite mellow by this time, and the wine was making them rather garrulous.

Mika had said very little during the dinner course, and the girls were wondering if she spoke much English, until she suddenly turned to Susan, saying in a soft-spoken voice, "You would like to go visit someone in another time and place, would you not? You have been thinking of this person for a very long time."

Susan, who was about to take another sip of wine, drew back from her wine glass and stared at the old woman. "Why, what can you mean?" she asked.

"Do not pretend you do not know what I mean," Mika replied staring intently at Susan. "You and your friend were talking about this person just today, and this person is still in your mind."

"Oh, come on, Susan, you know what she's talking about," Lynn said. "Remember, we were reminiscing about the concert we went to last year and you were saying how you wish you could re-live meeting you-know-who in Disneyland? Then you said how cool it would be to go back into the past and meet him before he became famous. She has you figured out." She giggled, forgetting about how she had scolded Susan for thinking of James.

"Please stop, Grandmere," said Marta, gently laying her hand on Mika's arm. "This lady wants no such thing. Leave this kind of thing for home."

"But she wants to go; I can see into her soul. She has wanted this for a very long time. She has something to find out and learn about herself in regard to this person. And, it awaits her in the past."

"What are you talking about?!" exclaimed Susan. "I think I've had too much wine."

"Are you talking about time travel or something like that?" Lynn interjected.

"Don't listen to my grandmother," said Marta. "She imagines things. She thinks she can see into people's souls."

"But Marta, you know I can," insisted Mika. "You know I can see into the souls of people. And this lady wants very much to meet this James person in the past. It has been in her heart for a very, very long time. She will learn something very important about herself by doing this."

"How can you know that? How did you even know his name?" asked Susan, her curiosity getting the better of her.

"My grandmother thinks she is all knowing as well as being able to read into people's souls," responded Marta shaking her head.

"So can you really send someone back in time?" asked Lynn, draining her glass of wine.

"That would be interesting," remarked Susan with a giggle. "Just imagine me popping into the Dusky Club, like fifty two years in the past, and there he is live and in person. Whoa!"

Marta was silent. Mika stared hard at Susan. "Would you want to go? It would only be for a short period of time, but I could arrange for you to go."

"Well, I sure as hell wouldn't want to go looking like the sixty-two year old I am now! He'd be what, twenty?" exclaimed Susan.

"You wouldn't have to go as you are now. You pick the age you want your physical body to be, and I will send you back that way."

Lynn and Susan looked at each other, neither of them knowing what to say.

"You should do it, Susan. Really, you should," said Lynn, thinking Susan might discover James wasn't the paragon she'd made him out to be in her mind. "She said you would learn something from it. And just think, you could be like seventeen again!"

"And what would I learn? That he wasn't as perfect as I've always thought he was? Oh come on, this is ridiculous! What would I say? And how could this even be possible?!" exclaimed Susan.

Lynn thought to herself, "Yeah, it would be great if you found out that he was a jerk..."

"It *is* possible," whispered Marta under her breath. "My grandmother can do many things others would think strange or impossible. She is much respected in Haiti for the things she can do."

"Well, I don't know what to even think any more," said Susan. "How does this work anyway? I just - poof - vanish into the past, and then what?"

"You go at a certain time and you return one week later at the same time. What you do while you are there is up to you," responded Marta. "My grandmother would take care that no harm came to you. If anything dangerous were to happen to you on the other side, you would return immediately."

"But what do I do about clothes and money and a place to stay and all that kind of stuff?" asked Susan.

"It would all be arranged; you would have what you need for one week," responded Marta.

Mika nodded, staring at Susan through half-closed eyes.

"Do it, Suz. Then you can come back and tell me everything that happened," said Lynn. To herself, she said, "And hopefully, you'll realize that what you have in the present is much better than anything you would have ever had with him..."

"This is just too darn crazy," said Susan.

"But do you want to do it?" asked Marta.

Mika's eyes were closed now, but her head kept nodding.

"Well...maybe," said Susan. "But what in the heck would I do or say if I suddenly just showed up? He probably wouldn't even look at me!" said Susan.

"Are you kidding me?" exclaimed Lynn. "The way you looked at seventeen would certainly have him looking at you!"

"Ha, ha," responded Susan. "But it would sure be nice to have that seventeen-year-old body back again, even if it was for only a week."

"Then do it!" said Lynn, suddenly feeling quite drunk.

"How?" asked Susan, Looking at Mika and then at Marta.

"You come to our cabin a few minutes before midnight, and we will have it all arranged," responded Marta. "It is actually very simple. And it is very safe. Don't worry."

Mika got up from the table with Marta following and they left the dining room.

"I didn't even say for sure I'd do it!" said Susan.

"You didn't have to say anything," responded Lynn. "The old lady knows. Are you scared?"

"I'm not scared. I just think we're going to go to their cabin and find out it's a bunch of hocus pocus."

"You should take your iPod, you know," remarked Lynn. "You could show him how famous he's going to be and let him listen to all the music he's going to write."

"You're as nuts as they are," said Susan. "Where in hell would I plug in an iPod in 1962 and in England? They don't even have the same type of plugs over there."

"Charge it up before you go," said Lynn.

"Oh geez!" said Susan, finishing up her wine. "Let's go watch the show in the main theater and let me think about this."

The two old friends stumbled out of the dining room, clinging to each other's arms and giggling.

Candles aren't allowed on cruise ships, but there were three candles burning in Marta and Mika's cabin when Lynn and Susan arrived at five minutes before midnight, all of them deep down in glass jars of the primary colors blue, red and yellow. There was an unmistakable odor of incense in the air, but neither of them could recognize what scent it was.

The door clicked shut behind them and Marta moved forward out of the shadows. Mika was hidden behind her.

"First a few things we need to know," said Marta, looking at Susan. "You want the body you had at age seventeen? That is no problem. Are there any other talents or characteristics you want to have or want to take with you?"

"Well, I'd like to take the knowledge and common sense I believe I now have. Other than the seventeen-year old body, I think I'd like to be able to play the piano...play by ear...play reading music...whatever, just be able to play incredibly well...and I want to be able to dance better than I was ever able to...double pirouettes no problem..."

"Suz!" Lynn exclaimed. "When are you going to have a chance to do double pirouettes at the Dusky Club?"

"You never know...Oh! And I want to be able to sing! ...Oh my gosh! I can't forget this! I want to have perfect 20/20 vision. I think I wore contacts when I was seventeen. It would be horrible to be all squinty-eyed and not be able to see him!"

Lynn shook her head, but then started to laugh as she thought of something herself. "You sure don't want it to be your time of the month either, right? Don't want to be having cramps. They might not sell Midol or Tampax in England."

"That is all fine. It is done. If there's nothing else, then lay down on the bed," Marta instructed Susan. "Lynn, sit on the floor beside her and hold her left hand."

Susan and Lynn silently did as they were told, emboldened by more wine prior to coming to the cabin.

"Are you sure you want to do this?" asked Lynn looking at Susan as she laid down on the bed.

"I'm not sure...I think so..." she responded. "I just don't know what I'll say to him. I'll probably get all tongue-tied or faint. That would be embarrassing! Maybe you should come with me."

"No thanks. I'm sure you can handle it all on your own. Just don't go falling in love or anything stupid like that."

"Well, that's unlikely! I'm only going to be there for seven days! What could happen in seven days anyway?"

Mika smiled from the shadows.

"I think we're both crazy," said Lynn.

"Totally," agreed Susan.

They both looked at Marta. Mika emerged from the shadows. She was wearing different garments and clutched a bag of what looked and smelled like strange herbs in her right hand.

"Relax and close your eyes," she instructed Susan.

Susan's eyes were suddenly as big as saucers.

"What's going to happen?" she asked.

"You will leave here in a few minutes. You will feel nothing. You will open your eyes and you will be in the Dusky Club in Brighton, England and the person you so wish to meet will be at a microphone singing. The rest will be up to you. You will be sitting on a stool next to a wall near the front of the club. In your purse will be a key to a room in a nearby hotel, where you will be staying. You will have money in your purse and you will be dressed in the fashion of the day. You will have spare clothes in your room for the week. That is all. As I said, the rest will be up to you."

Susan looked at Lynn, feeling a little frightened, but the wine had muddled her brain a bit and she just smiled.

"Okay, sure, let's go for it," she said from her prone position on the bed.

Just a few more things," said Mika. "Your friend here will be able to observe you on her iPhone. Marta will install an App on it. If she feels the desire or need to be with you, she can come to this cabin and we will transport her back. If she goes, however, she must return the same time as you. It is now near midnight on Friday. You will return next Friday precisely at midnight unless Lynn goes to bring you back sooner or unless you are in danger. If she does go back, you must be in agreement to return here sooner than next Friday and she will use the App on her iPhone to transport you both back...but you must agree to it. Once she is there, you must return together. And, as I said, should a situation occur where you are in danger, you will return immediately."

"And," added Marta, "When you return, all that happened to you in the past will become a dim memory to you. The same will be the case for those you meet or spend time with in the past. It is important that you know this."

Both Lynn and Susan looked at the clock next to the bed.

It was one minute before midnight. Mika began chanting and waving the bag of herbs over Susan's prone form.

Susan began to glow and become almost transparent.

"Oh my God, no Suz, no, no...*No!*" Lynn screamed as she looked at the clock, seeing the digital numbers as they registered midnight.

Suddenly, without further warning, Susan split into particles of light like sparkling confetti, and floated away up toward the ceiling and out from the sides of the bed.

Lynn fainted.

Chapter 3

In the Dusky Club

The first thing Susan noticed was the over-powering and choking smell of cigarette smoke. Her eyes were almost blinded by it as it hung like a fog throughout the club. She hastily put her hand up over her nose and mouth.

"Something wrong, luv?" asked a rather scruffy looking young man who had sidled up to the table she was sitting at. He was wearing a leather jacket and pants and had a cigarette dangling from the side of his mouth.

She drew back and shook her head.

"Why no, I'm fine," she responded. "Just a little smoky in here, that's all."

"Always smoky in here, luv," he said, moving his hand up to take a drag on the cigarette, then tilting his head back to blow it up into the air.

"Oh, that's just fabulous," she remarked. "I never considered that."

"Eh?" her companion said.

"Nothing."

"Not from here are you?"

"No. America, actually."

"Thought so. Accent, you know."

"Yeah, well…I can't help that. You're the one with the accent from my point of view."

He smiled. "Cheeky one, ain't you? Where did you come from, by the by? When I looked over here a minute ago, I swore Judy was sitting here, and now you are."

Susan blinked at him. "Actually, I've been here for about a half hour. You must be mistaken."

"Too much ale, perhaps," he responded, running his eyes over her from head to toe. "Want to join me in an ale? On me, of course."

"Um, no thanks. I probably won't stay too much longer." She thought fast. "The bus I took to get here was late, and I'm kind of tired after the airplane flight and all. Why don't you go find Judy; she must be around here somewhere."

"Right then; maybe I'll see you tomorrow." He winked at her and walked away.

Suddenly, she froze and squeezed her eyes shut. What had happened? Where was she? She was certainly on the cruise ship, probably in the piano bar, the usual hangout for her and Lynn. But, the smoke..."They don't smoke *this* much in the piano bar on the cruise ship!" she thought. "And that scruffy looking guy doesn't look like he belongs on a cruise ship."

Slowly, she opened her eyes and looked around the room.

Dingy. Smoky. Smelled like stale beer. The walls looked like they were made of brick or stone or a combination of both. They looked dank and dark, kind of like a dungeon. She didn't see any windows at all in the room. There were tall tables with stools sitting up against the walls. She was at one of them. Smaller tables were scattered in-between. They were all full of people, mostly girls.

She looked down at her lap and then her chest and arms to see what she was wearing. Holy crap! It looked like something out of the fifties... something like June Cleaver would wear on "Leave It to Beaver." It was a light pink, cotton seersucker dress, with a defined, belted waist and a scoop neckline. It had short sleeves with small bows at the ends. On her feet were dainty little sandals in a color to match the dress. Oh my God! She wondered what her hair looked like or if she had make-up on with silly pink lipstick to match the dress or a headband or bows in her hair. It would have made her laugh if she hadn't been so appalled.

She pulled her purse onto her lap and fished around for a compact or something that had a mirror in it. Impatiently, she pushed aside a pair of short, white gloves. Gloves!? What in the hell were gloves doing in her purse? When would she wear gloves here? Ah! There was a compact at the bottom of the purse. She took it out. Tentatively, she flipped it open and looked at herself. Thank goodness; no makeup or pink lipstick! She snapped it shut and tossed it back in the purse. She reached up and touched her hair. Thank goodness, no bows, headbands or hairspray. She wiggled her toes and looked down at them. Yes, they were her toes all right. She looked at her hands; yes, they were definitely her hands and thank god, no pink nail polish to match the dorky dress.

Then she felt a shudder go through her and looked toward the front of the room...

And there *he* was.

Live and in person.

Scruffy, with greasy hair and sweating under the lights.

In leather and a black t-shirt?

Really?

This was James?

Derek was singing.

"Life is treating me saaaaad...agony...I'm the type of bloke, who always used to joke...Now life is treating me saaaaad, agony...She's run away for sure; she even slammed the door...It's certainly a drag, agony..."

Whoa!

"I recall the best of times we had great fun...Why don't she know I never wanted her to run...as she done. Give her now to me, cause even she must see... alone without her I will be in agony..."

Her eyes became giant orbs on her face as her mouth formed into an "O." James was so close! Only about fifteen feet away from her, standing between Ian and Derek.

"I recall the best of times we had great fun. She must recall and decide we should be one, in the sun...Give her now to me, cause even she must see, alone without her I will be in agony...oh, my oh my, in agony oh yeah, such agony...tra la, la...tra, la, la..."

As the song ended, James wasn't looking her way, but Ian was. She saw him nudge James, who then turned his head to look in her direction, squinting his eyes in the bright lights above the stage area to get a better look through all the smoke.

"New girl in town to check out," she thought, shivering and pressing her back into the wall behind her, thinking to make herself smaller...or maybe even invisible. The roughness of the bricks and stone pressed into the back of her dress. The wall felt cool and somewhat damp.

"Either that, or I stand out like some kind of quirky oddball in this dress. Geez..."

Derek sat down on a stool in front of the microphone, guitar resting on his knees. He also had the greasy hair look and was wearing leather, as they all were. "One last song before a break," he said. "This one's called *"I Love My Baby,"* and he began singing.

"Well, I love my baby, all day long...she's sweet to me...oh, yes, she is..."

She was starting to feel a bit faint, thinking James might look over at her and their eyes might connect at any second, when there was a tap on her shoulder.

"Whatcha drinkin', dearie?" said a small girl with curly red hair and a dimple in her cheek. She was looking Susan up and down as if she couldn't believe what she was seeing.

Susan squirmed on the bar stool. "Oh!" was all she could say. This must be a waitress.

"Need to have a drink if you're sittin' at a table, ya know," she said.

"Um," Susan replied. "What's good to drink here? I haven't been here before."

"On holiday then? American?"

Susan nodded, feeling as if James and Ian were now looking at the oddly dressed "new bird," their eyes boring into the back of her head.

"I'm Susan," she said, extending her hand. "From California...the southern part...So if I need to have a drink, can you just bring me something like a glass of chardonnay?"

The redhead raised her eyebrows. "Shar...doe...what?" she asked.

"Oh, um...wine...You know, it's a white wine."

"We got port and a stout and ale, small beer, and I think Frank might have some kind of wine in an old dusty bottle under the bar, but we don't get much call for wine here, ya know."

Susan stared at her dumbly.

"I'm Sandra, by the way," said the redhead, feeling sorry for her. "You seem a little lost. Let me just get you a small beer, and if you don't like it, I'll see if that old bottle of wine is still under the bar...By the way, two of the guys in the band are giving you the look over, if you haven't noticed. I'll be back in a flash."

As Sandra sauntered off, she thought to herself that this American bird sure was dressed funny. Add a pair of gloves and a hat, and she'd be ready to go to church. She stuck out like a sore thumb. No wonder the boys in the band and some of the other guys in the club were all gawking at her. She wondered if Susan noticed.

Susan turned her head back toward the stage area.

Ian and James were on their guitars, Ian playing a solo tune, with James on bass. They were both looking at Derek.

Derek was singing, *"Well, I love my baby, all night long, she's a sweet treat to me. Oh yeah, she is... Well she's my honey because she knows I'm a needin' man...Day and night...night and day...I'm a needin' man...Oh yeah, I am..."*

James looked towards her as the song finished, but then girls on the other side of the room started yelling, "One more! One more!!"

James turned to look at them. Derek looked at Ian and said into the microphone. "Go Ian...How about *"Sigh in the Shadows?"*

The girls yelled their approval, and Ian stepped up to the microphone, lowering it to guitar-level, and started to play the instrumental song. James moved over to Derek and said something to him. Derek looked in Susan's direction then turned back to James and laughed as he said something back to him. Then he winked at James.

Susan was observing this with amused interest, wondering if Derek had been told to check out the new girl in the silly pink dress, when Sandra came back with a mug of beer that looked like it was all foam.

"There ya go, love. See whatcha think."

Susan took a sip, wiping the foam from her upper lip. It was pretty much all foam.

"Not bad," she lied. "Not bad at all. Hey, I don't know you money system very well; can you figure out what I owe you from what I have here?"

She opened her purse and pulled a bill out of one of the inside pockets.

"Lor!" exclaimed Sandra. "That ud be enough for six or seven beers!"

"Well, then, why don't you bring me the dusty wine bottle, if it's enough to cover it, and keep the change for yourself?"

"Sure, and that's awful good of you, love...I'll be back with the bottle in a bit...By the way," she added, just as *"Sigh in the Shadows"* ended, "I think you're gonna have some company."

She gave a big grin and turned to walk away.

"Ciggy?" said a voice over her shoulder.

Susan froze, the color draining from her face. Hairs stood up on the back of her neck. She knew that voice as well as she knew her own. She'd heard it thousands of times over the past fifty years, talking and singing. She held her breath as she slowly swiveled around on the bar stool.

And there he was, just a couple of feet away, leaning towards her over the tall table, one hand extended with a cigarette in it. He also had one dangling from the side of his mouth that was lit.

His dark hair looked greasy, but it might have just been sweat. His face was certainly shiny with it. He had on a black leather jacket over a ratty-looking black t-shirt. He put the hand without the cigarette in it up to his forehead and brushed his hair away, a gesture that drew her eyes to his. They were brown with amber flecks in them and they were smiling; his mouth also quirked in a grin.

"Cat got your tongue, luv?" he asked.

Thanks to the smoky room and dim lighting away from stage area, James didn't see Susan's face turn crimson as she stuttered, "No, of course not. You just startled me is all."

24

"Oh my God!" she thought to herself. "Those are the same words we said to each other in the Sleeping Beauty Castle, but…but that's in the future still!" She shook her head to clear it.

"Your accent…are you American?" he asked.

"Yes, California…the southern part…"

"Here on holiday then?"

"You could say that."

She was thinking to herself, "What can I say? What story can I make up? Think quick, Susan, think quick!"

"I'm here to meet some friends. We're…um…students…my Uncle back in the states is a history professor…we're um…on a history tour. I'm staying at a hotel just down the street. I was out walking around and heard music coming from here. I thought I'd check it out."

She was mumbling like an idiot, words tumbling out of her mouth at random. She was starting to feel faint. Looking into his gorgeous eyes made her feel weak in the knees. She was glad she was sitting down.

"And where are the other students?"

"Well, they're not here yet…they were, um, delayed…they should be here in a week…by next Friday…then we're off to Bath and…and Devon before heading to London."

Bath and Devon were the only other English cities she could think of on the spur of the moment, recalling the names from the English Regency romances she frequently read. How lame was that?!

"Ah, here for a week on your own then?"

"Yes, but I'm sure I'll find plenty to do. I plan on buying a guide book tomorrow." Oh geez! What made her say something so stupid?

"A guide book of Brighton?"

"And the surrounding area…yes."

He started to laugh. "Not much to see around here," he said. "Other than the Prince Regent's palace, I wouldn't say there's enough to take up a whole week or even a whole guide book."

"But, I'm very resourceful!" she quipped, again wanting to kick herself for all the stupid words spouting out of her mouth.

"Are you?" he asked, his eyes filled with amusement.

"Oh, yes!"

"So, you want the ciggy? I can light it for you."

"No thanks; don't you know that stuff can kill you?"

"Is that so? No, I haven't heard that. The commercials on telly say smoking is good for you. They make it glamorous like."

"Well, they're wrong, you know. They'll find out someday that it causes cancer. And it's also habit-forming and it makes your clothes and breath stink and..."

"Stop...stop...I'm thinking you don't approve of my smoking."

"I didn't say that."

"You did in so many words. You said it makes me smell bad."

She could see his lips quiver as if he was about to laugh out loud. It was hard for her to keep a straight face and she gave a sudden burst of laughter.

"Okay, okay...so I insinuated that it might make you smell bad... and well, have you ever kissed a person that's been smoking? Gross! Ick! And, quite frankly this whole place smells bad because of all the smoke...it's hard to breathe in here and my eyes are burning."

He dropped the unlit cigarette into the ashtray on the table and stubbed his own out.

"There, how's that?" he asked. "Wouldn't want to be kissing any-body with smoke breath."

She blanched, regretting the comment about kissing. What was wrong with her? There was nothing but nonsense coming out of her mouth! She was so nervous, she started playing with the silver chain of her necklace, fingering the silver ballet shoes that hung on it.

She swallowed. "Much better, thank you," she replied, ignoring his comment about smoke breath.

He stared at her intently. From a distance, she'd stood out from the crowd because of her pink dress up against the dark wall of the club. Up close, however, she stood out even more, despite the dim lighting. The dress was totally out of place, of course, but he looked beyond that. She was slender, and looked to have some very nice curves outlined by the form-fitting dress. Her skin was clear and flawless, and tanned by the sun. Her long blonde hair fell down her back almost to her waist; some of it spilled over her shoulders and arms. Her eyes were greenish in color, under thick lashes and nicely arched eyebrows. Her comment about kissing had drawn his eyes to her lips. Hmmm...they looked very kissable.

"Hey James! Time to get back up here and quit flirting with the new bird!" Derek yelled from the stage area.

"See you after the next set?" he asked, arching his eyebrows.

"I suppose so," she replied, her heart pounding so loud in her chest she could almost hear it.

"And may I know your name?"

"Oh, um, sure...it's Susan."

"Would you like to know mine?"

She almost choked. "Of course I would."

"It's James." He winked at her as he walked away, wondering if he'd be able to win a wager in regard to her. Too soon to tell. He'd need to stop by and talk to her some more after the next set.

"What's with guys winking here?" she wondered. She remembered the scruffy guy who tried to buy her an ale when she had first popped onto the bar stool a half hour earlier, then Derek winking at James after they'd looked over at her.

◡◡◠

"Here's the wine, luv!" Sandra said, as she set an empty drinking glass on the table with a dark colored bottle of wine. It was uncorked. "Go on and see whatcha think. Sorry we've no wine glasses here."

Susan poured a small amount from the bottle into the glass. It was a dark burgundy color.

"Red?" she remarked. "Hmmm...I usually only drink white, but I appreciate your getting this for me. Want the beer? It really isn't my kind of stuff."

"Can't drink on the job, luv, but thanks all the same...Hey, are you here on holiday with anyone?"

"No, like I just told James, the band guy, I'm waiting for some friends to arrive before we head off on a, um... history tour. I have a whole week to kill here. I'm planning on being my own tour guide."

"Well, if you want someone to maybe show you around tomorrow, like some shops and stuff, I have tomorrow morning free. It's Saturday, ya know. A lot of people come in from the countryside to shop, so there's a lot open."

"Hey, that's really nice of you. If you don't mind, I think I'll take you up on it. You show me around and I'll treat you to lunch. You name the place, okay?"

"Yeah, that sounds fine. I need to go and get more drinks, but I'll pop by later and we can set up a time to meet...By the way, see those girls on the other side of the room? No! Don't look right at them. Just listen to me...a little warning...they're all mad as hell at your being here...one of them, Hilary...used to be James's girlfriend at one time; at least she thought she was... has had her sights on him for weeks now since she lost some other band guy at another club. She'd planned on being back in James's bed tonight, but he's been paying attention to you instead of her."

"Oh, my God! You must be kidding! Why would she see me as a threat? I didn't ask him to come over to my table! And I most certainly have no intentions of being in his bed!"

"Doesn't matter. You're a real looker, all innocent looking and everything, and she's pretty used-up in appearance if you know what I mean, plus one of her arms is shorter than the other, lost part of it in a roller skating accident. She's probably envious."

"Well, she has nothing to worry about. You can go tell her if you want. And tell all of them I'm only going to be here for a week, so I'm no threat to her or to any of them. Geez!"

Sandra nodded and hustled away as Frank yelled her name.

Ian stepped up to the microphone and said, "Ready for more?"

The girls on the other side of the room screamed "Yes!"

While their attention was on the stage, Susan took a quick glance at them, trying to figure out which one was Hilary, but couldn't see clearly through the thick haze that permeated the room.

"Hilary," she thought to herself. "And with one arm shorter than the other. Was this a coincidence or was there another one-armed whore in James's life from an earlier time?"

She almost choked on her wine at the thought, recalling how James's second marriage in the future had ended in disaster after a woman named Hilary had taken him to the cleaners in a bitter divorce. But, that was still far, far into the future.

"Maybe I should go over and introduce myself."

The wine was making her brave, even though she hadn't drank very much of it yet.

"Potent stuff," she thought. Or, maybe she was still a little tipsy from all the wine she and Lynn had drank on the ship.

Not likely.

She was simply intoxicated at the mere thought of being here and having James talk to her. This was totally crazy. And, he said he was going to come back and talk to her some more after the next set! No wonder she felt half drunk.

Derek started to sing.

"We've known each other for a real long time... I shared a lot of things with you...But when you try and take away the girl that's mine...Well, that's when we're through... Stay away from my baby now...I ain't gonna tell you again... Yeah, I mean just what I say now...Stay away from my baby doll now...You need to listen to me, friend...That baby doll is all mine, so fine...But she's all mine..."

"Holy crap!" she thought. "...Stay away from my baby now? Did that jealous chick over there request that song?!"

She glanced across the room again. All the girls' attention was riveted on the stage, most of them with their eyes on Derek and Ian, but one very obviously staring at James.

"Must be *her*," Susan thought, feeling a miniscule twang of jealousy herself. "In his bed, huh...well, if she's his choice, he must not be very damn picky. Looks like she just climbed out of some gutter."

"God, I'm catty!" she scolded herself. And what was all this about being in someone's bed? This was the early sixties. Wasn't everybody all prim and proper in the sixties? She stole another look around the people in the club. Wow! The couple in the front corner looked like they were making out. What kind of place was this anyway?!

James looked in her direction and smiled. She smiled back and took a sip of wine, not glancing at Hilary to see if she noticed.

Derek continued singing.

"*I don't care if you wear the same shirt as me...Or drive the same kind of car...But you really gotta get something straight...Or it'll turn our friendship to hate... Stay away from my baby now...I ain't gonna tell you again...Yeah, stay away from my baby now...Listen to me, friend...Stay away from my baby now... Or friendship is at an end...Yeah, oh yeah...!*"

Susan tapped her feet on the rungs of her barstool, enjoying the music.

They finished the song and immediately went into another.

"*Ropes...My honey's got me tied up in ropes...And they're not the type so easy to see...Yeah, oh yeah, these ropes of love got a grip on me...Yeah, they do... Ropes, tight ropes...I just can't seem to escape from these ropes...Can't find another girl... to cut me free...Yeah, and oh, these tight ropes of love got such a grip on me, yeah, oh yeah...I should say to you pretty honey I can see you're quite sweet...I wish I could hug and kiss you, but I'm tied up in all of these ropes....*"

Susan poured herself another glass of wine and started to sing along, not noticing that James was looking at her again.

"*My honey's got me tied up in ropes...And they're not the type so easy to see... Yeah, oh yeah, these ropes of love got a hard grip on me, yeah, oh yeah they do...*"

She looked up at him. The song went on. He kept looking at her with an odd little grin on his face. Then he stared directly at her and winked again.

"*Please know that when I say to you...Your lips look so sweet...Just like candy... I wanna hold you and kiss them...But I just can't escape from all of these...ropes...*"

She choked at the words of the song related to lips and kissing, thinking about his smoke breath comment again, but didn't take her gaze away from him. He was still smiling at her.

Her heart was pounding insanely in her chest. She hoped she wasn't going to have a heart attack, but then she remembered she was in her seventeen-year-old body and not in the old lady one. She started playing with her necklace again; it was a nervous habit.

"This is *not* happening...it's not!" she told herself as the song ended. She glanced toward the other side of the room. All the girls were staring at her, some with shy smiles on their faces but some with dagger eyes.

"Oh my," she thought. "I'd hate to meet any of them in a dark alley."

James started into another song. "*Well, I got a honey crazy for me... Yeah, I got a honey won't let me be...Whoa, honey, honey, Arabella...Honey, honey, Arabella...Honey, honey, whoa, whoa, yeah oh yeah...*"

"Quit staring at me!" she wanted to yell at him. Chill bumps were all over her arms and she rubbed them as if she were cold...but she was certainly not cold.

One song followed another; she didn't know most of them as they weren't songs that had ever been recorded by the band, but she was enjoying every moment. Sandra came by every now and then to chat. She told her that most of the girls on the other side of the room thought it was really funny the way James was singling her out. A couple of them were thinking about coming over and saying hello. But, there were two, Hilary and her best friend, Sara, who were as mad as wet hens.

"Ha! Too bad for them..." Sandra said. She also said she told all of them that Susan would only be here for the week, which somewhat mollified the two jealous girls, but when James had so obviously looked at her during the "*Ropes*" song with the "sweet lips" line, Hilary was livid.

Derek was singing. "*Yeah...I'm gonna fall right down and sigh cause of you...I'm gonna fall right down and sigh cause of you...*"

The set ended and Sandra went off to fetch more drinks for the crowd. James took off his guitar and was heading towards Susan's table again, when Hilary approached him, grabbed his arm with one hand, then leaned up and whispered something in his ear.

Susan saw his eyebrows shoot up. He looked down at Hilary, shook his head and said something to her.

Hilary took a step away from him, hand on her hip. She tossed her head back with a smirk on her face, raised her one good arm and pointed at Susan.

Susan couldn't hear what she said to him, but it was very obviously something derogatory about her.

"Whoa boy," she thought.

James said something back to Hilary, then turned his back on her and came over to Susan's table.

"Your girlfriend?" Susan asked.

"Was at one time...wishes she was again," he responded. "Not going to happen..."

"That's sounds rather cold! Especially if she meant something to you before."

"At one time, I thought she was okay, but she's been hanging around being too pushy. Now, she's downright annoying!"

"So, what did she say about me?"

"About you?"

"Yeah, it was obvious! She pointed at me and said something to you."

"Something not very nice," was all he would say.

"Well, I was thinking to myself that I'd hate to meet her and her friends in a dark alley, that's for sure!"

"Don't worry about her. Let's forget her. Can I ask you something?"

"Sure."

"How did you know the words to *"Ropes?"* Have you heard it before?"

"Um, gee, I must have...not sure where. Why do you ask?"

Ian came up to the table then.

"Going to introduce me?" he asked.

"I'm Susan," she said, extending her hand, grateful for the change of subject.

"From America," added James. "California."

"Hallo," said Ian, looking her up and down, and trying to get her measure. He was pretty sure James was going to propose a wager on this little, innocent-looking American. She appeared fairly easy prey, but you could never tell with these foreign girls. And the way she was dressed; she looked like a nursery school marm. Might not be so easy after all...

Derek yelled from the stage area, "You bums get back up here; we've one more set!"

Ian took Susan's hand and shook it before turning and going back to the stage.

James looked at Derek and nodded his head, "Just a sec."

He turned back to Susan. "Just so you don't have to walk down any dark alleys, would you like to go out for a cup of coffee or something when we're done here? Then I could walk you back to your hotel."

How convenient, he mused, her staying in a hotel alone and all.

She hesitated. "Holy crap!" she thought. "What should I do, what should I do?"

"James, come on!" yelled Derek, strumming his guitar.

"Oh...okay...sure...that is, if you really want to...I mean...just for a cup of coffee..."

"When we announce the last song, have Sandra take you back behind the stage upstairs to the practice room. I'll meet you there."

And he was gone, back on the stage, slipping his guitar strap back over his shoulder. He leaned over and said something to Ian and Derek. Derek looked over at Susan, then he and Ian nodded their heads and laughed.

Derek started singing.

"Running to and fro, hard work...Working at the mail...Never fail...Get the mail...Yeah, some rotten deal...For just a meal...Ow! Too much funny business...Too much funny business...Too much funny business for me to work there again"

The club had been getting more and more crowded as the night wore on. People were drinking, laughing and singing along with the band. The girls on the other side of the room were getting boisterous and shouting requests.

"Say me...Talking to me...Tryin' to run me down...All over town...Sayin' she'll pay me again next week...Ow! Too much funny business...Too much funny business...Too much funny business for me to work there again..."

It was almost 1:00 a.m. when Ian finally stepped up to the microphone and said, 'This is our last number," and started singing.

"The sun is moving away...the end of another great day...While the sun light turns to night light...I'll be gone to stay...Kiss me now then I'll go...You'll miss me, that I do know...While the sun light turns to night light...I will go away..."

Sandra was busy picking up glasses when James caught her eye and motioned with his head for her to go over to Susan.

"Hey, so what's that about?" she asked.

"He said you'd take me behind the stage upstairs to the practice room. He's going to walk me back to my hotel so I don't get jumped in the alley by Hilary and Sara."

"Oh, ho!" she exclaimed. "So that's where the wind lies."

"No, no, no...Don't misunderstand. He might have ideas, but I'm not that kind of girl."

"Don't matter what kind of girl you are; if he wants you, he'll have you, you know."

"What in the hell are you talking about? I just met the guy for Christ sake!"

"Well, I've never been tempted his way, but I have to say those eyes are the dreamiest I've ever seen. They pull you in like a magnet...at least they do most girls. They say he's a real heart-breaker, you know, but once he decides he wants a girl, he always has her. Just crooks his finger, and down she goes."

"Down?"

"Yeah, on her back, ya know."

Susan gulped. "Well, he won't be breaking my heart or 'having' me! He's just taking me to coffee and walking me back to my hotel."

"Oh, so it's coffee too, is it? Well, just be on your guard, that's all I'm sayin', luv. What time should we meet tomorrow and where?"

"How about my hotel...you know the one down the street, the Claridon."

"Ooooo, the fanciest one in town, I'd say! Sure, and what time?"

"Well, since it's so late, how about 10:00 or is that still too early?"

"No, that'll be just fine. In the lobby then?"

"Yeah, sounds good."

The song was coming to an end.

"I'll feel the wind blow...Then watch the river flow...'fore I go away...Oh, yeah, I will go away...Perhaps there I will stay...But, I'm going anyway..."

The girls on the other side of the room were screaming now for more songs as Sandra led Susan up some stairs, out the front door, down an alley and into the room behind and above the stage area. The club itself was at basement level.

"Don't do anything I wouldn't do," she said with a quirky grin on her face and winked.

"What in the hell is it with all the winking?" Susan thought to herself again.

"See you tomorrow, Sandra," she said.

Sandra was a little worried as she walked away. Should she have warned her about how the boys make wagers? It was clear as day they'd made one on Susan for tonight. But, this American girl seemed like she had a good head on her shoulders. She figured she'd find out tomorrow if James had his way with her.

Chapter 4

The Wager

James was the first to come up from the stage into the practice room above, taking his guitar off as he entered the room. He picked up a towel that was lying on a chair and wiped the sweat off his face.

Susan was standing by the door leading in from the alley, her purse strap over one shoulder, the purse itself clutched tightly in both hands. She was trembling and hoped he wouldn't notice. She could barely fathom how she had got here. Everything had happened so fast. She'd expected to maybe watch him sing to a crowd of screaming girls, watch from afar, and just drink in the sight of him. But now, to be in a room alone with him, standing just a few feet away... It was overwhelming.

He threw the towel back onto the chair and glanced over at her as he shrugged off his leather jacket, pulled the black t-shirt up and over his head then reached for a dingy white, long-sleeved shirt that was hanging on a hook on the wall.

She looked like a frightened sparrow ready to take flight. Standing in her dress in the light of the practice room, she looked even lovelier than she had sitting at the table in the dim lights of the club. The pink dress fit tightly over nicely rounded breasts and was cinched in to show a trim waist. The skirt flared out at the hips and dropped down to a point just below her knees. Unlike the girls in the club, who were decked out in leather skirts halfway up their thighs, with loose-fitting blouses opened to reveal as much of their breasts as possible, this girl was a breath of fresh air. He had to stop himself from wondering what was hidden under the pretty dress.

Her eyes grew as big as saucers as he bared his chest and she inhaled a large quantity of air, holding it in her lungs before slowly exhaling as she watched him reach for the dingy white shirt. Holy crap! She thought she might faint. He was so overwhelmingly attractive. All she had dreamed of and fantasized him to be, only more. She felt as if a thousand butterflies had been let loose in her stomach and were beating their wings frantically trying to get out. She sensed her seventeen-year-old hormones begin to awaken and wondered what role they were going to play in her being here. It was a worrisome thought after what Sandra had told her about James always having his way with girls. Yikes!

"Ian and Derek are still down out front with the girls," he said, buttoning up the shirt then doing the buttons on each cuff.

"Is that where you're supposed to be?" she asked breathlessly, mesmerized by the sight of his hands and nimble fingers.

"No, I'm supposed to be here getting ready for our date," he responded looking up at her while he tucked his shirt into his leather pants.

"Our date?"

"Yeah, we can call it a date, you know."

She gathered herself together, thinking it was awfully presumptuous of him to assume he was taking her on an actual date.

"Hmmmm..." she said, letting her purse fall back to her side and folding her arms in front of her. "Just a short date for a cup of coffee is all."

He smiled at her, "Of course..."

A few minutes later, he had his gear packed and locked up in a chest that was bolted to the floor and wall.

"Keeping my stuff here for practice tomorrow. Phil, the owner, has a flat upstairs, so it's all safe and everything. Ready to go?"

"Sure."

He motioned her out the back door and down the side alley. Just as they were coming out of the alley, three of the girls who had been on other side of the room in the club, came out the front door of the Dusky and glanced in their direction.

"Well, well," Susan heard one of them say.

"Let's go," said James, as he grabbed her hand and pulled her down the street away from the club.

She adjusted the shoulder strap of her purse as it started to slide off her shoulder. His hand was warm and held hers tightly. She felt weak in the knees just thinking about it, hoping she wouldn't trip and fall flat on her face.

"Where are we going?" she asked.

"Away from here," he said as they swiftly turned a corner.

He looked behind them. No one was following.

"Do you always have to look over your shoulder like that?" she asked.

"Most nights," he said. "Some of the girls like to follow us and offer us, well, um...they follow us."

"I see," was all she could think to say.

A few blocks later, they came to an all-night coffee and tea shop.

"It's open all night for the sailors coming in on ships. Most of them go hang out at the pubs closer to the docks, but this is where they come if they just want a good cup of tea and some quiet. Brighton is a busy shipping port, you know."

When she didn't answer right away, he said, "Well of course you know, being a history buff and all."

'Yes, of course," she responded. Yikes! She hoped he didn't know a whole lot about history or that he wasn't going to ask her any questions about it. As they sat down, she started to feel nervous again and started playing with the silver ballet shoes on her necklace.

"And what's that?" he asked.

"What's what?"

"What's on the end of your necklace?"

"Oh! It's ballet shoes," she said, holding it out to show him. "They're pointe shoes, you know, toe shoes."

"So, are you a ballerina then?"

"Not really; I just take classes and teach sometimes, and I'm in a recital now and then. I always wanted to be a real ballerina, but I don't have the right physical attributes."

"Which means?"

"I'm not flat enough in the front." For what seemed like the millionth time, she wished she could unsay the words. She blushed.

"Oh," was his only response, not wanting to ask anything more when he saw her face tinge pink.

They spent the next hour talking over their coffee, Susan sharing stories and information about America and James telling her a bit about his life. Susan told him about losing her father at a young age and James talked about losing his mother when he was fifteen. She could tell it had affected him deeply. He sat staring into his coffee cup for a full minute before looking back up at her.

"I don't really talk about it much...when you told me about your father, it made me think about her...I still miss her," he said.

"I'm sure you do," she said reaching out instinctively to put her hand on his. She could sense his pain at the memory.

"Did your dad ever re-marry?" she asked.

"No desire to," he responded. "But, he's okay now. He loves music as much as I do. He taught me most of what I know. He's a good bloke."

She looked at her watch. "Hey, it's after 2:30! I need to meet Sandra at ten. She's going to take me shopping, and then I'm going to take her to lunch."

"You're going with Sandra tomorrow? I was thinking I could show you the sights," he said, sounding disappointed at her plans. Then he smiled to himself as he thought it was unlikely she'd be meeting Sandra anyway after spending the night with him. He was going to walk her to her hotel after all, and then…

"Well, she asked me, and I said I'd go. She seems like a really nice girl. I like her a lot."

"How about the afternoon? Would you like to come and hear us practice? Mindy comes to all the practices."

"Oh, you mean Derek's wife?" she blurted out before she could catch herself. She knew Derek would end up marrying a girl named Mindy.

He looked a little startled. "Well, no; she's not Derek's wife...yet that is. But he's pretty taken with her, you know."

"Oh, well, I was just guessing, I suppose. What time is your practice?"

"3:00. Then we take a break for dinner and come back to the club at 11:00 when we start our first set."

"Wow! That's really late to start!"

"That's because two other bands are on before us. We like being the last band because we can play as many sets as we want and as late as we want. The other bands only get an hour each."

"So...okay, maybe I'll come to your practice. I'll see how the day goes. How do I get back to my hotel from here? You took a lot of turns; I'm kinda lost."

He pushed some money onto the table and stood up. "Allow me to escort you, m'lady," he said, making a small bow.

"Thank you, kind sir," she responded, smiling shyly and giving a little curtsy.

She linked her arm in his, and they left the coffee shop.

Her hotel, as it turned out, was almost eight blocks away, a good ten minute walk. It was a tall building, almost the tallest in town, at ten stories. Built in the early 20's, it had an old-fashioned elegance and charm. They went into the lobby, stepping onto plush carpet, and Susan turned to go to the elevator, stopping for a moment to tell him good night.

"So, I might see you tomorrow then," she said.

"Oh, I'll just walk you up to your room, if that's okay," he said, starting towards the elevator.

"Actually, I can find my way to my room just fine, but thanks for asking," she said, stopping in the middle of the lobby next to some sofas and chairs.

"Are you sure?"

"It's very gallant of you to ask, Sir James, but a lady never allows a gentleman to escort her to her bedroom...and you *are* a gentleman, aren't you?"

She smiled up into his face.

"Sometimes," he responded, his eyes roving over her.

She shivered. "Well, I appreciate your being a true gentleman tonight then. It was very nice to meet you...and thank you for the coffee...I enjoyed talking to you."

"And I to you. Promise me you'll come to the practice tomorrow. Mindy will be there and you can get to know her. She's a great girl."

"I don't really know if I should. If all those girls were to find out..."

"Quit worrying about the other girls. I'm a gentleman; I can protect you, you know."

His eyes were laughing.

She couldn't help but laugh herself.

"Okay, okay...so I guess I'll come to your practice then. Will you sing a song to me?"

"But of course, m'lady. I'll sing something special for you. Can I kiss you goodnight?'

She looked up into his mesmerizing eyes and thought of everything Sandra had said about him. Oh, the temptation! A girl could drown in those eyes...She was torn between saying "yes" and "no, not yet." She'd only been here a few hours, and yet here she was in the lobby of a hotel with him wanting to come up to her room, and now wanting a kiss. She thought for a minute as he continued to look at her questioningly with his perfectly arched eyebrows raised.

"You may kiss my hand," she said impulsively, lifting it up towards his face.

"Are you teasing me?" he asked, the laughter still in his eyes along with something else that wasn't all that hard to recognize.

It was almost as if she could read his mind. Arrogant guy! He was thinking that it wouldn't take a whole lot to get her to take him up to her room and "surrender all." But, for some reason he wasn't pressuring her. She didn't know why, but she was very grateful for it. You don't hop in bed with somebody you only knew a few hours. At least she wouldn't contemplate such a thing. The thought made her knees feel weak again. Sounded like the girls at the club did it every night. Yikes!

It felt like a stomach punch as he took her hand in both of his and brought it up to his face. His lips lingered over the top of her hand, then kissed the knuckles on each one of her fingers. Very slowly, he turned her hand palm up, kissing each finger again, then softly pressed his lips on her palm as he looked up into her eyes. His lips moved up to kiss the inside of her wrist, while at the same time, he trailed the fingers of his other hand up the inside of her arm to the crook of her elbow. Her legs felt like they were made of jelly and were going to cave under her. Her breath caught and her lips parted in a small gasp. She turned her head away. Her unruly, young hormones were beginning to awaken.

Sensations were shooting through her from the tips of her fingers down to her toes, and she knew when she met his eyes again that he was aware of her response to him.

He gave a triumphant smile and said softly, "I'll just be walking you up to your room then." He started to pull her towards the elevator.

She let out a big exhale and stopped, planting her feet on the carpet. "No...oh, no thank you...that's quite all right..." She was trembling, and she knew he could see and feel it.

He stood staring at her, waiting for her to change her mind, but when no words were forthcoming, he said, "Until tomorrow then, m'lady." He looked disappointed and even slightly annoyed.

"Certainly, sir," she whispered as he released her hand and turned to walk away.

She was still looking at him as he got to the lobby door. He turned and gave another small bow before going out the door.

"I think I'm going to faint," she said to herself as she pushed the elevator button and grasped her necklace, twisting the chain back and forth between her trembling fingers.

Sandra was ten minutes late for their shopping expedition, saying she'd had to drop her mum off at the hair dressers for a tint.

"No worries," Susan said.

Sandra thought that a rather odd expression but ignored it, blurting out, "So...tell me about last night, love. I've been dying these hours to know what happened." She looked Susan over for some change in her attitude, but didn't see anything different about her. Today she was wearing another one of those "go to church" dresses, this time a pale blue one, with her hair tied in a ponytail that went down her back.

"Why such an intense interest?" asked Susan.

"Well, love, the odds were against you, you know, him being so experienced and all that, and you seeming so innocent and all."

"What are you talking about? What odds? You're just speaking figuratively, right?"

"Well, whatever that means, I'm sure I don't know," Sandra giggled. "No, you don't know, of course. The boys always make a wager when there's a new bird for James or Ian or Blue to...hmmm...how do I put this delicately...to, um...seduce...you know what I'm getting at?"

"A wager?!" Susan exclaimed. "Like a bet!? You've got to be kidding me! Who would bet on something like that? That's downright tacky!"

"Might be and that's for sure, but it doesn't mean they don't do it."

"What kind of wager do they make? What do they bet?"

"Well, things like who pays for dinner after a practice or who buys a round of ale for the band during a break between sets, that sort of thing."

"I see," murmured Susan, a strange expression coming over her face. If Lynn had been there, she would have seen the warning signs of some very unpleasant thoughts in regard to her future meeting with Sir James and the "boys."

"So, how long have they been doing this kind of thing?" asked Susan, sounding nonchalant, but secretly fuming inside.

"Pretty much since they started singing at the club, a few months ago, I'd say. The girls bet too, ya know."

"So you think people were betting about me?"

"Sure. We English love to wager, you know. I actually saw James, Ian and Derek whispering to each other and looking at you after James went over and talked to you the second time. Pretty sure they were making a wager."

"And what do you think the wager was exactly?"

Susan was becoming more incensed by the moment.

"As I said before, and warned you about last night, it most likely was whether James would get you into bed last night. He has no trouble at all getting girls into his bed after knowing them for just a few hours. And then, here you are staying in a hotel all by yourself and all."

"Well, he didn't! He didn't even come close!" Susan exclaimed, thinking about his kissing and just about gobbling up her hand.

"Really and truly? Did he at least kiss you?" Sandra asked.

Susan was about to lie and say "no," but said instead, "I gave him permission to kiss my hand is all."

"You what?!!!"

"I said I gave him permission to kiss my hand, so he kissed my hand. I thanked him for being a gentleman and shooed him off home."

"Whoa, ho! That's a funny one! Just wait 'til the boys find out about that! He'll be a laughing stock and that's for sure!" She bent over chuckling.

"Well, I'm sure not telling anyone, and you shouldn't either!"

"I'm not promising. I hope you don't mind. It serves him right, always being so cocky and sure of himself...So, why did you only let him kiss your hand? Just about all the girls think he's irresistible; they'd all die to have been in your shoes last night... Say... You're not prudish or a virgin or studying to be a nun or something are you? Or, or...You're not a girl who likes other girls better than guys?"

Susan's eyes opened wide. "Holy crap! No! I don't like girls better than guys! Geez! And I'm certainly not studying to be a nun!" she exclaimed. "And, no, I'm not a prude...and...and... I don't think I'm a virgin...I mean I'm not sure...I mean, I need to think..." She started to mumble. "I'm seventeen and it's June now and my birthday was in January, so I think I might be...but...geez! I never thought about that aspect!"

Sandra was looking at her like Susan had lost her senses. "How would you not know if you're a virgin? Have you done it or not?"

"Done what?"

"*It!* You know, the tumble in the sheets."

"What an expression! Well, no, I guess I haven't if you want me to be specific."

"Holy Jesu! If anyone knew that, the cost of the wager would be ten times higher!"

"Sandra! Please, please don't say anything about me being a virgin for Christ sake! This is downright embarrassing! But...I'm totally pissed about being part of a wager. That's just a low-down, dirty thing to do... to bet on getting a girl into...into...tumbling in the sheets, as you say. I could choke him for being part of something so, so...dastardly!"

"Well, that's a big word!"

"Yeah, well, it means worse than horrible...which is what this is... hmmmm...so he thinks he can tumble me with just a nod of his head or one of those 'looks' from his big bedroom eyes, does he...well, he'll find out how mistaken he is! I suppose if he lost last night's bet, there'll be another one on for tonight?"

"Of course there will be! Double the odds and all. And, if they find out you're a virgin, oh blimey, I can't even imagine what they'll wager!"

"You are NOT telling anyone that...promise!"

"Okay, I promise not to tell anyone you're as pure as the driven snow, but I won't promise not to say anything about the hand kissing. That's just too good to pass up, plus it's about time Mr. thinks-he-can-get-any-girl-he-wants, gets his just desserts, if you know what I mean."

Susan sighed. "Well, I wish you wouldn't, but on the other hand, it would be pretty funny to overhear what they all say when they find out. I'm supposed to go to the band practice this afternoon, you know. He made me promise I'd go. And you're right; it would serve him a good one if everyone knew he didn't get to first base with me, as the saying goes. And furthermore, if they find out that I just gave him permission to kiss my hand and it embarrasses him, that's just what he deserves!" She'd worked herself up to a feeling of indignant outrage again, thinking about being part of a bet.

"Well, now you know why he invited you to band practice," said Sandra. "Needs more opportunity to try and have his way with you...ha, ha...I'm a funny one, ain't I?"

"Yeah, you're a real bag of laughs."

"So are you going to the practice then?"

"But of course! Now that you told me all this, I wouldn't miss it for anything!"

"You have an evil look in your eye, I see."

"Really? Am I so transparent then? I'm actually just thinking."

"Plotting revenge, you mean?"

"Well, let's not put it that harshly, but, yes, I most certainly am. Wagering on a girl's virtue...despicable!"

Sandra led Susan out the lobby door and down the street.

"Most of the interesting shops are down by the waterfront. Parts of the waterfront are quite seedy, but where the cruising ships come in...we don't get many...there are some decent shops. Let's go; it's only about a kilometer if you're up for walking."

"I'm up for walking. I actually need to burn off some steam."

"What's that, luv?"

"Oh, nothing."

Susan and Sandra enjoyed a few hours walking through the shops, which sold everything from trinkets to high-end clothing and even furniture.

"Interesting place," remarked Susan. "Hey, I'm getting hungry; I didn't have any breakfast. Where do you think we should go for lunch?"

"Well, I actually thought of a place last night. It's down on the wharf. They have great sandwiches, and of course they have fish and chips, their specialty. But, if you're going to the band practice this afternoon, they'll probably send Mindy out to pick up fish and chips for dinner after the practice. James is gonna have to pay, ha, ha..."

"Did you really have to remind me of that wager business?" asked Susan.

"Oh, sorry, luv. Didn't mean to mention it again."

"Hmmmmm," was all Susan responded.

Lunch was so-so. Susan knew that England wasn't known for its culinary skills, so she expected bland food and she got bland food. It was filling enough, however, and she enjoyed Sandra's company. Sandra told her about her family, how she got the job at the Dusky and how she had a boyfriend from one of the other bands but was currently mad at him for making eyes at a girl she called "one of the groupie sluts" who hung around the club every night, hoping to sleep with one of the band members.

"Wow! And I thought everyone in England would be so prim and proper! You'd think this was the 90's or something!"

"What's that, love?" asked Sandra.

"Oh nothing," Susan replied, realizing she needed to guard her tongue better.

It was close to 2:30 when Susan got back to her hotel. She went upstairs to try and find something in her suitcase not too stupid looking to wear, and Sandra went off to the Dusky to make sure all the tables, glasses, etc., were in order for the night. Her off and on boyfriend was practicing before the boys and she was thinking of making up with him.

Susan knew Sandra would also likely spread the news about the hand kissing and cringed. She shouldn't have said anything. James would probably be livid as well as embarrassed. Maybe he'd kick her out of the practice, figuring the silly-ass American girl was a tease and just as annoying in a different way from Hilary. But she was still very offended about the wagering, and thought that he deserved a good set down.

"Well, I guess I'll find out," she thought to herself. "It'll just be an amazing experience to hear them practice...Oh, I wish Lynn was here to share this with me. I wonder if Ian would be after her like James seems to be after me...oh come on...calm down...he's not after you as a person...just to win a dumb bet...how humiliating is that?!"

She started to feel her temper rise again at the thought and raised her chin as she looked at herself in the mirror. Holy crap! She did look pretty damn good at seventeen! Long hair, nice eyes, a flawless complexion, thank god, no zits.... A small waist, but good size boobs.

Before she slipped her dress on, she looked at the tag in her bra. 32D...nice! She slipped a white dress she'd discovered in her suitcase over her head and twirled in front of the mirror. She'd decided to put the white "churchy" dress on to purposely look as peachy fresh and innocent as possible. Dare she say even "virginal?" She giggled.

The dress came to just below her knees. There was no visible cleavage, but sometimes keeping things like that hidden did more to draw a guy's imagination to what was underneath. And, a man's imagination was a powerful weapon, so she may as well use it.

Geez! Did women really used to wear these dresses? It seemed so long ago that it was hard to remember. She'd probably worn a dress like this herself at one time, long, long ago, like maybe in sixth grade. She laughed. In 1962 in real time, she was close to being in sixth grade.

She brushed out her hair, and as a last touch, she pinched her cheeks to brighten them up a little then smeared on some lip gloss, looking at the lipstick tube. Yardley Slicker? Wow! She always loved Yardley.

"Oh my god, do I have any *Oh de London*?" she wondered, digging through her purse for her favorite old perfume that had been discontinued in the mid 60's. It smelled so good, like a field of flowers.

Yes!

She liberally sprayed it on, even putting some in her hair, which she left hanging loose, swirling around her shoulders and down her back.

"We'll see how Sir James responds to this, won't we?" she said out loud as she winked at herself in the mirror before picking up her purse and locking the door behind her.

Susan walked into the Dusky just as Sandra was leaving.

"So, how'd it go with the boyfriend?" Susan asked.

"Not so bad," responded Sandra. Todd was jealous of Frank, which was pretty stupid on his part, so he thought he'd make *me* jealous. We'll work it out. How he even thought I'd look twice at the bartender beats me. ...So, I see you decided to come to the practice. I think Mindy's waiting by the back door to let you in. I'd walk you to the door, but I think you know where it is. None of the girls hiding in the alley this time of day."

She seemed anxious to be off. Susan wondered what story she'd told about the hand kissing event or if she kept her promise about the virgin thing. She felt heat flood her face at the thought of Sandra telling anybody about that!

Susan exited the club up the stairs and out the front door then went down the alley to the back door leading into the practice room. She knocked on the door. Seconds later it was opened by a pretty blond girl, who told her to come on in.

"Susan's here!" the blonde yelled.

The boys were in a corner of the room in what appeared to be a heated conversation, not quite an argument, but it sounded about to

49

escalate into one. At the sound of the blonde's voice, they all turned around, James glaring at Susan through what she thought were cold and angry eyes. They were burning into hers accusingly. It was obvious someone had told about the hand kissing and his failure to get into her bed the previous night.

"How dare him!" she thought. "*He's* the jerk who was crass enough to make a wager!" She was incensed at the thought.

James turned and said something to Derek. The blonde held her hand out to Susan, trying to draw her attention away from the boys.

"I'm Mindy," she said. "I'm glad you decided to come. Derek didn't think you'd show up..."

"Wouldn't show up?" Susan interrupted. "Why would that be?"

"Well...um...after last night and all..."

"What about last night and all?"

"Well...um..."

Derek stepped up to the microphone. "Testing, one, two...testing, one, two...Let's go boys...Hey, Min...here's one of our new ones; James wants to start with this one today for the new bird. I don't think it's a good idea but..."

Mindy and Susan raised their eyebrows. And the boys all broke into the song.

"*Oh my...oh yeah...oh my...oh yeah...Pretend that I am holding you...it's simple cause I know...I've pretended I was holding you so very, very, many times before...It's not really to pretend...but I'll have you, I'll have you in the end...yes, I will, I'll have you in end...oh my, oh yeah...*"

James was glaring fixedly at Susan as they sang, with a wicked gleam in his eye. He looked at her, she thought, as if he were a bird of prey, and she was ready to be caught and netted. She thought about what Sandra had said about him always having his way with girls... either sooner or later.

She, of course, knew the words to the song, and was livid. He thought he was going to "have her," did he? Well, he was much mistaken! The arrogant asshole! Who in the hell did he think he was anyway?!

"That's enough, damn it all!" she yelled as loud as she could over the music. "I'm outa here right now! ...How dare you...how dare you!"

she screamed over the guitars, staring James down. Her eyes were blazing and she was shaking with rage.

The music came to a sudden halt.

"Why whatever can you mean?" James said so softly that she had to strain her ears to hear him. He was looking down at his guitar and playing with the adjustments to the strings.

"You know damn well what I mean, you low-life, arrogant, jackass!" she yelled back before she could stop the words from coming out of her mouth. She was visibly trembling now.

The rest of the boys and Mindy were looking at her. They all turned their heads back to James, waiting for his response.

"I think we can go outside and discuss this," he said, taking off his guitar.

All heads turned back towards Susan.

"Oh no, we won't!" Susan said, standing her ground. "Everyone here can listen to what I have to say! Admit that you made a bet as to whether you'd get in my pants last night, you good for nothing who thinks he's so damn wonderful...Go ahead and admit it!"

She was in a fit of rage now.

James flung back, "So miss hoity-toity, cold-as-ice...what makes you think you're so abused to the whole world after making fun of me for kissing your hand and leaving me standing in the lobby of your hotel? Eh? What do *you* have to say to that? Thought it was pretty funny, didn't you? Trying to make a fool of me by spreading the word around and all!"

She tossed her head and her hair went flying off behind her shoulders. "I was totally pissed off when I heard about your stupid wager," she responded. "I believed you really were a gentleman, but gentlemen don't make wagers on a girl's virtue. I only told Sandra...And, I never made fun of you...so there! You...you conceited, worthless piece of shit!"

There was dead silence in the room. Mindy gasped and put her hand over her mouth.

Susan held her chin up and tossed her head again. "You owe me an apology," she said. "In fact, all you guys owe me an apology. She looked around the room. Betting on something like that isn't...nice!"

She could see Derek was trying as hard as he could not to laugh. James a "gentleman!" Where in the hell did this bird come from anyway? Nobody talked like that! But at the same time, he mused, she swore like one of the sailors down at the docks. Where had "little miss prissy" picked that up from?

"Sorry," mumbled Ian, turning around to fumble with his guitar strings.

"Sorry, luv," said Derek, still smirking and looking over at Mindy as if to say, "This is quite amusing."

"Fine! I'm sorry then...so, *so* sorry," said James sarcastically, looking away from her.

She glared at him. "Say it like you mean it or I'm leaving right now. You obviously don't want Miss cold-as-ice here anyway!"

She spun around on her heel and started to walk toward the door leading to the alley, then turned her head back and added, "So, what was I supposed to be, some kind of trophy you could say you'd won? Something you could add to your collection of cheap conquests? Do you carve notches on a wall somewhere to keep track? ...How *could* you...!!" Tears welled in her eyes and her voice was quavering. She moved towards the door again, wiping a hand across her eyes before any of the tears had a chance to roll down her face. She grasped her necklace and twisted the chain back and forth between shaking fingers. She was thinking that maybe this trip into the past had been a mistake.

He looked around at her, stung by her words and the forlorn look on her face. "Wait! ...Let's go outside for a minute so we can talk..."

Before she could respond, he'd moved in front of her and grabbed her by the arm then pushed her toward the door. He opened it and pulled her out into the alley.

As they left, Derek looked over at Mindy. "Mark my words, Min, that bird is trouble with a capital T."

Mindy thought he might be right. She'd seen James angry before, but never so quietly incensed. It was unusual for him to get so upset over a girl, especially since he could pick and choose amongst so many willing ones every night. His reaction to this American bird was interesting, to say the least.

Out in the alley, James backed Susan against the wall of the building. Her purse strap slipped off her shoulder. James put his hands on either side of her head and planted them on the wall. His face was inches from hers. The wall was cold against her back. For a full minute, he didn't say anything. They just glared into each other's eyes, trying to read what the other was thinking and trying to gain control over their emotions. Then James relaxed. Susan bit her lower lip and broke the eye contact. A stray tear rolled down her cheek.

James spoke softly, tilting her chin up with a finger of his hand, turning her face back toward his and looking into her eyes. He wiped the tear off her cheek with his thumb. Seeing her eyes tear up before they left the practice room and seeing one roll down her cheek made him come all undone. He hadn't meant to make her cry.

"You want me to say I'm sorry?" he said quietly. "Okay then...I'm sorry...I really *am* sorry...I shouldn't have agreed to the wager..."

He pushed off the wall and turned his back to her. She could sense the turmoil of his thoughts and his struggle to admit to any fault. Stubborn and proud were written all over him.

"I didn't know...I didn't know you were any different than the rest...I didn't know until we were at coffee...and you told me about your dad... and you listened to me when I talked about my mum...and you seemed to understand...to care...it was too late then...the bet had already been made."

"You didn't have to try and follow through to win it, you know!"

He turned around and looked at her full on.

"Maybe not...but when you played into the sir and lady thing, I thought maybe you were teasing me...you know...inviting me...flirting with me...And it didn't take much to get you to go out with me...And then in the lobby of your hotel, I could tell it would only have taken a bit more persuasion...It was obvious the way you responded to my kiss, even if it only was your hand."

"Of all the arrogant assumptions...!"

"Wait...stop...don't say any more. I told you I was sorry...I meant it...I truly am...can we call a truce, please?"

He looked deeply into her eyes. She bit her lip again, trying not to drown in the depths of his amber gaze. His eyes were hypnotic. Was this all a game? She'd only met him yesterday! Was he really sorry, or was he just a practiced flirt and heartbreaker as she'd been warned?

What the hell...why fight it...? Why not let the whole thing drop? She'd come here to be with him anyway, didn't she? And, here he was live, in person and up very close. Maybe too close for comfort even.

What exactly had she envisioned by coming here? What had she expected after meeting him? Holding hands and walks along a beach somewhere? For a whole week? Even though he was young, he was a man of the world. He'd been to Germany. He played in a band at clubs. Girls were falling all over him. And, based on the hand kissing and his wanting to come up to her hotel room last night, he was obviously virile and experienced in the bedroom. She swallowed. She was still in shock over him singling her out and talking to her at all!

"Well, okay...and maybe I shouldn't have told Sandra about the hand kissing...I didn't really think she was going to spill the beans on me with that..." She paused. "Well, actually, I *was* hoping she would spill the beans. I was very angry."

"Truce then?"

"Yeah, truce."

"So, can I ask you a question then?"

"And what's that?"

"Are you really a virgin?"

She stepped back, hands on her hips, her mouth forming a big "O," stunned that he would ask such a thing after he'd just made profuse apologies to her. Damn that Sandra anyway! What should she say? Holy crap! Her face tinged pink, but was quickly darkening to a bright red, thinking that this body she was in really was virginal.

"That's for me to know!" she responded.

"And for me to find out?" he quipped with a devilish twinkle in his eye.

She couldn't help it; she started to laugh.

"You're simply incorrigible!" she said. "Let's go back into your practice, but no more 'I'll have you,' okay?"

"Well, okay..."

He winked, took her hand and they went back in.

The boys all had their guitars on and were ready to start. They all looked away when James and Susan came back in. Mindy grabbed Susan's arm and said, "What was that all about?"

"Nothing. We called a truce," Susan replied.

Derek stepped back up to the microphone and started singing.

"Put down your arms and give it all to me (Tra la, la)...Put down your arms...you'll surrender, you'll see... (Tra la, la) yeah (Tra la la)...Use your lips for kissin' me...Sweetheart, that's just how it's gotta be (Ooh)..."

Susan shot James a look as if to say, "What the hell is all this 'surrender' stuff about?" He just smiled, shrugged his shoulders and shook his head as if to say, "Not my choice of a song."

"Hmphhh," she said to herself.

"So did you go to bed with him or not?" Mindy asked. "I don't really believe that hand kissing stuff."

"No, no and another *no!*" Susan exclaimed. "Is that all anybody thinks about? Don't people have platonic relationships around here?"

"And what would that mean exactly?"

"You know, just be friends...or just start out getting to know each other...talk, maybe hold hands, that kind of thing."

Mindy rolled her eyes. "Well, maybe in some circles, but not here, that's for sure. Derek and I were in the sheets a few hours after I met him. No shame in it...it's just the way it is...a really good way to get to know a bloke, you know...Most of the girls that come to the club come here looking for a tumble in the sheets with a nice bloke...Gotta take the opportunity when it's there or you can miss out, you know."

Susan stared back at her in bewildered disbelief. Derek kept singing.

"Don't look at me like that, "Mindy said. "We all have our weaknesses, you know. Derek just happens to be mine."

"And you'll end up marrying him someday," said Susan before she could stop the thought from coming out of her mouth.

Now Mindy raised her eyebrows. "And how exactly do you know that?"

"Because I have intuition, that's all. I can tell the way he looks at you."

"Really...and how does he look at me?"

"With love...and some lust thrown in, of course."

"Lust is the fun part. You should try it sometime. I didn't really hear what happened last night between you and James, but he was mad as a hornet's nest when he came in and all the boys were teasing him about just kissing your hand and nothing else. I think it was Sandra who told Derek out in the club. That's why Derek thought you might not show up. I didn't believe it. I've never known any girl to refuse James."

At first, Susan looked like she was going to go off into a tirade again about how "not nice" it was to make bets on a girl's virtue, but then she visibly relaxed.

"Oh...umm, yeah, well, let's just forget it for now, can we? Tell me something about yourself."

Susan and Mindy floated into friendly conversation and the practice wore on.

"*Shanna...You came and told me, girl...To let you be free, girl...You think he loves you better than me...So I might just let you go free...Run off with him... Run off with him,...*"Shanna...*Oh sweet, before you leave me now...I need you to know right now...That I adore you so...But should he adore you more...Run off with him...*"

Susan started to sing along, "*For my whole life...I've been waiting to find a girl...To want me as much as I want you...Oh, no, but when I find a girl that makes me glad...She steps on my heart and makes me sad...So, what am I, girl, what am I likely to do...oh, now, oh now, oh how...*"

Mindy was staring at her curiously. "How do you know the words to that song?" she asked.

Susan was startled out of singing.

"Oh...um...James was telling me about it last night...he sang some of it...I think...um...it's a really good song, isn't it? Who's Shanna, by the way?"

"Nobody I know," replied Mindy. "Just odd that you would know the words so good."

"Well, I guess I'm just an odd sort of person then," said Susan trying to change the subject. "So, how long does the practice session last? What happens after that?"

"Until about 5:00 or so. Then I'll go out and pick up fish and chips for everybody...tonight it's on James...then we'll sit around and talk some more, the other bands will come in and we'll listen to them before the boys go on. Sometimes Derek and me will slip off for some private time..."

"Hey, James's motioning to you," said Mindy.

Susan turned and looked at him.

"For you," he said, and the boys started to sing again.

"A taste of sugar...Tasting a lot sweeter than grapes..."

Oh my! She knew the words to the song, but dared not make it obvious. Instead, she just smiled. James sang in his clear voice.

"I think of our first kiss...And now...I can taste you on my lips once more... A taste of sugar...Tasting a lot sweeter than grapes."

She extended her arm and hand towards him then turned her palm upwards. He grinned back at her, sharing the private joke that no one else seemed to notice.

"I will come back, yes, you know I will come back...I'll come back for the taste of your cherry-red lips and you..."

It was slightly after 5:00 when practice was close to getting over. Derek gestured to Mindy and asked her to run out for the fish and chips. James said nothing as he reached in his pocket and handed over some money. Derek passed it on to Mindy, who headed toward the door motioning for Susan to go with her.

Derek elbowed James. "Eh, are we on for the same bet for Tuesday supper then? Triple the odds due to her being a virgin, so it'll be supper and two rounds of ale."

"For tonight?" asked Ian. "You think he can pull it off tonight then?"

"I'm having no part of this," interjected James. "You make your own wagers, but keep me out of it."

He turned on his heel and walked away.

"Losing your touch?" Derek said teasingly after him. Both Derek and Ian laughed.

Mindy and Susan were shortly back with a large sack of fish, chips, malt vinegar and lots of American ketchup. The boys loved ketchup.

Mindy said Derek put it on just about everything. They all sat cross-legged on the floor, except for Susan, who had her legs to the side due to wearing a dress, with the feast in the middle. Mindy, who was wearing pair of jeans, sat next to Derek, and James nodded his head at Susan to come sit next to him. She felt as if she were in heaven.

They ate and talked, asking Susan questions about America, while she asked them questions about Brighton and England. She tried to slant her questions towards history to fit her story of being a history student, but the topic didn't get much response, so she gave it up in favor of more interesting subjects like music, the all-consuming passion of the boys.

"So, whatca think of us and our music?" asked Ian. "How does it compare to America? Do you think we're as good as Elvis?"

"Far better," she responded. "You're going to be famous someday, you know."

"And how would you know that?" he asked.

"As I told Mindy earlier, I have intuition. The only thing is...you've got to lose that greasy-hair, scruffy look. You all look like you haven't washed your hair in a month."

"Wait just a minute! We cultivate this look, you know!" exclaimed Ian. "It's the Elvis look with the hair and all. We put stuff in it to make it look this way!"

"You sound like Jimmie, now, always tellin' us we need to clean ourselves up a bit...look presentable and all," said Derek.

"Well, no offense or anything, but to me it just looks like you haven't washed your hair in a month. What girl would want to run her hands through a guy's greasy, dirty hair?

"Are you saying you want to run your fingers through my hair, then?" quipped James.

She turned to glare at him. "No, I didn't say anything at all about running my fingers through your hair."

"If I washed it up all nice and didn't put stuff on it, would you run your fingers through my hair?"

"You're being ridiculous."

"Well, would you?" asked Ian.

She rolled her eyes. "I was just saying it would look a lot nicer is all. You can still have the scruffy look with clean hair."

"But it *is* clean," said Derek. "We just put stuff in it."

"Well, then quit putting stuff in it!"

"If I quit putting stuff in it, will you run your fingers through my hair then?" asked James again.

"You're all making fun of me, aren't you?"

"No luv," said Derek. "We'd never make fun of you. Don't want to get on your wrong side, do we James?"

James shook his head. "Hot temper is what she has."

"I do not!"

"Might be hot in other ways," mumbled Ian.

"I beg your pardon...what did you say?" she asked.

"Nothing."

"Speaking of feeling hot, let's go take a little nap before we have to go on," Derek said, helping Mindy to stand up.

'I'm off to get some guitar strings," said Ian. "Come along with me," he said, looking at Blue.

"A nap sounds good to me," said Susan.

James raised his eyebrows at her. "Am I invited?" he asked.

"Go home and wash your hair," was her response, as she got up, flung her purse over her shoulder and went out the door. "See you later."

The club was crowded and smoky, and Susan had to push her way to the front where Mindy was saving a stool for her at the same table she'd been at yesterday.

"Cor! And I'd almost given up on you!" Mindy said.

"I went back to my hotel after the practice, fell asleep and woke up late. I didn't realize what time it was."

Mindy looked at her, again wondering why she chose to wear those ridiculous dresses when everyone else was in leather or something more casual. Mindy wore jeans most of the time. She thought that maybe Susan was some kind of rich girl, like maybe one who'd gone to what they call a "finishing school," where the daughters of wealthy parents are sent to obtain the ladylike skills needed to be part of the upper classes. She sure didn't fit in here, that was for sure. James was playing with fire if he was playing with a little rich girl.

"Well, here come the boys now," she said with a smile, forgetting about Susan, as her eyes rested on Derek.

Susan looked at James. He was wearing a leather jacket again, but this time he had on the dingy white shirt instead of the black t-shirt. He still had the greasy hair. "So much for any fingers in his hair later on," she thought then immediately halted her line of thinking. She was *not* going to be tempted by him; she was *not!* They started singing.

"Well now, when your hands begin to clap...And your fingers start to tap... And your feet start to shuffle all around...Your senses float away...You begin to twist and sway..."

The next two songs she knew, and had to stop herself from singing along. It was really annoying, knowing the words to the songs so well, but having to keep her mouth shut. She knew Mindy was looking at her, possibly waiting for a slip-up. It was obvious that she had sensed something odd.

"La de da, da, da...La de da, da, da...It's not only how you look that stills my heart...It's not only how you kiss that rips me all apart...Uh, oh...oh no... so many days and nights go by...I sit by my phone at home and I sigh because of you...Just what am I supposed to do...I just can't quit my love, because honey, it's always you...Always you..."

The boys played three sets, and as the last song ended, James leaned over and said something to Ian and Derek and they began playing again. Mindy nudged Susan. "James's going to sing something special to you now. I can tell. Derek was waving at me to have you pay attention." James started singing.

"I know I'm gonna fall... Gonna fall for you...I know I'm gonna fall so far in love with you...You're just too sweet...and so dear...I'm gonna fall so far in love with you..."

Mindy smirked. "Hey, I know the words to this song. Listen up good." She reached out and swiveled Susan's stool around so she was directly facing James.

His eyes pierced hers as he sang.

"So now you gotta hug me tight...Make it happen tonight...Sweetheart, you gotta let it show..."

Susan froze, numb in her seat at the words, *"Make it happen tonight..."* This was all happening way, way too fast for her to even think straight. She started fingering the chain of her necklace and bit her lip. She'd only met him last night. She'd only come here to meet him, and maybe look into his eyes or something.

Something? She hadn't really given any thought to what would happen *after* she met him. There he was, a very sexy young man, at a time in his life where girls were crawling all over him, hoping to get in his bed, even if it was just for one night.

And here she was, lost in a storm of her conflicting emotions without enough time to think what she should do or where this might lead. She crossed her arms over her chest and swiveled her stool so she faced away from James. She felt the heat creep into her face.

"Loving you is what I really want to do...I need you for the whole of the night..."

"Whoa!" said Mindy, "He has it bad for you. That's what happens when a bloke don't get what he wants right off; he gets all obsessed and stuck on it. He's sure stuck on you. You shouldn't torture him so much, you know. Go on ahead and 'make it happen tonight,' as he's singing to you."

"Torture him?!" exclaimed Susan. "I just met him last night! We went out for coffee and talked is all..."

"And he took you back to your hotel and you brushed him off... and you came to practice today all dollied up and not only brushed him off, but you put him down and in his place...and you teased him about his hair so he went home and washed it."

"He did? He went home after practice and washed his hair? Then why is it still all so greasy looking?"

"Because the boys refused to go on with him looking so tidy. They even made him put on his regular old, dingy shirt and take off the clean white one he had on. They make fun of him always wanting to look more neat and clean. They like to look teddy-boy tough, ya know."

A weak, "Oh," was all Susan could think to say.

Mindy swiveled Susan's stool back around so she was facing James again.

James was completely turned towards her as he continued singing, his eyes searching hers questioningly.

"So now you gotta hug me tight…Make it happen tonight…Sweetheart, you gotta let it show…Loving you is what I really want to do…I need you for the whole of the night…"

She couldn't think of anything to say as the song ended. She had six nights left. Should she give in as Mindy suggested and make it happen tonight? No! She was *not* about to be manipulated! If and when she decided to give in, it would be her choice, not his!

But then she wondered just how long it would take before she let her defenses down. Just one hole in her defenses and she knew she was doomed to *make it happen tonight*. On top of that, her seventeen-year-old hormones were playing havoc with her body and its response to him. They were jumping up and down in anticipation. She slapped them down. To be alone with him would be downright dangerous. Oh, she shouldn't have come here! This was all getting too complicated. She wished Lynn was here to give her advice!

"So, are ya gonna do it then?" asked Mindy.

"Do what?"

"Ya know, make it happen tonight and all. Enjoy a tumble in the sheets."

"No! Most definitely not! I'm not that kind of girl!"

Mindy looked at her curiously. "So, and don't tell me it's true, but are you really all virginal and all?"

Susan turned a deep shade of pink. "What if I am?"

"Well, if you are, I'm thinking you'll need a little instruction for tonight then."

"Instruction??!! I don't need any instruction! And I'm not tumbling in any sheets tonight!"

"Ha! That's what you think," her hormones whispered. She angrily shooed them away; they were getting to be annoying.

Mindy contemplated the situation for a few seconds, but decided to ignore Susan's comments about not making it happen tonight. She figured James would end up having his way with her sooner or later, and if this strange American really was untouched, she needed to know a few things.

"So, then," Mindy said as she leaned in close to Susan's ear, where she proceeded to explain a few of the basics, making Susan's face turn even pinker. "Got all that?"

Susan nodded. "Um, yes...thank you for the tips..." thinking to herself, "Oh geez, and here I am getting sex ed and I'm technically sixty-two years old! How crazy is that??!!"

Chapter 5

Mel

"Well, see you around," said Mindy, pushing herself up from the stool next to Susan. She started to say something else, but decided against it. She just smiled, then turned and walked away. It was so obvious Susan would soon surrender to James. Susan just didn't know it yet.

Susan looked over at the girls on the other side of the room, who were all deadly silent, glaring at her. James didn't notice as he took off his guitar and walked over to her.

"Come watch me pack my gear up and then we can get out of here," he said. He took her hand and they stepped up onto the stage area where all the boys were unplugging their instruments and carrying everything to the practice room upstairs before taking them out to their cars.

One of the girls from the other side of the room came up to the front and said loudly, "Us English girls not good enough for you anymore, Jimmie? Prefer the American whore to us, do ya?"

James spun around. "Get yourself out of here, Sara. What I do is none of your business."

"Well, it is when my best friend is having her heart broken over you."

"You mean Hilary? She doesn't have a heart. She just wanted me to increase her consequence so she could climb the ladder to a more popular bloke with more money. You know that as well as I do."

"You didn't seem to mind her so much when she gave herself to you...in fact..."

"Stop, Sara...just because the bloke with the other band decided he didn't want her anymore, doesn't mean she can come running back to me. She sickens me. I don't even know why you decided to be her friend other than you feel sorry for her."

Sara turned to Susan. "Just wait, little American girl...just you wait until he's sick of you. It always happens you know...he's had just about every girl that was in the room tonight at one time or another."

"Get out!" yelled James.

Derek looked over at Sara. "Better leave, Sara," he advised.

She glared at Susan with hatred so intense, that Susan took a few steps backward and almost knocked over a speaker. Sara smirked, then turned and walked away.

"Watch your back, little girl," she flung over her shoulder. "Hilary won't let this drop, you know."

Susan, shaken by the encounter, was at a loss for words.

"I'm sorry," said James, motioning for her to follow him upstairs into the practice room. "Please don't worry yourself with anything she said. I made a big mistake when I hooked up with Hilary. It looks like I'm going to be regretting it a lot longer. Sara's not such a bad person, in fact she's quite nice. Ian goes out with her from time to time. She should never have become friends with Hilary. It's Hilary that's tellin' her what to do and say."

Susan sighed. "That's okay," she said. "She just kind of frightened me, that's all."

James and the boys had to make several trips out to their cars with all their gear. They wouldn't be playing at the club again until Tuesday, so they generally took their stuff home in case they wanted to get together somewhere else or in case they individually wanted to work out a new tune. Their Dusky nights were Tuesday, Friday and Saturday, which meant James would have all day Sunday and Monday off.

James opened the passenger door of his car and Susan got in. He got in the other side and started it up.

"Mind if we stop off at my house before we head out somewhere else so I can drop my gear off?" James asked.

"Why no, of course not," she replied. "Where else are we going tonight?"

"Well, first I thought I might freshen up a bit, you know wash the stuff out of my hair..."

She turned and looked at him. "Are you doing that for me?"

"Yeah...I guess I am."

"I'm flattered...thank you."

"Actually, I was hoping maybe later you'd run your fingers through my hair."

"Hmmmm...Were you? ...I knew there would be an ulterior motive."

"I also thought we could head down to the docks and peek in some clubs there."

"Sounds fine to me."

The first thing Susan noticed when they walked in the front door and James switched on the light was the piano up against the back wall of the main room. James saw her looking at it.

"Yeah, that's the piano my dad taught me to play on. My mum used to play it too. They'd sit there on that bench and play tunes together."

"Oh, how sweet! Making music together. That must have been very special for you."

"It was. My dad still sits there and plays the same tunes, mostly American ragtime...you know, Scott Joplin...Hey, I'm gonna run upstairs real fast like, run my head under some water and make a quick change. Make yourself at home; I'll only be a few minutes."

She smiled, looked around and sat down in a big armchair. The room smelled faintly of tobacco smoke, like pipe smoke. It was much nicer than the cigarette smell from the club.

After a minute, she stood up and went over to the piano. She sat down wondering if she really could now play. Had Mika given her the gift? "Might as well test it out," she thought. "Hmmm...I wonder if I know anything by heart..."

She put her hands on the keys and started playing. "*Moonlight Sonata*" came flowing out of her hands as they moved across the keyboard. She closed her eyes, and with a deep and gratified sigh, played on. This was great!

As she finished, she heard clapping behind her and spun around on the piano bench. An older man in a bathrobe was looking at her intently with a pleasant smile on his face.

"Very nice, very nice indeed," he said, coming over and extending his hand. "You must be the American girl James told me about. I'm his dad, Melvin. Just call me Mel."

"Oh! I'm so, so sorry!" she said contritely. "I didn't realize anyone else was at home...James never said...I just wasn't thinking...I must have woke you up!"

"No matter at all, dear. I'm a light sleeper, and I found your playing quite delightful. Might you want to play something else for me?"

"Oh no...no...I'm not very good you see..."

"There's some sheet music in the piano bench. Get up a moment and let me get it."

He came over to the piano bench as she stood up. He opened it and took out some sheets of music and set them up on the piano.

"Have you ever played any Scott Joplin?" he asked.

"Um...no...I don't believe I have," she answered.

"Well, since I'm up and you're here...where is James by the way?"

"He went upstairs to wash that horrible greasy stuff out of his hair... oh geez...I shouldn't have said that. I suppose it's all the rage and everything...but I didn't mean to be insulting."

"No need to apologize; I think it's quite appalling myself and actually, so does James. ...Well, while we're waiting, why don't you come sit down on the piano bench and we'll play this together?"

"Oh my! I really couldn't...I mean shouldn't...I'm sure I'm not near good enough."

"Of course you are; now come and sit down with me. I'll play the right hand, the hard part..." He grinned at her. "You just play the left hand, and I'll do the foot pedals."

He sat down on the piano bench invitingly. She shrugged her shoulders. "Oh well...here goes," she thought. "I hope I don't make a fool of myself."

"Ready then?"

Both of their hands hit the keys at once, Mel's fingers flying and Susan's playing rather tentatively.

"Give it more gusto!" said Mel. "Come on now; I know you can!"

She read the music and played, doing her best to follow his lead, and soon found that she was having fun. This was actually quite fabulous, being able to play the piano. Mel flipped the pages of music as the song went on. It was *"The Entertainer,"* Susan recognized, thinking of the movie in which it was the featured song. Mel and Susan were both laughing as the tune ended.

They heard clapping behind them. For the second time, Susan spun around on the piano bench and there was James.

His hair looked clean and fresh, but was still a little damp. He wore dark trousers and a long-sleeved shirt, and looked excessively handsome. He shook his head in an attempt to dry his hair and Susan stifled a gasp. This was the James she remembered falling in love with from afar at a concert in August, 1964, a concert that hadn't even happened yet.

And here he was in front of her now, young and exuberant, his career and world-shattering popularity on the brink of happening. For all his sexual innuendos and outrageous flirting with her, he still looked so open, honest and innocent. So...so...darn desirable! Damn it all! She shook her head to try and clear her thoughts.

Mel was observing Susan looking at James and James looking at Susan. It was easy to see the attraction between them. In fact, he could almost feel it crackling in the air.

"Trying to steal my girl away from me, are ya Dad?" James asked.

"Sure and why not!" responded Mel. "She's a fine piano player and very pretty on top of it."

James grinned. "Yeah, she is very pretty; I haven't told her yet."

Susan blushed and started fingering the silver ballet shoes on her necklace.

"Say, play a tune with James, will you?" said Mel, getting up from the piano bench and looking at Susan. "Come on over here, Jimmie, and make some music with your new girlfriend."

Susan almost choked. She was his new girlfriend, was she? Just how much had James told his dad about her anyway? She hadn't even been here that long!

James came over and sat down, flipping through the music on top of the piano. They were sitting so close together that his thigh was touching hers. It sent uncontrollable shivers down her spine. She moved over an inch, but there was no more room on the piano bench.

"Ah! *'The American Beauty Rag'*...sounds like a good one," he smiled at her.

He placed the music so they could both see it and started to play. She joined in. Mel tapped his foot along in time to the music. As it ended, they all clapped.

"Very nice," complimented Mel. "You'll come back and play sometime again, won't you?"

"Well, maybe I will..." She looked at James as she slid off the piano bench and stood up.

"Yeah, Dad, I'll bring her back sometime soon."

"Excuse me," Susan said. "But, may I use your bathroom, please?"

"Oh, sure," responded Mel, pointing. "Right up the stairs there, door on your left at the top."

Susan thanked him and went up the stairs. Both James and Mel heard the bathroom door close.

"So then, you told me this morning you'd met an American girl last night at the club, who I can only assume is this Susan here. A delightful little thing. How old is she?" asked Mel.

"Didn't ask, Dad, but you have to be eighteen to get into the club, you know," James responded.

"Well, she doesn't look that old to me. Too fresh and innocent looking. And that dress she's wearing; looks like she's ready to attend a church service. She must have really stood out in the club."

"Yeah, she did. Ian noticed her right off and pointed her out to me. It was really odd. One minute she wasn't there, and then all of a sudden she was. Almost like she appeared out of nowhere."

"Well, I guess if she was in the club, she must be at least eighteen, but it concerns me with you and your way with the girls. The ones you and the boys hang around with have all been around the block, you know what I'm saying? This one looks untouched."

"Yeah, she rather does." James was remembering his conversation with her out in the alley at the practice, where she all but admitted that she was virginal.

"So where in America is she from? Are her parents with her?"

"She's from California, and no, her parents aren't with her. Her dad passed away when she was seven. She's a student, college I think, here on a history tour with a group of other students. The others, though, are delayed in getting here."

"So, she's here all alone?" Mel sounded shocked.

"That's what she tells me. I'm volunteering to protect her until the others arrive."

"You protect her?!! She needs protected *from* you!"

"Now, Dad, I can be a gentleman if I want to."

"Well, that's the question then; do you *want* to?"

Just then, they heard Susan coming down the stairs.

Mel turned to James, lowering his voice and said, "She seems a good girl, Jimmie. Don't be misbehaving with her, okay."

"Sure thing, Dad."

Susan went to pick up her purse, thinking about James's dad. She really liked him. She hoped they'd be able to come back sometime during the week and see him again. Playing the piano was fun. She wondered if she could play *"Fur Elise."*

"We're off then, Dad," said James. "Thanks for entertaining my girl."

She looked at him. He'd called her "my girl" twice now. This was just getting downright ridiculous! She shook her head as if to clear her thoughts.

Susan and James left and got back into his car.

"So, where exactly are we going," she asked.

"I thought we'd drive down to the wharf, kinda near where you and Sandra were today. There's a couple clubs down there that have other bands that sing later than we do, some of them all night. A lot of the sailors off the ships come in and join in the singing. Anyone who's there can jump up and sing."

"Oh, like karaoke?" she asked.

"What's that?"

"Oh, something they do in America where people go up and sing in bars."

She thought, "There I go again; blurting out something from the future that makes no sense to him."

James parked the car down by the wharf and they walked up and down a few streets, past a few clubs and bars with the sound of music drifting out the doors. They went into the next one, where James was greeted by a few friends he knew. He introduced Susan to them and they all sat together at a small table near the back. James's friends were looking at him a little oddly. Susan thought it was probably because he'd lost his usual scruffy look and they were finding it amusing. It was also, no doubt, due to the way she was dressed. She didn't see any other girls in the room dressed like June Cleaver.

Various people were taking the stage to sing at the front of the bar, none of them very good singers, but the music wasn't so bad. James's friends urged him to go up and sing, but he refused, not wanting to leave Susan alone with strangers. After about a half hour and drinking a mug of beer, Susan looked at her watch and said, "Oh gee! It's after 2:30 already! I should be getting back. You keep me up too late!"

They said goodbye to James's friends and left the bar, James holding Susan's hand. It felt really good to her, but she knew she was on dangerous territory with him. It gave her chill bumps.

When they were in the car, James asked, "So can I see you tomorrow? I mean, today that is...I was thinking maybe we could go on a picnic."

"A picnic sounds nice," she immediately answered. "But where is there around here to go on a picnic?"

"Actually, I was thinking we could drive out to my Auntie Annabelle's cottage. I used to spend time there when I was a lad. I don't visit her as much anymore, but I have a lot of nice memories of the place. It's about twenty five kilometers north of here...in the countryside, you know...there's a hill overlooking a pond my brother and I used to swim in. The hill has a big tree we used to climb up. We could picnic under the tree."

"Hmmmm..." Susan thought. "Out in the country...sitting under a tree on a blanket...having a picnic..." It sounded incredibly romantic, but at the same time very risky for her and her virtue. She almost laughed at that. How much "virtue" did a sixty-two-year-old woman who's been married for forty-four years have left anyway? Aside from having the seventeen-year-old body, that is. But then again, she figured if Auntie Annabelle was there, she'd be safe enough.

"Something funny?" James asked turning to look at her.

"No, nothing at all. I was just thinking I haven't been on a picnic in a long time. It sounds like fun. I could have the hotel pack up a basket for us."

"I have a hamper at home; I could throw some things in."

"Okay, then let's surprise each other. You pack a basket and I'll pack a basket."

"There's also a shop on the way out of town that has fresh-baked bread and homemade cheeses, if you have an interest."

"Oh yes! That sounds wonderful! I'm getting hungry right now thinking about it."

"You want to get something to eat now then?"

"No, no...I'm not all *that* hungry...I was just thinking of fresh-baked bread. There's nothing like it! I make it all the time at home in my bread machine."

"Bread machine? What's a bread machine?"

"Oh...it's something we have in America, like a little oven is all," she responded, wanting to slap herself again at her careless words.

"You like to cook then?"

"I love it! I like inventing new recipes."

He looked at her with his eyebrows raised. "You're the first girl I've ever met who said she loves to cook let alone knows how to do it enough to invent new recipes."

"Really? How odd..." She thought to herself, "Best change the subject before I start talking about microwaves."

"So...what time do we want to leave for the picnic?" she asked.

"How about I pick you up at 10:00?'

"You sure you don't want to sleep in longer?"

"I'm sure."

As they pulled up to the hotel, Susan said, "You can just drop me at the curb," but as she started to open the door, James put his hand on her arm and said, "No, I'm walking you in and you wait right there while I come around and open the door for you. Wouldn't be very gentleman-like to just let you hop out on your own."

"It's what we do in America."

"Well, it's not what *I* do. When you're with me, you wait for me to open the door for you. It's gentlemanly, you know. Remember, okay?"

He turned off the car and slipped the keys in his pocket. "Stay right there." He came around to the other side of the car and opened the door for her then held out his hand to help her out."

"I'm impressed, Sir James," she said smiling, "but you're only walking me to the lobby, you know."

He opened the lobby door for her, but before she could protest, had pulled her across the foyer to the elevator where he pushed the "up" button. The doors immediately opened and he tugged her in.

"What floor?" he asked.

"Four," she responded with a quiver in her voice. The words of the song he had sung to her beat in her head..."*Make it happen tonight...*" Oh, no, no, no...!

Her hormones were leaping with joy. She did her best to ignore them.

Neither of them said anything until they reached the fourth floor and stepped out. Susan didn't move from where she'd come out of the elevator.

"I can find my way from here."

"What room number?"

"You don't need to know that."

"But I'm picking you up for our picnic in just a few hours."

"You're picking me up in the lobby. Besides, I heard your dad tell you I was a good girl and that you should behave yourself," she added.

"I am behaving myself."

He started to walk one way down the hallway.

"No, this way," she said, turning the other direction. "Room 4027."

They arrived at her door. She made no move to get the key out of her purse. He looked at her with his eyebrows raised.

"You're not coming in, if that's what you're thinking," she said. Then she suddenly thought of something else and blurted out, "You didn't make another wager did you?"

"No, no!" he assured her, raising both hands in the air. "I didn't want any part of it."

"Well, you're still not coming in my room…"

"Then how can I properly kiss you goodnight?" he asked.

"Right here in the hallway will be just fine."

"But it's so public a place."

"Not very public at 3:00 in the morning." She looked up at him, suddenly feeling shy. Her heart was beating wildly.

"And what makes you think I *want* you to kiss me goodnight? You know…you just about knocked my legs out from under me with that hand kissing last night…"

"Did I?" he asked with a rueful grin on his face. His eyes were twinkling with amusement. "Then I'm thinking you rather *do* want me to kiss you goodnight."

"So...he knew...he knew how it affected me," she thought, heat flooding her face.

As the memory of that kiss rolled through her head again, he brought one of her hands to his lips, turned it over and gently kissed her palm just as he had the night before. Again, just like the night before, shivers raced down her arms and back all the way down to her toes.

His eyes never left hers as he slowly and gently kissed the inside of her wrist, followed by a trail of gentle kisses up her arm to the inside of her elbow. His eyes had become dark, and the amber highlights in them were like tiny flames as his pupils enlarged. His lips were so very warm and soft. She had a momentary thought of them kissing her all over. Her eyes closed as a deep sigh escaped her. Oh my God; it was as if he was starting to make love to her in the hallway! Her purse strap slipped off her shoulder and her purse thudded on the carpeted floor.

He tilted up her chin with one finger and she opened her eyes. He could clearly see the passion burning in them, knowing how close he was to having her surrender.

In ordinary circumstances with other girls, it would have been mere moments before they'd be in bed together, but for some reason, he stopped himself from pursuing that avenue, waiting for her to make the suggestion.

Maybe it was what his dad had said. Maybe it was the thought that she really was a virgin, although he doubted that was even possible. Maybe it was because, after being with her and getting to know her, he didn't want to spoil it by taking advantage or scaring her.

He had to admit that he was captivated by her. No, it was more than that even. It was as if she'd cast some kind of spell on him from the first moment he'd laid eyes on her in the club. And although he craved her body lying under his, he also wanted more from her than just her physical self. Maybe that was why he wasn't pressuring her to open her door.

Whatever the reason, he didn't press her further to let him into her room. Instead, he leaned forward and kissed her lips very tenderly and softly, brushing his own lips back and forth across hers, while at the same time placing his hands on each side of her waist and pulling her in closer.

She pressed her hands against his chest when his kiss deepened and became more demanding. As his tongue slid into her mouth exploring and tasting her, she was tempted to wrap her arms around his neck and pull him more tightly into her. A stray hand reached up and she ran her fingers through his hair, her other hand curling into a ball as she crushed a handful of his shirt.

He smelled so wonderful and his hair was so soft and silky in her fingers. The feel of his hands caressing her and pulling her into him set her on the verge of losing all sense.

She made a little sound of pleasure as his lips left hers for a moment and he moved them to the side of her neck to taste her skin. He moved his tongue over her delicate collarbone then lightly bit down the side of her neck before fiercely claiming her mouth again as his kiss turned hungry.

Her mouth tasted so sweet and her full breasts pressed up against his chest. He felt on fire. His arms wrapped around her tighter and his hands roamed up and down her back pressing her even closer into him.

Her knees were ready to buckle under her. Oh, God, she wanted more of this! Her seventeen-year-old body was on fire with uncontrollable want and need as she felt his hardness pressing against her belly, but her aged mind was sending out loud warning signals. Another minute of this and she'd be opening her hotel room door and dragging him inside.

As these conflicting thoughts registered in her mind, she abruptly pushed him away and stepped back, ending the kiss. Their eyes locked together. There was no humor or laughter in them now, only wonderment and the thought of some deeper feeling that neither of them could define quite yet.

James stepped away and raised his eyebrows again, looking towards her hotel room door, while at the same time picking up her purse and handing it to her. Slowly and breathlessly, she shook her head at him.

He stepped back, breathing heavily, and made a small bow to her. She released a huge sigh.

"Thank you for being a real, true gentleman tonight," she said so softly he could barely hear her.

The memory of his kisses and his lips and his eyes as they had looked into hers flooded her mind and she could feel a tightness in her lower belly as well as a throbbing lower down. Her hormones were holding their breath, waiting for her to change her mind about letting him in her room.

"My lady," he said as he turned and walked back down the hall.

If she had only known it, he was thinking about their picnic in just a few hours and how she wouldn't be able to hold out much longer. He smiled to himself in anticipation. She would most certainly surrender; he had no doubt about it.

She fished in her purse for her key and was opening her door when she saw him go into the elevator. He didn't look back at her. She went into her room, closed the door, flung her purse onto the floor, leaned against the back of the door, and slowly slid down until she was sitting on the floor, her back against the door.

"Holy crap," she said. "I'm doomed for sure now. Oh my God! He is one hot and irresistible guy!" She tugged on her necklace nervously. "Well, at least," she thought to herself with a smile, "I didn't make it happen tonight!"

Her hormones sighed despondently, but then chuckled as they thought about the picnic and the opportunities tomorrow would present.

Lynn had been checking the App on her iPhone periodically since Susan had been sent off into the past. She was a little shocked when James had singled Susan out within minutes of her arrival, but then again, Susan was like a magnet to guys in the club in her seventeen-year-old body, her California girl tan, long blonde hair and, of course, the dorky dress. She smiled in amusement when Susan stuck out her hand for James to kiss it in the lobby of the hotel, knowing Susan was overwhelmed at the attention he was paying her.

She had been extremely upset, however, to later learn that a wager had been made on Susan's virtue. In fact, she was still steaming mad about it.

Susan was no match for James and his beguiling ways, and she wished there was some way to communicate with her and warn her against him. Lynn had also heard what Sara said about James having just about every girl who came to the club and thought Susan was right at the afternoon practice when she accused James of wanting to just carve another notch in the wall with her in regard to the wager business.

A wager! A bet!! How hideous was that??!!

The guy took arrogance to a whole new level, and she was certain Susan was his newest prey. The fact that she'd resisted him the first night only meant he would increase his efforts on the next one. And then when she heard the song James had sang to Susan…"*Make it happen tonight…*"

Well, that took the cake!

Lynn was starting to feel that this whole trip into the past was a big mistake. She and Susan had been close to drunk at dinner when they'd met the ladies from Haiti. She could hardly recall the conversation, but thought she might have played a major role in convincing Susan to take the journey. What was it Mika had said? That Susan would learn something important from this trip? Was Susan going to learn that James was nothing more than a shallow, self-indulgent jerk who screwed every girl in sight then discarded them like used up toys?

If so, Susan was going to be badly hurt, and she really hadn't meant for her very best friend in the world to get hurt.

Yes, this going into the past was definitely a mistake. Susan needed to get over her "James thing" some other way. She didn't belong with him. She belonged back in the present with her husband, who worshiped the ground she walked on. Lynn thought this was almost like cheating, and if James had his way with her, it *would* be cheating.

Oh my! Why had she encouraged Susan in this craziness??!!

It was 9:00 at night in the Caribbean as Lynn turned on her iPhone and touched the App Mika had installed to check on Susan again. The scene in the hallway outside Susan's hotel room door unfolded in front of her. Lynn's eyes opened wide.

"Oh Suz," she cringed, "What are you getting yourself into? And you've only been there a little over twenty four hours! Kissing already?" And not only lip kissing, but all that hand and arm kissing! He looked like he was gobbling her up.

She started pacing the floor, wishing there was some way she could communicate with Susan. What was going to happen next? It looked like Susan was on the brink of letting him in her hotel room door. She'd seen the look on his face, knowing he was plotting Susan's surrender, and she knew it probably wouldn't take much. She vowed to keep a close watch on events, telling herself again that this whole trip into the past was a mistake.

Lynn was very uneasy.

Chapter 6

The Picnic

The picnic basket wasn't in the closet in the hall where James thought it was.

"Dad, do you know where the picnic hamper is?" he asked, looking back over his shoulder as Mel came down the stairs.

"Picnic hamper? Let me think. Haven't seen it in a while, I don't believe. Might be out in the potting shed."

He headed through the kitchen toward the back door leading out to a small enclosed garden. To the side of the yard was a wood potting shed containing garden tools, pots and a bench. Mel spotted the picnic basket beneath the bench.

"Ah, here we are!" he said triumphantly, producing the basket.

James took it from him. "Thanks, now I just need to find some things to fill it with."

"Going on a picnic, are you?"

"Yeah, thought we'd head out to the countryside."

"You and your new American girlfriend?"

"Yeah, but I don't know I'd say she's my girlfriend...at least not yet."

"Nice girl."

"Yeah, Dad, I think so too. So, any ideas what I should take on a picnic?"

"Let's see..." He opened the refrigerator. "Here's the rest of the roast chicken I made last night, some shaved ham...oh, and here, let me pack up some of these oatmeal cookies I baked just this morning...tomatoes I just picked...take a couple of these to slice up... and a couple of bottles of orange soda, can't do without that!" He started opening the kitchen cabinets. "Just in case, take this tin of potted meat and here's a box of rye crisps..."

"Enough, Dad! All this could feed a crowd; it's only going to be the two of us, you know."

"Well, don't want you to go hungry...country air and all, you know. Works up an appetite. So, where in the countryside are you thinking of going?"

James responded casually, not really wanting to be specific, "Oh, you know, out by Auntie Annabelle's cottage, you know the hill where we used to go with Mum years ago. We used to picnic there all the time, remember?"

"Annabelle's cottage, eh?"

"The hill above the cottage, yeah."

"That's a long way to go for a picnic."

"Not really, less than an hour drive is all."

"You know I took Annabelle to go visit her sister over in King's Head last Friday. Not picking her back up again until next Sunday."

"Yeah, I think you might've mentioned something about that."

Mel stared hard at James.

"James, now listen to me; I believe the girl is an innocent if you get my meaning. Does she know where you're taking her?"

"Not yet; I was going to make it a surprise."

"Did you hear what I just said? I wasn't born yesterday, you know. That girl is a sweet thing and not like the others you chase around with."

"I know that, Dad."

"So what's with taking her out to Annabelle's when Annabelle isn't there?"

James folded his arms over his chest. "We're getting to know each other better, is all."

"Is it? I was young like you myself, you know. I know what it's like to have your nether parts think for you instead of your brain, and I can see that's what it is with you."

James looked contrite. "I can do my own thinking, Dad."

"Maybe so, but don't you go breaking that poor girl's heart, you understand me? You get what you want from her and break her heart, you answer to me for it. Clear?"

"Yeah, perfectly clear."

"I don't feel as if you're heeding a word I'm saying."

"I hear you loud and clear… But you don't understand."

"What exactly is it I don't understand?"

James looked down at the floor, intently observing the toes of his shoes. "There's something about her…I don't know what it is…She's not like other girls…She's sophisticated like…and she talks to me and listens to me like she really cares what I'm saying…I can't explain it… It's like it happened so sudden, overnight like…I think she's already got a little piece of my own heart, you see."

Mel contemplated that statement for a few seconds then said, "Has she then? I suppose that's something new for you?"

James looked up. "Yeah, it is."

He picked up the picnic hamper and headed toward the door. "See ya, Dad…and thanks for filling up the basket."

As the door closed behind him, Mel shook his head, a worried expression on his face.

"Love at first sight, eh?" he mused.

Then he thought, "For some reason, I don't see this ending well. I hope that poor girl can hold her own against him…but I won't hold my breath about it. She looks like a fresh peach, ready to be plucked off the tree…and James will likely bruise her badly…Oh Sherry…I wish you were still here…"

James was prompt to pick Susan up at 10:00. She was waiting for him in the lobby of the hotel, a straw sun hat in one hand, her purse slung over her shoulder and a large picnic hamper at her feet. James came over and gave her a quick kiss on the cheek.

"Ready luv?" he asked.

"As ready as you are," she replied. "Are you tired at all?"

"Not a bit. I had to get up early to look around for the picnic hamper, then scrounge around for something to put in it. My Dad helped me pack. He put in some of his special oatmeal cookies that he baked this morning and a bunch of other stuff. There's some roast chicken, shaved ham, some tomatoes from the garden and bottles of orange soda. He loves orange soda. Too much really, and there's still the shop on the way out of town that has the fresh bread and cheese I was telling you about last night."

"Oh, oatmeal cookies! They're my favorite! And, I have plenty of stuff too; the hotel packed three bottles of wine, two white and one red. I wasn't sure if you liked wine or not or what kind you liked. One of the whites is sweet, a Muscat, and the other is dry, a Chardonnay. Chardonnay is my favorite! Then they put in some pastries, a bunch of grapes, a large container of fresh strawberries...I just love strawberries; they're my favorite! There's some other stuff, but I don't know what it is. Maybe some chocolates."

"And are chocolates your favorite as well?" He was teasing her.

"No, not at all. Are you making fun of me for having so many favorites? What do you like? Are you a picky eater?"

"My Mum always used to say I was, but I don't think so. She was a great cook, but so is my dad. Are you ready to go?"

"Yeah, let's. Take the picnic hamper, please. It's awfully heavy with all that wine. I don't even know if I should drink any wine with you..."

"And why would that be?" he asked.

"Well...it might make me reckless...or, or I might lose my inhibitions..."

"And then what happens?"

"Well, likely something that shouldn't happen."

He looked at her intently, thinking of what his dad had said about her being "an innocent."

"I'll never cross the line if you don't want me to, Susan. Believe me, okay? What happens today will all be up to you."

She froze. "Oh, that's just great," she thought, wincing. "Put it all on me, as if I have any control when it comes to you...!"

84

Her hormones were clapping excitedly. "Hooray! We're in charge now!" they chuckled.

She looked into his eyes. "I don't even know how to respond to that, you know."

He just shrugged his shoulders then leaned over to pick up the picnic basket. She set the sun hat on her head and they went out the lobby doors.

As he opened the car door for her, she almost felt faint. Really? Up to her? The day was going to be up to her? Oh my! After those kisses, what was next? More kisses...and then? Certainly not back to holding hands! And, on top of everything else, she had her young, teenage body to deal with that was responding to him physically like a cat in heat. Where, oh where, was Lynn when she needed her?

Then she thought to herself, "At least Auntie Annabelle will be there. A chaperone will be a good thing. Keep things from getting out of hand. I think I'm going to like Auntie Annabelle...and I think I'll stick to her like glue."

"You're no fun at all," whispered her hormones.

It was four o'clock in the morning on the ship and Lynn couldn't sleep. She had watched Susan as James kissed her in the hallway and as she slid down the back of her hotel room door onto the floor after James had left her the night before, and she thought something was about to happen that Susan would regret.

Things were moving way too fast. She could sense that Susan was confused at the speed of events. She knew that Susan was a romantic, probably thinking she'd go back, meet James, he'd sing to her and they'd walk down English lanes or something holding, hands for seven days.

As she looked into her iPhone for the tenth time in the last twelve hours, she saw them in the lobby of Susan's hotel. They were talking. She heard James say that whatever happened today was going to be up to her. After that kiss in the hallway last night, what exactly was that supposed to mean?!

Then, it dawned on her. She'd heard what James's dad had said to him in regard to Auntie Annabelle not being at the cottage and she knew James was intending to have his way with Susan even if she didn't. He was well aware she couldn't resist him. All he'd have to do was crook his finger.

"Suz! Pay attention!" Lynn cringed, thinking that was pretty damn arrogant of him, and knowing that Susan was doomed. She had seen the desire burning in Susan's eyes and her reaction to his kiss. It was pretty much all over for her. What would happen after James had his way with her? Would he just take her back to her hotel, drop her off and carve another notch on a wall somewhere?

Lynn toyed with the idea of going to Marta and Mika and asking to be sent back. Susan looked confused and vulnerable, and she wanted to cry thinking how hurt she was going to be once James bedded her then discarded her. But, what would she be able to do? How could she stop what was about to happen anyway? Susan would never listen to her and would likely be upset at her interference.

Then she started to laugh. Being an old lady and having been married for forty-four years, Susan was quite experienced in the act of lovemaking. Their "girl talk" over the years sometimes strayed into that subject area. It was easy to see that once Susan gave in, James was going to be in for the surprise of his life. Forty-four years of experience combined with a seventeen-year old body – what a combination! What would he think? She chuckled again and tried to forget about the "cheating" aspect of the situation.

James and Susan stopped at the shop that had fresh baked bread on the way out of Brighton and bought way too much stuff, considering the things they already had in the two picnic hampers. They bought a loaf of French bread, a baguette and a bag of Kaiser rolls. They couldn't resist the cheeses either and ended up with Brie, some Swiss and a chunk of sharp white cheddar.

"This is enough for a picnic for a dozen people!" said Susan as they left the shop, bags in their arms.

"Well, maybe we'll just need to go on another picnic," James responded.

They got back into the car and continued on their journey, out to the country and Auntie Annabelle's cottage. It took them forty-five minutes.

The cottage was set back from the country road in what appeared to be a pasture of wild flowers, blue bells, hollyhocks, daisies and lupines. Susan stepped out of the car when James opened the door for her. "This is beautiful!" she said, looking at the cottage. It was bordered by roses. "Is your Aunt expecting us?"

"Ummm...Actually, no, she's not... She's not here, you see. My dad took her to visit her sister in King's Head. He picked her up on Friday and he won't be picking her up to come back until next Sunday.

She spun her head around to look at him. "You didn't tell me she wasn't going to be here!" she said accusingly, panic rising inside of her.

He shrugged his shoulders. "You didn't ask, you know."

She took a deep breath then exhaled. This was bad, very, very bad. She felt doomed in one sense of the word, but there was also a tense excitement stirring in her stomach, giving her butterflies and chill bumps on her arms. Her hormones were cheering wildly and her heart was pounding in her chest so hard, she almost thought she could hear it.

She thought of what James had said in the hotel lobby before they left and closed her eyes for a moment, taking a deep breath. Up to her...up to her... Holy crap! If it was up to her seventeen-year old body, she didn't stand a chance! She could already feel the stirrings of some-thing in her lower regions and blushed at the thought.

James grabbed one of the picnic hampers and a bag from the car and headed up to the front door of the cottage. He set everything down, went around the side of the house and returned with a key. "Glad she keeps it in the same spot," he said.

He opened the door and motioned for her to go inside. Just as he started to close the door behind them, a fluffy black and white tuxedo cat raced inside and brushed against her legs.

"Oh! A kitty! Is this your Aunt's kitty?" she asked, picking up the cat and holding it in her arms. "I just adore cats!"

He didn't look very pleased. "Yeah, that's Buttons. She doesn't like me." And, as if to prove what he said, he looked over at Buttons, who hissed at him, jumped out of Susan's arms then up onto a chair.

"So, what did you do to her to make her not like you?"

"Nothing. I think she likes girls and hates guys is all. I'm not very fond of cats anyway, so I don't really care if she likes me or not."

"Well, that's not very nice," she said, going over to rub Buttons on her head. Buttons turned on her purr motor, looking over at James as if to say, "I don't care if you like me either! I like this new lady."

Susan looked around and saw a neat and tidy living room area, with a piano against one of the walls. "Does your Auntie play the piano?" she asked.

"Of course! She's my dad's sister. They're all musical, you know. Let's take these things into the kitchen," he added. "And look in the hampers to see what we have. Then we can decide what to take up the hill for our picnic."

He set the picnic hamper down on the kitchen table by a window, followed by the bag with bread. He then went back out to the car to retrieve the other basket and the remaining bag. When he came back, Susan was unpacking the first hamper, which was the one from the hotel.

"Wow! They sure packed a lot of stuff. It's going to be hard to decide what to take on our picnic, but I'm just about starving to death now."

"Let me show you around first, just so you know where the loo is and all, then we'll pack up some of this stuff and head up the hill for our picnic."

He led her out of the kitchen and pointed across the way, off the living room, to a bathroom. Next to it was a door that opened into a bedroom with a large four poster bed. "That was my Mum and Dad's room when they came to stay here, but when Mum died, my Dad didn't come here much anymore, so when my brother, Chad, and I came to visit, that was our room."

Just then, Buttons ran into the room and jumped up on the bed. She turned in a couple of circles before laying down and putting her head down on her paws.

"Scat!" James yelled at her, trying to chase her off the bed. "You don't belong on the bed!"

Buttons just lifted her head for a minute and started at him, but she didn't budge.

"She's okay there," said Susan. "In fact, my cat sleeps on my bed with me every night."

"Well, *she* won't be sleeping there tonight..." he started to say.

Susan looked at him quizzically, and he immediately changed the subject.

"Up here," he said, pointing her up a set of stairs next to the bathroom. They started up the stairs.

At the top were two other bedrooms. "My Dad built these after Auntie Annabelle's husband died. She had a son and his wife move back in with her, who stayed downstairs for a few months before getting their own place. Auntie's bedroom is up here. She uses the other bedroom for her sewing. She takes in sewing jobs from time to time."

They went back downstairs and into the kitchen where they sorted through the hampers and bags, putting the excess food away in the small refrigerator in the corner of the kitchen. "Plenty more for later, that's for sure," said James.

He grabbed a blanket and tucked it under his arm. Susan searched through the cabinets and drawers and found a couple of wine glasses and a corkscrew to open the wine. She grabbed the bottle of Chardonnay, the glasses and the corkscrew. She had re-packed one of the hampers with some of the food and they headed out the door, up the hill to a spot under a big, tall, leafy tree. They could see the cottage down below. James set down the hamper and spread out the blanket.

"Time for our banquet." He motioned to Susan to sit down beside him. She lowered herself down and reached for the hamper.

"But first the wine," she said.

Expertly, she used the corkscrew to open the bottle and poured them each a generous portion.

"To our picnic," she said raising her glass.

He bumped his glass against hers. "Yes, m'lady, to our picnic." They smiled into each other's eyes.

They sipped, then dug into the picnic hamper and ate ravenously as if they hadn't eaten in days.

Chapter 7

The Pond

They were both sleepy after drinking the glass of wine and eating a large amount of the baguette, brie, shaved ham and grapes. They both lay back against the tree trunk, empty wine glasses in hand. Their eyes started to close when James said, "Would you like to see the pond?"

Susan's eyes fluttered open and she said sleepily, "Sure," and sat up.

James stood up, took her hand and pulled her up. "It's down the path this way. Chad and I used to swim in it during the summers we stayed here."

He led her by the hand down a narrow path bordered by ferns, to a small pond surrounded by large boulders. There were overgrown trees on each side. A small waterfall cascaded into the pond between two of the boulders, making the scene idyllic.

"I haven't been here in ages," he said gazing around.

"Is the water very cold?" she asked.

"Shouldn't be this time of year," he responded. "Go ahead and stick your toe in."

She slipped off her sandals, set them down on the pebbles by the shore of the pond, and tentatively put one foot into the water. It was chilly, but not uncomfortably cold. On a warm day like this one, it wouldn't even be too cold to swim in.

The pebbles beneath the water were smooth and somewhat slimy with algae. She stepped in with her other foot, but as she did so, she started to lose her balance and was just about to fall full into the water, when James grabbed her arm and pulled her back. As she spun around, the front of her body thudded against his chest, and within a second, he had wrapped his arms tightly around her and crushed his mouth down on hers.

Her response to his kiss was immediate, all her pent up emotions from the previous night exploding into uncontrollable desire. She returned his kiss with a passion she didn't even know she had, reaching both arms up to twine around his neck. Her hands moved up to the back of his head and she ran her fingers frantically through his hair, scraping her fingernails on his scalp. He groaned as their kiss became intense and he shot his tongue into her mouth, teasing and probing.

He cupped one of her breasts in his hand and she responded by thrusting her hips into his and rubbing against him. He moved his hands down to her bottom and pulled her even closer. She could feel his pulsing arousal against her stomach and the beginning wetness between her legs. A throbbing need began deep in her belly then slowly moved down to her most private parts, leaving her almost breathless with want.

Her hormones were in a drunken stupor, while her aged and mature mind fled into the depths of the pond.

Their kiss became an erotic play of lips and tongues. Their hearts were beating wildly against each other. He covered her neck with kisses and small bites then took her earlobe between his teeth and tugged gently before swirling his tongue inside her ear, making her almost swoon.

She reached between them down to the front of his trousers and squeezed the pulsating bulge that was begging for release. He reached a hand behind her head, grasping a handful of her hair and pulled her face towards his again, kissing her once more.

James was the first to draw back and look down at her, his lips parted, his eyes smoldering and dark with flickering amber highlights.

They were both breathing heavily. Her lips felt swollen from his kisses. His eyes locked onto hers. She knew the next move was up to her. He'd said so when they left for the picnic this morning.

But did she even have a choice? She knew there was no point in fighting against this; she wanted him to possess her, and it was far too late for either of them to call a halt to the inevitable. All rational thoughts fled from her head as he squeezed her bottom, pulling her back into him. She could feel his throbbing manhood, imagining how it would feel inside her, and the last of any rational thoughts flew from her brain.

"Take me back to the cottage and make love to me," she whispered huskily.

There was no need for him to respond. She bent down and retrieved her sandals. He took her hand and they raced back up the path, bypassing the blanket and the remnants of their picnic, then down the hill to the cottage. When they got inside, they wordlessly headed back to the bedroom, where James kicked the door shut behind them.

There wasn't any slow, seductive removal of clothes. Both quickly and eagerly stripped down to nakedness, James on one side of the bed and Susan on the other. The only thing Susan still had on was her necklace. The ballerina shoes hung down between her bare breasts. Buttons jumped down off the bed then up onto the window sill, turning her head away. James and Susan met in the middle of the bed, both on their knees, and embraced with a need so powerful that it made them dizzy.

They kissed again, this time more slowly and sensuously, running their hands over each other's skin, feeling, touching, exploring. He cupped both of her full breasts in his hands and rubbed his thumbs over her nipples. They instantly hardened. She reached down and grasped his erect shaft in one hand and gently tugged on it. He groaned, moving one of his hands down between her thighs, feeling her wet heat and expertly fingering the most sensitive part of her. She gasped, parting her thighs to give him better access.

"Oh my God!" Susan suddenly thought. "Am I a virgin or not? How can he even possibly think I am after I told him to make love to me, stripped down naked without a second thought, and now I'm doing this? What's it feel like to be a virgin anyway? I don't remember!"

She would have laughed in different circumstances, but this wasn't the moment. Her mind was in a whirl and she was throbbing for the want of him inside her as he continued to stroke the nub of her desire, making her slicker and wetter. She begged him to stop, thinking she might explode right then and there.

Slowly, he removed his hand from between her thighs and laid her back onto the pillows, his body held slightly above hers. His lips claimed hers again.

As he kissed her, instinct took over and she spread her legs beneath him. He lowered one of his hands down between them and stroked her again. She scraped her fingernails down his back in eager anticipation and slightly lifted her hips. She was ready. He grasped his manhood and prepared to enter her, then suddenly stopped, looking full into her face.

"Are you sure this is what you want?" he asked softly.

"I've never wanted anything more," she whispered as she raised her hips up to receive him.

To the surprise of them both, he met a barrier partway in and pulled back, amazement on his face.

"Are you really then...are you...have you never done this before?"

She thought for a moment, then shook her head. "No, I don't believe I have."

"I don't want to hurt you. I've never encountered...that is to say...I've never experienced..."

Her only response was to frantically thrust her hips up to meet him again as she grasped his bottom and pulled him down into her in one swift movement. He moaned in pleasure as he broke through her barrier and her tight sheath enveloped him. He paused for a moment, looking down at her. Her eyes were closed. Slowly, he pulled partially out and slowly pushed in again. She opened her eyes, staring into his and reached up to cup his cheek in her hand, softly moaning as he repeated his thrust. She wrapped her arms around his neck and her legs around his back, urging him on.

But, he needed no urging as he began stroking back and forth inside her in a sensual rhythm. She flung her arms outwards, tilting her hips up to allow him to go deeper. He kissed and suckled her breasts as she clutched the hair on the nape of his neck. She met each and every one of his thrusts, feeling the spasms of her climax beginning deep inside her. She reached down between them to fondle his balls then screamed out his name as they both reached their peak. He collapsed on top of her, rolled them onto their sides and smothered her face with soft and feathery kisses.

She ran her fingers through his hair once more as they looked into each other's eyes, their chests heaving from the exertion of their first encounter. As they began to caress each other again, James's maleness sprung back to life and they enjoyed each other again, this time more slowly. Then, sheer exhaustion overcame them both and they fell asleep in each other's arms.

They slept and made love several times more through the late afternoon and night. Buttons paid little attention from her perch on the window sill.

Susan's hormones smiled contentedly.

It was 10:00 in the morning on the ship when Lynn woke up. Even that was early for her, but she felt as if something was nudging at her brain and telling her to wake up. She needed a Diet Coke and there wasn't any in the cabin. She sat up, thinking to get dressed, when she saw her iPhone and thought she should check in on Susan. It was Sunday and would be mid-afternoon in England, around 3:00. When she turned it on, however, all she could see was a wooden door. She waited a minute or two then checked the volume to see if she could hear anything, but there was no sound. Then the phone picture changed to show a black and white cat sitting in a window. It was licking one of its paws. It looked just like Susan's cat in the present named Checkers! What was Checkers doing back in the past and what could the door mean?

It certainly wasn't Susan's hotel room door. Where was Susan? Where was James?

A sick feeling came into the pit of her stomach.

❧

Birds were singing outside the window when Susan woke up, feeling languid and satiated from a night of lovemaking. She looked over at James, still asleep, his long lashes sweeping over his cheeks, his hair tousled on the pillow. Quietly, she got out of bed and slipped a wrapper on that she'd found hanging on a hook on the back of the bathroom door. She tied the belt around her waist and silently padded out of the bedroom, closing the door softly behind her. Buttons silently followed, then pawed at the kitchen door to be let out.

"Oh look, Buttons," she said as she opened the door. "Here comes the sun!"

Sunlight began streaming across the kitchen table and floor as she opened the refrigerator to see what might be in it to concoct for breakfast. Ah yes, eggs, more than a dozen or so, in a large, blue bowl, a dish of butter and a glass bottle of milk. Omelet or French toast? She looked in the cabinets for maple syrup, but couldn't find any. Then she spied the strawberries. French toast with some confectioner's sugar and strawberries. Perfect!

She found the French bread they'd bought yesterday in one of the bags from the shop, pulled it out and sliced half of the loaf. She then whipped a few eggs with milk and put some butter in a cast iron skillet that was sitting on the stove. She sliced some strawberries into another bowl. She thought of going in the bedroom and waking James up, but then laughed to herself as she knew what the outcome of that would be. And, she was really hungry and figured he would be too. They hadn't eaten anything since their picnic the previous afternoon. She decided to just wait for him to wake up on his own.

In the meantime, she found a coffeepot and made some coffee. While it was brewing, she opened the back door and stepped down onto a small porch then down a step into a garden bursting to the seams with a variety of vegetables and herbs…tomatoes, lettuce, cabbages, squash, peppers, eggplant, oregano, basil, mint, thyme, sage and more. She pinched a leaf off a basil plant and sniffed it. Fabulous! She heard the back door open behind her and turned around. James was standing on the porch, squinting his eyes against the sun with a hand shading his eyes. He'd pulled his trousers on, but was shirtless and looked marvelous to her, his hair still unkempt.

They both smiled at each other at the same time, warm memories of the previous day and night still fresh in their minds.

"Morning, luv," he said, coming over and planting a kiss on her upturned mouth.

"Morning," she said, wrapping her arms around his neck and looking up into his eyes. "I'll have breakfast ready in a flash if you're hungry. Coffee's already made."

"That's what woke me up, you know, the smell of coffee. I'd love breakfast. What are you making?"

"French toast with fresh strawberries."

"Mmmmm…sounds wonderful."

He released her from the embrace, and they went back in the kitchen where she lit the gas burner to melt the butter in the skillet. The kitchen door was left open, and Buttons came back in, rubbing her cheeks against Susan's legs. James ignored her.

"So, I guess I'll find out how good of cook you really are," he said teasingly.

"I'm very good, you'll find," she responded, reaching down to scratch the cat's head.

"You seem to be good at a lot of things."

"That's because I am, but you're the real talent here, you know. Go over to the piano and play me a tune while I make the French toast."

"Yes, m'lady, as you wish. And why don't you put that darned cat outside? She shouldn't be in the kitchen while you're cooking, you know."

"She can be wherever she wants to be, isn't that right, Buttons?" she responded, pouring a small saucer of milk and setting it on the floor.

James glowered at them both, but went into the other room.

As she dipped the French bread into the egg mixture and placed it in the skillet, he sat down on the piano bench and randomly played bits and pieces of tunes. The French toast was soon done and she added some salt to the remaining eggs and milk, then whipped them into scrambled eggs. They sat down at the kitchen table to eat.

"Wonderful," he said, smiling over at her. "Best I've ever had."

"Have you had French toast before then?" she asked.

"Never," he said.

"Well, no wonder it's the best then!"

As she was washing up the dishes, James went back over the piano and began picking out more tunes. As she raised her cup to take a sip of coffee, he began to play a tune that she knew so startling well that she gasped and dropped the cup on the floor. It was the beginning notes of *"All My Kisses."* It had been her favorite song for fifty years. The fine porcelain cup shattered and coffee went flying all over.

"Oh no, no!" she yelled. "Look what I've done!"

James leaped up from the piano bench, running over to her as she dropped down to the floor on her knees and began to gather the pieces of the cup.

She was trying to hold back tears, but couldn't quite do it. A large teardrop ran down her cheek and she reached up with one hand to brush it away. James joined her on the floor, reaching to pick up other pieces of the broken cup.

"Hey now, what's this?" he asked, as he saw her brush away the tear.

"Oh, I just feel so bad breaking the cup. It's probably one of your Aunt's best or most favorite or…"

"No, now stop…" He reached up to cup her face in one hand. "She won't care…really, it doesn't matter."

"But, I was so clumsy, and…"

She thought to herself, "Oh…this isn't about the cup at all…it was hearing that song!"

"It's not important. We can always get her a new one if you like."

"And where would we get a new one?"

"Well, we could go into to Little Dippington," he said. "It's just a ways down the road and they have quite a few shops there. Auntie goes there all the time for most of her stuff. A lot of her friends live there."

She sat back on her heels, then stood up and put the broken cup pieces in the trash.

"Okay, then, but first let me finish cleaning up this mess and wash the rest of the dishes. I'll sweep up what I can and scrub the floor when we get back."

"I'll go get the broom, and I'll help you with the floor later."

"Are you kidding me? Men don't know how to scrub floors properly. Just go get the broom...And don't you dare scare Buttons with it," she added, seeing James looking at the cat menacingly from the corner of his eye.

After the floor was swept and the dishes put away, Susan went into the bathroom to wash her face and use the loo. When she was done, she looked into the mirror above the sink and stared silently at what she saw.

"What are you doing here?" she asked herself. "Oh! Why did you decide to even do this and come here?!"

Hearing the beginning notes of her favorite song, the one she had cried herself to sleep listening to every night for years on end, stung her to the quick. She put her hands up to her cheeks and took a deep breath. She wondered if James was just starting on the song or if he'd finished just the tune but not the words. Should she ask him about it? Should she help him with the words? No! No changing history! She'd just have to wait and see. She thought she might ask him to play it again...Her mind was swirling as she came out of the bathroom.

This was all becoming overwhelming to her. She didn't even know if she really wanted to be here. She'd been an out of control wanton the day before, and felt almost shamed about it. Seeds of doubt were planting themselves in her mind. She wished again that Lynn was here. And, as an afterthought, she said to herself, "He doesn't even like cats!"

Chapter 8

Little Dippington

The village of Little Dippington was less than a kilometer from Auntie Annabelle's cottage, so James and Susan decided to walk. The morning was glorious, not a cloud in the sky, and it was warm enough but not too warm to enjoy walking. They strolled hand-in-hand along the side of the country lane, taking their time to stop and pick wild flax and daisies along the way.

They arrived late morning in the village, and upon James's insistence, went first to a shop that sold a variety of household items, including tea cups, pitchers, cream pots and sugar bowls.

A bell tinkled above the door as they entered the shop and a rosy-cheeked woman with a broad smile greeted them.

"Is that you, James?" she asked, looking over the top of a pair of spectacles perched on her nose.

"Is that you, Emily?" he responded.

"Well, I say, dearie, haven't laid eyes on you in an age. Are you still playing music with your mates in Brighton? Your Auntie said you were getting pretty popular."

"Well, as to that, can't say we're all that popular, but we're doing all right. Got a gig at the Dusky, better than our last gig."

"Oh, and who's your lady friend here? Going to introduce me?"

"Of course! Emily, this is Susan, a history student from America, and Susan, this is Emily, one of Auntie Annabelle's long-time and best of friends."

"Pleased to meet you, dear," said Emily, extending her hand.

Susan held out her own, and Emily took it in both of hers. "Lovely little thing," she said to James, turning to look at him. "What brings you into Little Dippington today?"

"Thought we'd look to buy Auntie a new teacup and just browse around the village."

"And where is Annabelle? Did she come with you, or is her arthritis acting up again?"

"Arthritis acting up again."

"Och, well, tell her I said hallo, dearie, will you?"

"Of course, Emily. So, show us one of your best teacups, will you?"

"Sure thing, and right over here."

She led them over to some shelves at the back of the shop, pointing to the ones on the top shelf. "Those are the prettiest, I think. Nice size too." She left them as an elderly woman entered from a room in back of the shop, holding out a frail hand and pointing it at Susan.

Neither James or Susan noticed her.

"So, which one do you fancy?" James asked.

"I like the one with hummingbirds on it," she replied.

He took it down from the shelf and handed it to her.

"Oh yes!" she exclaimed. "This is lovely!"

They both walked over to the counter, where Emily was talking quietly to the old woman, but as Susan was opening her purse to take out some money to pay for the cup, James stepped in front of her and handed some bills to Emily.

"Excellent choice," said Emily, wrapping the cup in tissue, placing it in a bag and handing it back to James. "Hope to see you again soon. Nice meeting you, dear. I hope you enjoy your visit to England and that Annabelle makes you some of her excellent scones."

Susan glanced at James then turned back to Emily. "I hope so too. Very nice meeting you."

"Och! Wait just a minute," Emily exclaimed, suddenly thinking of something. "I have a bit of leftover kidney for Buttons. Let me run upstairs and fetch it real quick." She bustled off to the back of the shop, up a set of stairs, and was soon back with a small sack. She handed it to Susan. "Buttons loves kidney. I hope she enjoys it!"

"Why, how thoughtful of you!" Susan said, glancing over her shoulder at James. "Buttons will be very grateful, I'm sure." She slipped the sack into her purse.

James and Susan headed towards the door.

"Wait!" croaked the old woman in a hoarse voice, pointing a finger at Susan again.

"Ye should no be here, ye know!"

James and Susan stared at her.

"I know who ye are. I can help ye...I can help ye get back now... Ye should go back now...You'll break his heart, you know..." The old lady's voice trailed off as Emily grabbed her arm and turned her around toward the back of the shop.

Susan had frozen at her words.

"Come along, Granny," Emily said to the old woman. She turned to Susan. "Don't mind her words now. She's gone a bit daft in her old age. Imagines all sorts of strange things. Thinks she can see into the future and all." She shook her head as she led Granny away.

Susan was rooted to the spot. James took her hand and they left the shop.

When they got outside, Susan turned to James and asked, "Why did you make Emily think your Aunt was at home, and who was that old lady?"

He looked at her sheepishly. "Well, word spreads fast in a small village, and the people here can be pretty prim and proper. No reason to start unnecessary gossip..."

"Or to make them think I'm a scarlet woman, is that it?"

"Ummm....yes...let's just leave it at that, okay?"

"Fine with me. But, who was that old lady? Did you hear what she said?"

"She's a looney one; that she is. She's Emily's Granny; must be close to a hundred by now. Everyone in the village says she has 'the sight.' You know, she can see into people's souls and tell the future, that sort of stuff. All nonsense, of course."

"Oh...of course... So, why did you go ahead and pay for the cup? I'm the one who broke it; I should have paid for it."

He shrugged. "I just thought I would, that's all. No need to spend your money. Oh, look over there! It's Simon's art studio; I wonder if he's in today. Want to take a look?"

"Sure."

They walked across the street and entered a small shop with landscape paintings displayed in the front window. As they entered, a tall bearded man peeked at them from behind an easel, bushy eyebrows raised.

"Eh, Jimmie, is that you? Haven't laid eyes on you in an age. Still attending art school? Still playing in a band? Done any good artwork lately?"

"Slow down, Simon; you're asking too many questions all at once. Yes, it's me. No, I'm not still in art school, and I haven't done any sketching or painting lately, but I've been playing music with Derek. We're getting pretty popular, actually."

Susan grinned at that.

"Music, eh? Well, that's a form of art after all, isn't it?"

"For sure it is...by the by, this is a friend of mine, Susan. Susan, this is Simon. He used to give me bits of canvas to paint on when I was young. Got me interested in art, actually."

"Nice to meet you," said Susan, extending her hand.

Simon grasped it firmly and shook it up and down. "Pleased to meet you too. Are you an artist as well?"

"Actually, she's a history student, here on a tour. The other students got delayed, so she has a few days free before she's to join them," responded James.

Susan looked at James, a tad annoyed that he answered Simon's question for her.

"To answer your question, Simon, I'm not much of an artist, but I do love to draw. I like drawing people. Pencil, sometimes charcoal or pastels, but I've also done a bit of painting, not very much though," Susan said.

"Ah, a fellow artist!" exclaimed Simon. "Always good to meet a fellow artist."

"You didn't tell me you liked to draw," said James, looking at her wonderingly.

"You never asked," she replied.

"What about we pick up some tablets and pencils then go back to the cottage and do some drawing?"

"Oh, that would be fabulous! I'd enjoy that, really!"

Simon looked at them both curiously, sensing something more than a mere friendship between them. There was something in the way they looked at each other. He couldn't put his finger on it, but being an artist, he was more sensitive and aware of body language than most. He sensed attraction bubbling between them. Aw, romance...

"I'll get some things for you, then," said Simon, standing up and going to a room in the back of the studio. He returned a moment later with two large sketch pads and a handful of pencils.

"Will these do?" he asked.

James reached into his pocket, asking what he owed.

"Nothing, nothing," said Simon. "My pleasure. Enjoy some drawing. Fine day for it outdoors."

"Generous of you, Simon," said James. "Appreciate it."

Simon nodded and smiled as they left the shop. "Something very cozy going on between those two," he thought to himself.

"Where to next?" asked James, looking up and down the street.

"Are we going back to Brighton today?"

"I wasn't planning on it. I don't have to be back until tomorrow, you know. We only play on Tuesday, Friday and Saturday. I kinda thought you might want to stay out here."

"Well, put that way, I think I would like to stay, even though we're being so wicked and probably shouldn't be here at all."

"I'm enjoying being wicked, aren't you?"

She blushed.

"Well, if we're not going back today, is there any place that sells clothing, something like shorts and tops or something like that? This is the second day I've been in this dress."

"You haven't been in the dress all that much," he quipped.

She nudged him with her elbow, blushing again. "You're incorrigible," she said.

"Do you mind?"

"No, not really."

They walked further down the street and shortly came to a shop with clothing displayed in the front window. Just before they went in, Susan looked over her shoulder down the street to see Emily's Granny standing in the open front door of the shop, staring at her. A shiver went down her spine. What had the old lady meant when she said Susan would "break his heart?" She turned away and they went into the store.

The shop had both men's and women's apparel, most of it more suited to older people, but Susan spotted an emerald green, silky-looking dress that didn't look too dowdy. There weren't any shorts or tops, just dresses, skirts and blouses.

"Oooo, feel this dress!" she exclaimed, running her hands down it. "So, so slinky and soft."

James reached out and touched it. "Very nice," he remarked. "Do you want it then?"

"I need to try it on."

They both looked around the shop for a salesperson, but didn't see anyone at first. From behind a nearby clothes rack, out popped a short dark-haired woman with her hair up in a bun. "Need to try that on, dearie?" she asked, a handful of pins in her mouth.

"Um, yes, I'd like to," said Susan.

"Just a minute then. I was pinning up a hem on a skirt for someone. Let me get rid of these pins."

She bustled off and returned a minute later. "This way, dearie."

Susan followed her to a small curtained area at the back of the shop.

"Need any help?"

"No, thanks; I think I'll be fine."

She slipped behind the curtain, took off the sundress she's been wearing for two days, and pulled the silky dress up and over her hips, wiggling into it. There were a short row of buttons on the back that were hard to do up by herself, but the dress fit perfectly. It was a brilliant emerald green in color, with a scalloped neck, gathered bust and a waist that clung to her nicely, flaring out at the hips. A tiny bit of cleavage poked out the neckline. The feel of it against her skin was delicious. She pranced out from behind the curtain and twirled in front of James and the saleslady.

"What do you think?"

"Lovely!" the saleslady said.

"You look beautiful," said James.

"In that case, I'll take it," said Susan.

She went back behind the curtain and changed back into her sundress, coming back out with the green silky dress draped over her arm. She walked over to the counter with the dress, opening her purse and saying, "So how much do I owe you?" when James pushed in front of her again and said, "Yes, how much is the dress, then? I'll be paying for it."

When the saleslady stated the price, James blanched, but pulled bills out of his pocket the same time Susan pulled some out of her purse.

"No," said Susan. "I'm paying for this. It's a dress for me; I have plenty of money and you don't need to keep paying for everything."

"But I do, you know," he said, pushing his money onto the counter.

"No, you don't," she insisted, pushing his money back towards him and placing her own on the counter. "You already paid for the cup I broke."

He pressed his hand down on top of hers as she was pushing her money towards the saleslady.

"I said I was paying for it, which means I'm paying for it and you're not. Is that not clear or something?"

She suddenly sensed he was angry and looked up at his face. Not clear? What in the hell was that supposed to mean?

And then she saw he *was* angry. She could see his eyes narrowed as he looked her straight in the face, unblinking. She'd seen that look before; it was when she'd first walked into the practice room after the hand kissing incident.

"But," she started to say.

"But, nothing. Haven't you been listening? Haven't I made myself clear?" His voice was calm, but cold.

Slowly, he lifted his hand off hers and she drew her money back towards her and put it back in her purse. She looked contrite but felt furious inside.

"Well, this is a side of him I wasn't expecting," she thought to herself, fuming. Controlling. And, as Lynn would have told him if she'd been here, she wasn't a person to be controlled or bossed around.

She found her temper begin to rise higher. No man had ever told her what she could or couldn't do, not even when she was seventeen. In fact, never! She'd always had one of those rebellious natures, and was used to getting her own way. She felt like saying "just never mind!" about the dress and stomping out of the shop.

Without any further words, the saleslady rung up the purchase, folded the dress between tissue paper, placed it in a box and handed it to James. He put it under his arm, took Susan by the elbow and they left the shop.

When they got outside, she spun around to look at him and shook her elbow free, stepping away from him a few feet and planting her hands on her hips.

"And what was that all about?" she asked, sarcasm heavy in her voice.

"It's not your place to pay for things when you're with me," he said. "If you want or need something, you let me know and I'll take care of it. You're *not* to spend your money! Do you understand me?"

"But I have plenty of money, and I know you probably don't, so why all the fuss?"

"Is that what girls do in America then? Humiliate their guy by paying for everything?"

"Humiliate? What in the hell are you talking about? It's a simple fact that I have the money to pay for whatever shit I want!" Her voice was raised.

"Well, then you need to learn that's not the way it's done here. When you're with me, I'm the one who pays for everything, including what you may need or want. And quit the swearing! It's not ladylike. I'm not letting you pay for anything and you better understand that. And, maybe you don't always get what you want!"

His voice was rising even higher than hers. People who were walking by slowed down to try and eavesdrop on the conversation.

"Oh really...I better understand that?!!..." she fumed to herself. And here he was on his way to becoming a millionaire and didn't even know it!

Then, she paused, looking down at the ground for a minute, tapping her foot on the cobblestone street while she tried to gather her wits about her and calm down. It would be pretty stupid and embarrassing to make a scene in the middle of the street. This was the early sixties after all. Women's Lib hadn't happened yet. Unless a woman was single or divorced and needed to work a job, she stayed home, kept house and made babies.

She suddenly realized that she had stepped over the line for the period of time she was in. She shouldn't even have gone into the shop to look for anything. Her sundress was just fine. She could have just washed it in the sink or something. She'd forced him out of pride to pay for something he probably couldn't afford right now. She felt terrible.

"I wasn't thinking," she said meekly. "I didn't really need another dress..." She looked up at him, tears brimming in her eyes. "Should we take it back?"

"No; you looked beautiful in it," he said, the anger instantly fading from his eyes as he saw her tears. If it was one thing he couldn't abide, it was a woman's tears. "I want you to put it on when we get back to the cottage, then we can take our pads and pencils, go sit up under the tree and sketch."

"Oh James," she said, looking into his eyes. "Thank you..."

He smiled, took her hand, and they walked back to the cottage.

Chapter 9

Falling in Love

When they got back, there was no sign of Buttons. Susan diced up the kidneys then put them on a small plate on the back porch, knowing she would find it eventually.

Before Susan slipped on her new dress, she remembered the kitchen floor, took out a bucket and some soap and filled the bucket with water. James had gone into the bathroom and when he came out, she was on her hands and knees scrubbing the floor.

'What a lovely picture you make with your bum in the air like that," he quipped.

She turned around, scrub brush in hand, "Oh really? You sure know how to flatter a girl, don't you? Grab that mop over there and dry the floor as I rinse."

"I thought you said men were bad at floor scrubbing. Besides, cleaning is girl's work."

"I'm not asking you to scrub, just mop it off. I figure you'll be able to manage that. And, it's *not* girl's work! Your dad cleans, doesn't he?"

"Yes, m'lady," he said, going to the closet without another word and taking out the mop.

When the floor was done, Susan slipped into her new dress, had James button her up in the back, and they headed out the door up the hill to where they'd had their picnic the day before. The blanket and remnants of yesterday's picnic were still there.

"Looks like we forgot to come back and pick up," James remarked.

"Hmmm...well, we know the reason for that now, don't we?" she said, smiling up at him. "Look! We still have a half bottle of wine left. Let's kill it off."

She divided the remaining wine between the two glasses she found lying on their sides on the blanket.

"Okay, your turn to make up a toast," she said.

"To more of yesterday," he said teasingly.

"Pretty single-minded aren't you?" she responded, clinking her glass up against his. "But, I suppose I can agree to that..."

Her hormones yawned and stretched, waking up.

James handed her one of the sketch pads and picked up one of the pencils he'd laid down on the blanket. She accepted the pad and reached down to pick up one of the other pencils.

"So, what's your subject going to be then?" he asked.

"Why you, of course," she responded. "I can do your profile if you turn sideways to me. How about you? What do you want to draw?"

"Hmmm...Nature, I think...trees, sky, clouds..." He opened his sketch pad and started making sweeping strokes across the paper.

She studied his profile intently for a moment, then put her own pencil to work. They drew silently and companionably for about twenty minutes, when Susan said, "Okay, see what you think," as she passed her sketch pad over to him.

"Hey, that's quite good!" he said. "Where did you learn to draw?" He handed her sketch pad back to her.

"My grandfather taught me. He does landscapes and still life, but I've always liked to draw people. I thought at one time I'd like to be a portrait painter."

"I thought you wanted to be a ballerina. Remember, when you showed me your necklace?"

"My bosom is too big for a ballerina as I was trying to tell you, but I'd still like to be one. I love to dance!"

"I don't mind your bosom being too big," he said wickedly.

"There you go again with your one track mind..."

He tossed his sketch pad and pencil down near the bottom of the blanket, leaned over and pushed her down on her back as her own sketch pad and pencil went flying. He brought his lips down on hers and began running his hands up and down the sides of her silky dress.

"Mmmmm...lovely, I do like this dress..." he said kissing her neck and throat.

Her arms snaked around his neck and she pulled him closer.

"Maybe we should go back to the cottage," she whispered seductively.

He looked into her eyes with his own half-closed. "Shall we then..." he agreed.

They stood up, gathered up the sketch pads and pencils and shoved them into the picnic hamper that had been left behind the day before. Susan put in the wine glasses and they both folded up the blanket then headed back to the cottage, eager anticipation vibrating through their bodies.

They didn't even make it to the bedroom. James sat on the sofa and beckoned Susan to him. She put her hands on her hips and shook her head.

"Wait just a minute," she said, as she slowly reached back to undo a few buttons of the dress then pulled it up and over her head. She then pulled down the straps of her bra and pushed it down to her waist then over her hips, taking her panties down at the same time until she stood naked in front of him with only her necklace dangling down between her breasts, her eyes burning brightly. She reached up and let her hair loose from the clip she'd fastened it up in. It cascaded down to her waist. She cupped her breasts in her hands and wiggled her hips seductively.

"Wow!" she thought to herself, knowing she was wet and ready for him. "These seventeen-year-old hormones are something else! I'd almost forgotten what it was like to be so horny all the time. It's almost embarrassing! I can't seem to get enough of him! Lucky guy!"

Her hormones smiled lazily. They'd been somewhat quiet lately. Probably because they were worn out and satiated from so much love making the previous afternoon and night.

She could see his arousal pushing against his trousers, walked over to release it, straddled him and slid down on top until he was fully buried inside her. He leaned his head back and let out a moan before grabbing her hips and working her up and down on his erection. She closed her eyes and threw her own head back, enjoying the sheer ecstasy of their movement. It wasn't long before they both reached the inevitable and powerful release and Susan collapsed onto him, wrapping her arms around his neck, her loose hair tumbling down her back and across his shoulders. Both of them were moist with sweat and slightly panting from their exertion.

James pushed her back slightly away from him, holding her by her shoulders, a warm smile on his face.

"That was quite aggressive of you...Have you no shame, m'lady?" he asked, teasingly.

She smiled back at him. "Where you're concerned, sir, none whatsoever..."

She eased herself off him and slipped the dress back on, this time with no undergarments...just in case they decided on more of the same later. She knew all he had to do was crook his finger.

She was indeed, shameless.

A short time later, after tidying up the cottage, Susan decided to take a bath, ran hot water into the claw foot tub and immersed herself in the warmth with a sigh. Buttons had come back, trotted into the bathroom with her and was sitting on the toilet seat. Susan's limbs were still like limp rubber after her last intimate encounter and she sighed deeply as she slid down into the water until it touched her chin. She closed her eyes, feeling as if she could fall asleep in the comfort of the bath. Slowly, she began washing herself with the rose-scented soap that was sitting on a small table by the tub, luxuriating in the slinky feel and wonderful smell of the soap on her skin. When she was done washing, she lowered her head back into the water, wetting her hair, then raised up using the same soap to wash it, as she hadn't been able to find any shampoo.

"Don't have shampoo or conditioner here?" she asked Buttons.

"Mrow," the cat responded.

"Well, whatever that means..." Susan said.

After leaning back and rinsing the soap out of her hair, she got out of the tub, wrapped a towel around her and walked back out into the main room. James was fast asleep on the couch, his hands pressed together under one cheek. The sight of him took her breath away as she continued to drink him in.

She was in love. There was no doubt about it. She had felt the emotion creep up on her from the moment she first laid eyes on him three days before. It was a feeling that started in the pit of her stomach and moved up into her chest, making her feel almost faint. Knowing she only had four days left to be with him, near him, holding him...tears stung her eyes and she rubbed them away quickly.

She turned and went into the bedroom, putting the green dress back on, then went out into the kitchen. It was late afternoon, time to think about dinner. Methodically, she started opening cabinets to see what was there. She then took a quick inventory of the refrigerator, where there were still numerous items left over from their picnic hampers and what they'd bought the day before.

"Ah," she thought, "Chicken; I can do something with Mel's leftover roast chicken..." She took it out and began removing the skin and bones, placing the pieces of meat into a large pan she'd found, saving a few pieces for Buttons, and added some olive oil she'd discovered in one of the cabinets. She looked out the window into the garden and remembered the basil she'd seen that morning. She went out into the garden, snipped several sprigs of basil, then some oregano and pulled an onion and a garlic bulb out of the ground. She removed the papery skin from the onion and garlic, chopped them on a cutting board and added them to the pan. With a pair of scissors, she snipped the basil and oregano and sprinkled it on top. She then took the tomatoes James's dad had given them, diced them, put them on top of everything else, lit the gas burner to low and put a lid on the pan. She found linguine pasta in another cabinet and set the package on the counter. In the refrigerator, she found some Romano cheese that was already grated and set it on the counter next to the pasta.

"Hmmm..." she thought, "I can turn the rest of the French bread into garlic toast and maybe make a salad. Auntie Annabelle appears to have a taste for Italian food based on her pantry items and garden."

James came into the kitchen then, just as the chicken and toma-toes were beginning to simmer.

"What are you making?" he asked, still looking a big sleepy-eyed.

"Italian food," she replied. "It appears your Aunt must like it. There's all sorts of stuff in her pantry to make it with."

He nodded. "Her husband was stationed in Italy during the war and he came back with all kinds of recipes and a love of Italian food. She learned how to cook it, and even her garden has all the herbs and things like garlic that she uses to cook Italian. My mum and dad used to come here all the time for her famous Italian feasts."

"Well, that explains it then. Do you like Italian food?"

"Love it...if it's good...Is yours going to be good?"

She put her hands on her hips, pretending to be insulted. "What do you think? You liked the French toast well enough this morning."

"That I did. But, I would probably have liked it even you'd burned it."

They both laughed, then James suddenly became silent. He looked at her standing at the stove. She had one of Auntie Annabelle's aprons tied around her waist and a spot of tomato juice on her cheek. She lifted the lid on the chicken, gave a quick stir with a large spoon, then put the lid back on and lowered the heat. He came over and wrapped his arms around her from behind, nuzzling the back of her neck. He pulled her tighter against him.

"I love you," he said into her ear. "I think I've loved you from the moment I saw you."

She froze. Those had been her own exact thoughts. A shiver went down her spine all the way to her toes. That feeling seemed to happen a lot around him. She turned slowly to face him and lifted a hand to brush the hair off his forehead.

"Oh James," she murmured, gazing deeply into his eyes, "I love you so much it hurts. It feels like I've loved you my whole life." Tears welled in her eyes as she laid her head on his shoulder. "Actually, I *have* loved you my whole life," she thought to herself. "Haven't I?"

He pushed her back for a moment, wiped the tomato juice off her face and gathered her closer to him. "I feel that I can't even hold you close enough..." Gently, he stroked her back as she sighed contentedly. He then slowly inched the skirt of her dress up and squeezed her bare bottom. Her face was buried into his shoulder. "Here we go again," she smiled.

"Oh my, yes!" giggled her hormones.

∽⟲

It was late morning on Monday, when Lynn switched on her iPhone and tapped into the App Marta had installed. James and Susan were in the kitchen in the cottage, Susan standing in front of the stove stirring something in a large pan. She saw James enter the room and come up behind her.

Where were they? This certainly wasn't Susan's hotel room, that's for sure! They must be at James's house or somebody's house. She laughed. It figured Susan would be in the kitchen. Lynn knew Susan had a passion for cooking.

Lynn listened to their conversation, a worried expression coming over her face.

"Okay, this is worse than bad," Lynn thought to herself. "What to do...what to do...She's so caught up in the moment, she doesn't even know what she's saying. She obviously surrendered to him...but, they're in love already? Oh my God!"

After only a few moments contemplation, and another peek into her iPhone that reflected a way too sensual moment between the two new lovers, she flicked off the phone and made her way to Marta and Mika's cabin. Time to throw a wrench in this before the craziness went any further.

Susan didn't belong with James! She belonged back home with her husband!

Chapter 10

Lynn Goes Back

"Believe in love at first sight?" asked a very familiar voice, as Lynn was fussing with her iPhone, trying to figure out why it didn't work anymore.

"Huh...what..." she mumbled looking up from her lap.

Ian, only a few feet away and leaning one elbow on the table she was sitting at, looked at her questioningly.

If she'd been paying attention for the past five minutes instead of poking at her iPhone, she would have realized that she'd materialized onto the same bar stool that Susan had been on just three nights previous.

She was in the Dusky Club. It was just past midnight on Monday night and Ian was subbing in for the lead guitarist for "The Stingers," and there was a break between sets. Right before the end of the last song, one of the other band members had elbowed Ian and motioned over to where Lynn was sitting.

As the music ended, he said, "Looks a bit like that other American bird that James went so gaga over last Friday and Saturday nights when you were playing. I was back with the bartender, and Sandra was babbling about how the regular girls were having fits and starts over his attention to her."

Ian looked intently over at Lynn.

She was wearing her own June Cleaver-style dress in a pale shade of yellow, which set off her suntan. She stood out like a ray of sunshine in the room, with her golden hair and generously endowed body. She had a yellow ribbon in her hair. Ian felt a familiar stirring in his loins as he took her in from head to toe. Where in the hell had she come from? Was she one of Susan's fellow students come to meet her for the history tour? Maybe she had just arrived earlier than Susan was expecting her? Susan said the other students would be arriving on Friday and then they'd all be going off to somewhere else for their tour.

The longer he looked at her, her sandaled foot swinging back and forth as she concentrated on something in her lap, the more he felt drawn to her. What exactly was it about these American girls that made them so desirable?

Ian had been the first one to notice Susan last Friday, and was ready to make his move on her, when James cut him out. No matter. This girl was much more in his style. Susan looked like some kind of frightened bird as James made his attempts to pursue her. This girl looked ripe and ready for the plucking. Voluptuous and just waiting to be caressed.

"Wager on?" asked the other Stinger band member.

"For tonight?" Ian asked.

"Of course! That's always the wager isn't it?"

"You're on then."

"Good luck, mate. Hope she's not like that other American bird, flighty as hell and not willing to put out on the first or even second try as I heard."

Lynn recovered from her initial shock at seeing Ian so close and personal. She quickly shoved her iPhone in her purse and glanced around the club.

"I...I...don't know what I think of love at first sight," she said, sounding very innocent and at the same time startled at his question.

"Well...I never really thought much about it either...until now..." Ian said, pulling another stool up to the table and looking at her.

She had the most gorgeous brown eyes. They were like chocolate and reflected a deep passionate nature. He was very intrigued.

Lynn thought to herself, "Oh geez, I wasn't expecting this! I came here to rescue Susan from her stupid self and now here I am confronted with...confronted with...Oh my God...my own silly daydream that I don't even really care about any more...my own opportunity to know the guy I used to dream about when I was what? Fourteen years old?"

Ian put both of his elbows on the table and tilted his head at her. "Cuppa after the last set, luv?" he asked.

"Cup of what?" she inquired.

"Whatever you like...tea...coffee...or me..."

She blushed furiously. This was ridiculous! What a trite and stupid pick up line to boot!

"How did I come to be here like this?" she asked herself. Where was Susan? Should she ask? She was supposed to be one of the history students, wasn't she? She couldn't really remember. She hadn't paid that much attention to what Susan had told James. Oh geez! She needed to remember!

"You?" she muttered under her breath.

"Well, just think about it, luv," he said as he walked back up to the front of the club and slipped his guitar strap back over his shoulder and winked at her.

"Winking...what was it that Susan was saying about winking," she asked herself.

Ian started singing, looking at her with an inviting smile on his face.

"I saw her sitting on the bar stool... with a yellow ribbon in her ponytail..."

"Oh my God!" she thought," her instinctively passionate nature making her feel warm all over. I came here to rescue Susan, but I think I'm going to be the one who needs rescuing!"

As James began to kiss her, Susan pushed him away and said, "Now look here, sir, I have dinner on the stove and don't want to be distracted and burn everything. Go twiddle at the piano some more and entertain me."

He reluctantly let her go then went over and sat down at the piano.

"Any special requests?" he asked.

"Whatever you want. We've got about twenty minutes until every-thing will be ready," she said, stirring the chicken again, cutting lettuce for the salad and slicing up the rest of the French bread to make garlic toast.

When she was done, she walked over to a cabinet next to the piano.

"What's this?" she asked, opening the top of the cabinet to reveal a record player. "Oh, are there any records?"

"I think there's some underneath in the cabinet."

She bent over and opened the cabinet doors. "Oh, look! There's lots of records here...Let's see what she has..."

He leaned over and looked into the cabinet with her.

"Look!" she exclaimed, "Here's one of my favorites..."*Sleeping Beauty*" by Tchaikovsky. Have you ever heard the "*Sleeping Beauty Waltz*?"

"Why don't you play it then?"

"Actually, I can dance for you to this. I love this music!"

"Ah, are you going to be my personal little ballerina then? Go ahead and put it on and dance for me."

"First, I need to warm up. You can play me some plie music...slow... an adagio...4/4 measure...four sets of sixteen counts. Think you can do that?"

"Actually, my dad played music for a dance studio once. When he was sick one time, I had to go take his place. I hated it."

"You won't play plies for me?"

"Of course I'll play plies for you. How's this?"

He started to play.

"Wait, wait...let me grab a kitchen chair...you need a four count intro..."

She kicked off her sandals, dragged a kitchen chair near the piano and stood in first position, arms in low fifth. "Okay, go ahead," she said.

At the intro, she placed her left hand hand gracefully on the back of the chair and moved her right arm in a port de bras and began. Demi, demi, grand plie, port de bras forward, back bend, move into second position. She moved with poise, her eyes half closed, totally enveloped in the music as he played for her.

He glanced over at her appreciatively, thinking how fluid her movements were. His heart tightened in his chest. What could be more beautiful than watching this?

He continued playing, and she turned to put her other hand on the chair, back in first position. She repeated the movements on the other side, ending in a releve (up on the balls of her feet) in a tight fifth with both arms overhead.

He stared at her silently.

She took the Sleeping Beauty record out of the sleeve, put it on the record player, turned it on and placed the needle on the record.

"Okay, watch..." she said, as the entre to the waltz blared throughout the room.

Balance forward, balance back, repeat, soutnou turn. The skirt of the green silky dress swirled outward as she turned. She started moving around the room to the music, totally taken over by the melody.

As the music began to repeat itself, she began to sing..."*I love you... you danced with me once upon a dream...When I saw you...the sparks in your eyes were so familiar to me... So I'm sure it's true...that first love is rarely what it seems...but now I'm with you... I know what is true...You'll hold me again... just as you did then...upon a dream...*"

She kept moving, turning, spinning, waltzing, until the music ended and she placed her hand on his shoulder in a ponche arabesque.

Memories of being in the Sleeping Beauty Castle when she was sixteen years old and had encountered an older James, rushed through her veins. She remembered singing the same *"Once Upon a Dream"* song at his insistence and then running away when he proposed they leave Disneyland together. She shivered at the memory.

James was speechless. He pulled her onto his lap on the piano bench and held her close. "That was so lovely," he whispered in her ear, still astounded.

She kissed his cheek, extracted herself from his arms and jumped up, dragging the chair back into the kitchen with her.

"Time for dinner, sweetheart," she said.

If Lynn was one thing, she was practical. As Ian sang and threw inviting looks in her direction, she evaluated the whole situation. Here she was living out a crazy fantasy she wasn't even sure she wanted to be in. She had four nights to live it. Unlike Susan, who was like a scared little kitten, Lynn always had her two feet planted firmly on the ground. She knew a bet had been made about her and Ian, just like a bet had been made on Susan.

"So what," she thought, being pragmatic. If she decided to go for it, she didn't think she'd have to fool around with that virgin thing either. She was pretty sure the preacher's son had taken care of that; she just didn't remember exactly when.

The set ended and Ian came back over to her table.

"So, do we have a date then?" He drawled.

"Mmmmm...I suppose so," she said. "Any particular place you have in mind?"

"Your hotel room?"

"Well, that's pretty darn blunt!"

"No reason to beat around the bush, is there? I find you very attractive...much more attractive than your American friend...I assume you're a friend of the other American bird who came in here Friday night and sent James into a tizzy."

"Oh! That American girl...Susan...Yes, I'm her best friend, actually. I came here to rescue her...I mean, join her. We're here for a history tour, I think...I mean, yes, we *are* here for a history tour."

"So, are all the students just popping in here one at a time then? Your friend told James that everybody else was to join up on Friday."

"Um, well, they're meeting us in London on Friday...the rest of them, I mean...just a little change in plans. I decided to pop in early, as you said, because I had a feeling Susan was getting herself into trouble."

"With James you mean?"

"Um, yeah, with James. She's a virgin you know." The words were out of her mouth before she could stop them.

Ian raised his eyebrows. "Well, I doubt she is any longer."

"Yeah, that's what I'm worried about. Do you happen to know where she is? When I went to the hotel room, there was no sign of her, and the front desk said they hadn't seen her since yesterday morning. She had them pack a picnic basket, which I thought was a little odd."

"No idea where she is, but must be with James, of course. So, about our date?"

"Can we start a little slower, please? I'm not saying 'no' to the hotel room for some time later, but I'm not a loose girl, you know. I'm a serious student of history." She tried to keep a straight face.

"Are you then? Tell me something historic."

She laughed out loud.

"Go back up on stage and play me a song," she said. "Something to win a lady over to your wicked ways."

"I'll do my best," he said, pushing away from the table and going back on stage.

"Young girl...sweet girl...got my head in a whirl...can't get you out of my heart..."

Just as James and Susan were finishing up dinner, the telephone in the main room rang. James didn't make a move to answer it.

"Don't you think you should answer?" she asked. "It could be your dad or something."

James hesitated just a second, then got up and went into the other room to answer the phone. He made it on the fifth ring. He didn't seem very anxious to talk to his dad if that was who was calling.

"Hallo."

"Hello, James? This is Dad."

"Yeah, Dad."

"So sorry to disturb you, but Derek called a bit ago and said it was important to get a hold of you. Seems some bloke named Ryan Graystein wants to hear you and the boys play tomorrow morning for an hour or so at some recording studio down in South Brighton. Might be an opportunity, you know. Sounds like it's an audition for making a record."

"Ryan Graystein? Tomorrow morning?"

"That's what Derek said. He wanted to make sure you'd be there. 10:00 on South Audley Road."

"I'll be there, but say, Dad, can I drop off Susan to stay with you while I'm there? It's right on the way to South Brighton and her hotel is quite a ways north."

There was a moment of silence on the other end.

"Of course, I'd be delighted to have her."

"Something wrong, Dad?"

"You both stay the night together at Annabelle's last night then?"

It was James's turn to be silent.

"Yeah, we did."

"And you're still there? Staying another night also?"

"Yeah."

"You heard what I said about her, didn't you?"

"Yeah; you were right." He lowered his voice. "She was innocent."

"But not anymore?"

"No, not anymore."

"We'll talk more about it tomorrow, then."

"Talk about what?"

"I said, we'll talk more about it tomorrow."

"Sure, Dad. See you tomorrow, then."

"Good night, James...and tell Susan good night too."

"Bye, Dad."

James went back into the kitchen, sat back down at the table and lifted his wine glass. "This calls for a toast," he said. "We've been requested to audition for a bloke named Ryan Graystein."

Susan almost choked on the piece of chicken she'd just put into her mouth. She chewed, swallowed and picked up her wine glass, clinking it against his.

"That's fabulous!" she said. "Oh, James, you're an incredible talent!! I just know you're going to be famous! This is just the start; you wait and see."

He grinned from ear to ear. "I hope you're right then," he said. "So, here's to our being famous!"

They each took a sip of wine.

126

James looked at Susan tenderly. How wonderful to have someone believe in him so much. She was like a rock, so sure of his future and success. It made his heart melt.

"Thing is, we need to leave early tomorrow morning and you can't come to the audition. I asked my dad if it was okay to drop you at the house, and he said it would be fine. I should only be gone a couple of hours at most."

She looked at him across the top of her wine glass. "Well, that sounds fine to me. I really like your dad...but...now that we've um... you know...and he knows we've been here overnight alone..." She blushed.

"Dad won't hold you responsible. He'll be blaming me for what happened anyway. What do you say we go do some more 'you know' right now?"

"Not before the dishes are done and everything put away."

She tipped her wine glass, sipped the last of the wine and got up from the table, carrying her plate. She put it in the sink and turned around to go back and get his, but he was blocking her way. Before she could utter a sound, he'd scooped her up in his arms and carried her into the bedroom.

"The dishes can wait," he said, tossing her onto the bed and pushing Buttons off onto the floor.

She smiled up at him and opened her arms.

As Lynn watched and listened to Ian sing, she started thinking back to the time when she had a huge crush on him. "Might as well live in the moment," she thought. He had a sensitive look about him and she remembered he'd always been called the "quiet one."

"Well," she thought, "He might be quiet, but he certainly wasn't shy with girls!"

She wondered if she was doing the right thing, letting him flirt with her so outrageously and with such bold innuendos. She was giving him back everything he was throwing her way. How wicked of her!

And what fun!

No sign of Susan, and she knew she wasn't likely to come across her tonight, so why not enjoy herself? No one would ever know...Ian was looking at her intently as he sang. Her mind wandering back to the past, she found that she rather enjoyed it.

Sandra came over just then, a tray balanced in one hand, plucked a glass of dark brown stuff off the tray and set it on the table in front of Lynn.

"Compliments of Ian," she said with a wink.

Lynn picked up the glass and sniffed. "What is this?" she asked.

"Why ale, of course. Ain't you ever had ale before?"

"I've had beer, but not ale. Is it the same?"

"Pretty much, but we have small beer too. Hey, you're an American too, ain't you? There was another American girl in here Friday and Saturday. Nice girl, name of Susan. I'm sorta getting to be her friend. You wouldn't be part of her history group, would ya?"

"Yes, yes, I am. In fact, I came here looking for her. She wasn't in her hotel room, so I thought she might be here."

"Ha! Not likely...She's off with one of the blokes who plays in the band Friday, Saturday and tomorrow. Ian plays with them regular-like too, but he sometimes fills in for other bands who need a good guitarist. He's the best actually...in high demand."

"No surprise to me!" thought Lynn.

"You wouldn't happen to know where the bloke from the other band would be with Susan, would you?"

"James, you mean? No clue. Probably has her off somewhere private like."

"That's what worries me."

"No need to worry; he's a good bloke."

"Well, I'm not so sure of that, but never mind. Thanks for bringing the drink."

"No worries, luv," Sandra giggled. "Your friend, Susan taught me that phrase. I've been usin' it a lot! Well, enjoy yourself," she said, walking off to deliver the other drinks on her tray.

Lynn made an executive decision and decided to forget about Susan for the rest of the night. She took a sip of the ale, making a face at the bitter taste, then smiled at Ian, who had finished playing the last set for the night and was coming over to her table. Oh, yes! She was going to enjoy the night...

After Ian packed up his gear, he and Lynn headed down to the pubs by the dock, where they chatted amicably for two hours. They hopped from pub to pub, listening to the music and sharing family history and experiences. It wasn't long before they felt they'd known each other for much longer than a few hours.

"Time to go to your hotel then?" Ian asked, leaning back in his chair with his booted feet and legs stretched out in front of him.

He looked fabulous to Lynn in his relaxed pose. Very sexy, in fact. The beer she'd been drinking had also most likely affected her vision and perception of him.

"I think I'd like that," she said.

He stood up, threw some money on the table, grabbed her hand and they headed out the door.

When they reached the hotel, Ian grabbed his acoustic guitar out of the boot of the car and took it with him into the hotel. Lynn pressed the elevator button for the fourth floor. As soon as they entered the hotel room, Lynn reached for the light switch. Ian put out his hand and stopped her as he closed and locked the door behind them, leaning his guitar against the wall next to it.

"Full moon shining through the window. No reason to waste the moonlight, is there?" he asked softly, putting his arms around her waist from behind and nibbling at her neck.

"Mmmmmm..." she sighed as he unzipped the back of her dress.

It slithered to the floor.

He pushed the bra straps down her arms, then reached around to tweak the nipples of her breasts.

"Oh!" she squealed breathlessly.

He then turned her around and brought his mouth down on her breasts, suckling her until she felt she would go wild with wanting him.

She pushed her panties down over her hips and used her feet to pull them the rest of the way off and onto the floor.

"Let's get in the bed," she whispered.

"Yes, let's," he said, kissing her full on the mouth and pushing her backwards.

She sprawled onto the bed on her back and watched him remove all of his clothes. She could see in the moonlight that he was ready for her and opened her arms to receive him on top of her. But instead, he brought his head to her collar bone and licked his way down her chest to her belly button, teasing and taunting her all the way. His head and tongue went lower, then even lower.

"I plan on pleasuring you first, luv," he said in a husky voice. "Lay back and enjoy it."

As his tongue reached her most private and sensitive nether parts, she let out a moan and grabbed his hair.

A pang of guilt washed over her but only briefly. She was definitely letting Ian win the wager...

Chapter 11

Susan and Mel

James and Susan left Annabelle's cottage at 8:30 after a hasty cup of coffee, not waking up in time for breakfast. Just as they were walking out the door, Susan remembered the pastries that the hotel had packed in the picnic hamper and grabbed them out of the bread box where she'd put them on Sunday. She also took the leftover chicken from the previous night, thinking that maybe James's dad would like it for dinner. She set down a saucer of milk and the pieces of chicken she'd saved for Buttons on the back porch. They hastened out the door and to the car.

They ate the pastries on the way and James dropped Susan off with just enough time to load his gear into the boot of Derek's car and take off for the recording studio. Derek had been waiting out front, as they were going to South Brighton together and leaving James's car with Mel.

James threw a quick "hello" to his dad, who was out back of the townhouse in the small garden, but took time to give Susan a rather long and romantic kiss.

"I love you," James said softly with his hand on her cheek.

"I love you too," Susan said, meeting his eyes.

He patted her teasingly on the bottom then went out the door. She wondered if Mel had noticed and blushed.

Susan stood awkwardly behind him in the garden. Mel was kneeling on a small rubber pad, weeding around the tomato plants. He pushed back off the pad, stood up and smiled.

"Welcome back," he said cheerfully.

The awkwardness of the situation instantly vanished. She smiled back at him.

"Thank you," she said. "I hope I'm not imposing on your morning or anything."

"No, no, dear...not at all. No plans at all for today. Why don't we go inside and I'll brew up some coffee for us?"

"That sounds great. We only had time for a quick cup before we left..." Her voice trailed off and she blushed furiously.

Mel pretended not to notice and turned away toward the stove to reach for the coffee pot.

"So, what did you think of the countryside?" he asked, trying for a neutral topic of conversation.

"It's beautiful, and the cottage is so quaint. We had a picnic under this wonderful tree at the top of the hill above the cottage, then James showed me the pond where he and Chad used to go swim..." She stopped dead.

"The pond, eh? Yeah, we all liked swimming in that pond. Sherry and I used to watch the boys swim there all the time."

Susan had her eyes cast down, not sure of what to say next. She bit her lip.

"Don't think I hold you responsible for anything that happened," he said, touching her gently on the arm. "I knew what it would be the minute James told me where he was taking you and knowing Annabelle wasn't going to be there."

"Oh, but...he...he told me before we left that what happened on the picnic would be all up to me...he said..."

"It doesn't matter what he said. He knew you were ripe for the plucking, if you'll pardon the expression. It was easy to see what an innocent you were."

Mel poured two cups of coffee and they both sat down at the kitchen table.

"Well, I'm not innocent anymore," she said, tears stinging her eyes. "You must think I'm no better than those other girls at the club..."

"I don't think anything of the sort about you. You're nothing like those other girls."

"But, I'd always thought I'd save myself for...you know...stay innocent until...But...I wasn't any better than those girls when it came to... to... resisting."

"Susan, I doubt you could have resisted if you'd wanted to. James is very persuasive. He had his mind set on having you. You would have given in eventually, if not Sunday, then the day after or the day after that."

She gave a large sigh. "You're probably right, but it doesn't make me feel any better about it."

"So, do you love each other then? I overheard what you said to each other. Obviously, it would seem like too short of a time for two people to fall in love, but it was that quick with my Sherry and me. Love at first sight, it was. We were a lot older, but I can see the way you two look at each other...And, I also saw the way he just kissed you before he left...tender like."

She looked at him shyly. "I believe that, yes, we do love each other. Oh yes, Mel, I *really* do...but it won't work..."

"But? What do you mean that it won't work? Now that he's taken your innocence, James will do the right thing by you, you know..."

Her eyes flew open at his last remark, but she decided to ignore it.

"Ummm...So, can I help you out in the garden," she asked, abruptly changing the subject and hoping he would say "yes."

"I'm just weeding."

"I know how to weed. James might have told you that I live with my grandparents. They have an acre of land and my grandfather grows everything. I love to be in the garden with my hands in the dirt."

"Then come on out," he said.

They both headed out the back door and started work, Susan telling Mel all about her grandparents, how they grew up during the depression and were very frugal, which included growing all their own vegetables and fruit as well as owning chickens jointly with a neighbor for eggs and sometimes roast chicken.

"I also love to cook. My grandmother taught me to cook, but I drew the line at plucking chickens. I brought you the leftovers from our dinner last night, by the way."

"My, my...a girl of many talents; I just might decide to fall in love with you myself and steal you away from James."

She threw her head back and laughed. "You can try. I think I love you a little bit too."

"Sounds like your grandparents raised you then?"

"Yes; my father passed away when I was seven, so my mother, brother and I moved in with grandma and grandpa."

"And here James was thinking you were an heiress or something."

"Why would he think that?"

"Dunno. Probably the way you talk, genteel and sophisticated like. And your clothes look pretty fine too."

"Well, I'm certainly no heiress, that's for sure! But, I can't say I lack for anything either. My, um...Uncle, the history professor...paid for this trip. He has a lot more money than my grandparents. This is just a special trip since I've graduated high school. My grandfather expects me to go to college when I get back."

"So, you'll be going back then?"

"Um, yes...I'll have to go back...after the history tour, that is."

"When do you leave on the tour?"

"This Friday. Midnight actually." The words were out of her mouth before she thought about them.

"Midnight?" Odd time to be leaving for anything. I thought James told me the rest of the students were coming here?"

"Well, um...change of plans...There's a charter bus...it's doing a turn-around from London. Gets in I think around 11:00 and then I'm off at midnight. I'll sleep on the bus on the way back to London then the rest of the students will join me and we'll continue on..." She was rattling off whatever came into her head, realizing home lame it must sound.

Mel sat back on his heels and stared keenly at her for a minute. He sensed she wasn't being totally truthful or was hiding something.

"Still seems rather odd. Why are the other students in London and you're here?"

She looked away at a bird that was sitting on the top of the fence. "Oh, look! A robin!" she said, pointing to the fence.

Mel looked up at the bird, realizing she was trying to change the subject yet again.

"Yes, very pretty bird, isn't it?"

"So, Mel, I have an idea. What would you think if I made a nice dinner for you and James after the practice this afternoon? He told me you love to cook just like your sister, Annabelle, so maybe you could lend a hand?"

"Well, that's very nice of you... sounds like a fine idea. I haven't made a meal for more than myself in a long time. I rather enjoy cooking a good meal."

She clapped her hands together. "Let's plan a menu then." She looked around the garden. "Hmmm...lettuce and tomatoes for salad, green beans for a vegetable...I think this will be a lot of fun! Would it be possible for you to take me to a store to buy some other stuff?"

"What are you thinking you might need then?"

"I was thinking something really nice, like a prime rib. Is there a butcher shop around here?"

"Not sure what a prime rib is; could you mean a beef roast?"

"Yes, a type of beef roast, but a really, really good beef roast. And, mashed potatoes...and I could make some bread...and for dessert..."

"Slow down, young lady! You're getting pretty fancy for us."

"It's not fancy. I just want to do something special. And...I have money to pay for the beef roast and a few other things we'll need."

"Can't let you pay for our food now and a beef roast is pretty dear..."

"Please? Please let me...James said the same thing when I tried to pay for this dress. He got quite angry with me about it."

"Not your place to pay for things, you know, being a lady and all."

"But, I have all this money that I'm supposed to be spending on my trip. This is just for a special dinner. Please let me pay for it."

"Well, I shouldn't, you know."

She ran to get her purse and came back holding out a fistful of bills. "Here, take this and you can be the one who pays for the roast and other stuff so it won't look like a lady is paying. Please, Mel?"

Reluctantly, he took it and shoved the bills in his pocket. Susan looked at the clock. It was getting on to noon. "Oh! Look at the time! James could be back any minute now!"

Just as the words came out of her mouth, the telephone rang. It was James. He was still at the recording studio and Ian was missing. They hadn't been able to find him the night before to tell him about the audition and he hadn't been home. Derek knew he'd played with The Stingers and had just got a hold of one of the band members who said Ian had gone off with some American girl. They were trying to hunt him down. James asked Mel if he could drop Susan off at the 3:00 practice later in case it took longer to find Ian. He asked if maybe Ian had called there, but Mel told him "no."

"Well, that certainly gives us time to put a dinner together, doesn't it?" Mel said, smiling at Susan, adding, "According to James, Ian didn't show up at the audition today. I wonder where he could be off to? James said he left the club last night with some American girl."

Susan froze. "An American girl?" she asked, a puzzled expression on her face.

"That's what he said. Could it be one of your history student friends?"

Susan thought to herself, "It must be Lynn. She probably saw me on her iPhone. Why did she decide to come, unless..."

Mel interrupted her thoughts. "Well, now we have time to get our dinner planned," he said again.

"Yes! And for me to make bread…making bread is an adventure in itself. But, can we go to the butcher's now?"

"You're twisting my arm on this, but okay, let's go."

The butcher shop was only a few minutes away. It was actually a small grocery store with a butcher counter. After discussing the merits of one type of beef roast over another, Susan selected what she felt most closely resembled a prime rib. It was pricey, but she'd given plenty of money to Mel to pay for it along with the other items she needed – potatoes, cream, vanilla, yeast, flour, eggs and extra butter. She was going to try her hand at Creme Brulee for dessert, hoping she remembered the correct amount of ingredients.

"All set," she said, as she and Mel walked out of the store, bags in tow.

When they got back and unloaded the bags, Susan got to work on the bread. Mel sat at the table watching her, a bemused expression on his face. "You really look like you know what you're doing there."

"That's because I do," she said, stirring the yeast into hot water and measuring flour into a large bowl. Working from memory, she added the other ingredients, stirred the dough until it formed into a big ball then slammed it onto the table that she'd dusted with flour. She began kneading.

"When I'm done, I'll put this in a greased bowl and in a few hours… I'll probably be gone at the practice…you'll need to punch it down, put it into the loaf pans and re-cover it, okay? We can bake it when I get back."

He was observing her actions with great interest. "Of course. You remind me of Sherry standing there like that."

"Does it make you sad?"

"No; rather brings back fond memories, it does."

"Well, that's good then. So, if I go outside and pick some beans, can you start peeling the potatoes? We can just put them in a pot of cold water for now."

He got up and filled a pan with water, brought it back to the table with the bag of potatoes and a peeler and started to work. She came back into the kitchen with a large bowl of green beans, sat down next to him and started trimming them. They talked more as they worked side-by-side then both went back outside to pick some lettuce and tomatoes for the salad. By the time they'd finished working on the salad and Susan whipped up a vinaigrette, it was after 2:30.

"I hope they found Ian," Mel remarked.

Susan didn't know what to say, thinking that the American girl Ian had met was probably Lynn.

"Um…what else did James say about the American girl?"

"Nothing really; he just said Ian didn't get word about the audition last night and they were trying to find him. He thought he'd probably gone off somewhere with the American girl he met at the club."

Susan remained calm. She was about to say something, but stopped, thinking she could too easily get trapped in more lies. "Must be Lynn here then for sure," she thought. "Especially if Ian is missing." She almost laughed, wondering what they'd been up to.

"Ready to go, then?" asked Mel.

She nodded, grabbed her purse, gave him a few more instructions regarding dinner preparation and they headed out the door.

"Oh wait!" he said going back into the house. "Let me get some of my oatmeal cookies. You can take them in for the boys. They always seem to enjoy them."

Lynn and Ian fell asleep only for brief, short intervals between their bouts of lovemaking, Ian showing Lynn some unusual delights he'd learned in Germany, where he said there was sex on every street corner, and Lynn giving him the pleasures only a very knowledgeable and experienced woman would know about. He didn't question her expertise.

"Hungry, love?" he asked, as they laid back on the pillows, smoking their way through a pack of cigarettes.

"I could use a Coke, that's for sure," she replied.

"Well, let's see what we can ring up from room service then." He picked up the phone and dialed the front desk. "Glad you're staying in such a posh hotel," he remarked as the phone was ringing on the other end.

"Oh, hallo, this is room 4027. Could you bring us up a couple of Cokes, some chips and a couple of sandwiches, do ya think?" He paused. "Turkey, chicken or whatever is fine. Thanks then."

He turned to Lynn, "Fifteen to twenty minutes." He leaned over the side of the bed and reached for his guitar then started strumming and plucking out different melodies. Lynn leaned back, a Cheshire cat grin on her face. "This is quite fabulous," she thought to herself. "Oh my yes, quite fabulous…"

Ian slipped on his boxer shorts as a knock sounded on the door. He opened it and accepted the tray being proffered by a hotel service person.

"Ta," he said, giving the boy a tip.

"Ta to you," the boy responded.

Ian carried the tray over to the bed where he and Lynn sat enjoying the food.

"I should check in with Derek," he said looking at the clock on the night stand. "It's almost noon and I want to make sure we're still on for practice this afternoon."

Derek's Aunt answered the phone and told him there was a search party out looking for him then told him about the audition in South Brighton. He hung up and leaped out of the bed, pulling his clothes on as fast as he could and explaining to Lynn about the audition at the recording studio.

"Stay here, luv, and get a bit of sleep. I'll come pick you up and bring you to the practice in a couple of hours." He leaned over and gave her a big smacking kiss good bye. "You can stay just like that if you want," he said teasingly, eyeballing her nakedness through the sheets. "We might have some extra time before practice."

She laid back, smiled and lit another cigarette. "I'll look forward to it," she said.

Chapter 12

Susan and Lynn Reunited

Mel dropped Susan off in front of the club shortly before 3:00. She looped her purse over her neck so the strap hung across her chest then she took the plate of cookies from him.

"Thanks," she yelled over her shoulder as she headed down the side alley to the practice room door. "See you later for dinner! And, don't forget I'm helping you make it, okay?"

"Sure thing," Mel replied out the car window as he slowly pulled away.

Halfway down the alley, leaning up against the wall, she spotted two girls. As she got closer, one of them pushed away from the wall, moved directly in her path and stopped, arms crossed over her chest.

"Well, look here, Sara," said Hilary, "If it ain't the little American bird Jimmie's been messing around with..."

Sara pushed off the wall to stand beside Hilary, totally blocking Susan's path.

"Pretty little thing," said Sara sarcastically.

"Yeah, maybe I could mess up that pretty little face a bit," said Hilary, revealing a razor knife gripped in her right hand.

Sara drew back. "Hilary! You didn't say anything about cutting her up. I thought we were just going to mess with her head a bit, scare her, ya know."

"I think I'm gonna enjoy messing her up a whole lot more with this," Hilary said, waving the blade in the air and circling around to the other side of Susan so she was on one side and Sara on the other. "See if Jimmie wants her then with her face all messed up…"

Susan dropped the plate of cookies and backed against the wall of the club. The plate shattered and cookies rolled in every direction.

"Why, how sweet…bringing cookies to the boys…too bad they're all ruined now."

Hilary advanced toward Susan.

Susan screamed and dodged to the right just as Hilary slashed forward towards her face with the blade.

Sara grabbed Hilary's arm. "Stop it, Hil!" she yelled. "This is going too far! I don't want no part of this!"

"Why you traitor!" Hilary screamed, turning to wave the blade at Sara. "Ain't you my friend or what?"

"Not if you're gonna be stupid and do something like this!"

"Let go my arm! I only gots the one, you know!"

"No! I'm not going to let you do this! I just felt sorry for you, getting your heart broken and all."

Hilary wrenched her arm free from Sara's grasp and went to slash her blade at Sara, but missed as Sara ducked out of the way, surprised outrage on her face.

"You've gone daft!" she yelled at Hilary.

"Think so, do ya?" Hilary screamed, rushing at Sara again.

Susan pushed away from the wall, grabbing Hilary's arm that held the blade. She spun her around. Hilary tripped and fell to the ground. This time Sara screamed. The door to the practice room burst open and James came running out, followed by Ian and Lynn.

Hilary was on her knees, pushing herself up, the razor knife still clutched in her fist. "I'll mess up you both!" she yelled.

James and Ian ran forward, James grabbing one of Hilary's arms and Ian the other, which was just a stump from the elbow up. The razor knife clattered to the ground as James twisted her wrist.

"I hate you, you bastard!" she screamed, spitting at him.

"Go tell Derek to call the bobbies," Ian yelled to Lynn.

Ian pulled both of Hilary's upper arms behind her back and pinned her face first against the wall. She continued to scream obscenities.

Susan rushed into James's arms, her heart beating wildly. He crushed her to him.

"It's all right now...It'll be all right..." he whispered into her hair.

She was still trembling as she looked up at him. "I can't believe she could hate me so much. I never did anything to her...She was going to cut up my face...!"

Sara overheard. "Don't matter...she had it in for you from the first. I just never thought she'd get so extreme like."

"You're supposed to be my friend!" Hilary screamed when she heard Sara's words.

"Not no more," said Sara. "You crossed the line, you did...and you lied to me and tricked me..."

At that moment, Susan looked over James's shoulder and saw Lynn coming out of the door to the practice room, her eyes as big as saucers. "Lynn?" she exclaimed. "Lynn, is that you?"

Susan flew out of James's arms and ran to Lynn, enveloping her in a giant bear hug. "Oh Lynn! Lynn! What are you doing here? How did you get here? How long have you been here?!!"

"Hey, slow down. Let's go inside and I'll tell you all about it."

James came up to both of them. "Well, I know who's important now, don't I?" he quipped.

"Oh, James! You wouldn't know," said Susan contritely. "This is my very best friend in the whole world, Lynn. Lynn, this is...well...I guess you know who this is...I mean, maybe you don't...this is *him*!"

Lynn started laughing and everyone except Ian, who was still holding Hilary against the wall, and Sara still standing next to Hilary, went down the alley and into the practice room. The police arrived shortly thereafter, taking Hilary away. Sara had offered more apologies to Ian while they were waiting then left to go home. Ian came back into the practice room.

"Well, that's all taken care of then," he said to the whole room in general.

"In that case, let's forget about it and start to play," said Derek, putting the guitar strap over his head.

"The first one here is for the girls, especially my girl..." He winked at Mindy, who had settled herself cross-legged style on the floor in her jeans. Lynn and Susan sat down in similar fashion next to her with their legs tucked to the side due to wearing dresses, but they didn't have a chance to say anything to each other as the song started.

"To see, touch and hold her...makes me know how much I love her...Every time I see her grin...makes me feel I need to win ...to win her love for me...is what my life needs to be...and it will...and it will...and it will..."

Mindy sighed as she listened to the lyrics, her and Derek having a silent conversation with no words as they looked at each other. James was looking at Susan and she was looking intently back at him with her lips slightly parted. Lynn could almost feel Susan's heart beating wildly in her chest just by looking at her. This was worse than she thought. Oh my, oh my!

The boys moved into the next song. Ian was signing, looking at Lynn. It was the same song he'd sang in the club the night before.

"Well, I saw her sitting on the bar stool... a yellow ribbon in her ponytail...
Susan nudged her. "Ha, ha...looks like this one's for you."

"She caught my eye in an instant...Well how 'bout that...Whatha think... I'm amazed...Whoa! Sweet thing...oh my, such a sweet thing...She's such a, such a sweet thing..."

Lynn gave her "the look," meaning "you've got to be kidding me," and then laughed, remembering the yellow June Cleaver ribbon she'd had in her hair the night before when she had "materialized" into the Dusky Club.

Susan laughed, wondering what had happened between Lynn and Ian last night.

The boys played and sang several more songs then James motioned to Susan to come up next to him. "Sing with me, will you luv?"

"Me?" she asked, a startled expression on her face. "I can't sing!"

"Oh yes you can!" yelled Lynn, elbowing Susan and saying under her breath, "Remember, you asked to be able to sing, so I'm sure you can sing."

"Come on, luv," James beckoned to her. "You sang me that once upon a dream song just last night, remember?"

She took a deep breath and stood up, then went to stand next to him by the microphone. Hopefully, she wouldn't embarrass herself. "What are we singing?" she asked nervously.

144

He pinned a paper with some lyrics to the music stand in front of him, and pulled a tall stool over for her to sit on in front of the microphone.

"Just listen to me sing the first verse or two, then join in when I repeat it."

She sat, her feet up on the rungs of the stool and he began singing, looking deeply into her eyes. She looked at the song pinned to the music stand. Oh yes! She knew this song so well. She had dreamed her whole life about him singing just these words to her...

"I saw stars in the sky but I never saw them shining...no, I didn't see them before...not before you..."

Tears welled in her eyes, but she didn't break hers away from his as she joined in.

"And there was sunshine...and beautiful sweet peas...that sent out fragrance reminding of you... There were birds all around...but I never heard their chirping...no, I didn't hear them before...not before you...not before you..."

As the song reached the final notes, Susan stood up and executed a perfect triple pirouette, smirking at Lynn as she landed in a solid fourth position.

James leaned over to give Susan a kiss, pulling her forcefully into his arms. It quickly turned into a rather long kiss until Ian and Derek cleared their throats rather loudly. "Enough already..." Derek muttered.

Susan blushed, then went and sat back down next to Lynn and Mindy. The boys broke into the last song for the practice.

"What in hell are you doing here?" Susan asked Lynn, finally having the opportunity to talk to her.

"What are you doing, period?!" Lynn asked. "You're getting in way to deep. We need to get out of here and now! You don't belong here! You shouldn't be with him and doing all those things you're doing..." She pulled out her iPhone.

Mindy looked over at them curiously.

"So what's that then?" she asked.

"Oh...just an American transistor radio," Lynn said, tucking it back into her purse. "Battery just went dead."

She turned back to Susan. "Really, Suz, this is ridiculous! You've got to know that. You can't stay here, so what are you doing fooling around with him like this? You just wanted to meet him and now you're probably having sex with him every five minutes like some kind of bunny rabbit all in love and everything!"

Mindy looked back and forth between the two of them. "So what's so wrong about having sex every five minutes and being in love?" she asked pointedly. She gave a big, huge grin to Susan. "So, you let him have his way with you, did you? Good for you!"

Lynn looked at Mindy. "No! Not good for her at all! She wasn't supposed to fall in love. We have to leave on Friday no matter what, and I think it would be better to leave now before things get worse."

"Worse? What's so bad about having sex and being in love?"

"Nothing is *wrong* with being in love, as long as you're in love with the right person...and at the right time," Lynn said, turning to scowl at Susan. Lynn wasn't very good at scowling, making Susan want to laugh.

"You can't always pick the right time, you know...it just happens," said Mindy.

"Oh, I know that, but this is different. She shouldn't be sleeping with him, and she shouldn't be in love! Once we leave, we can never come back...and that's the problem here."

Mindy sat back and contemplated what Lynn had said.

"Well, of course you have to come back after your history tour!" said Mindy, turning towards Susan. "It'll break his heart in million pieces if you don't come back."

Susan looked down. "I'd like to come back..." she muttered to herself.

"Well, you know darn well you can't! You know there's no history tour! You know you made it all up!" Lynn said.

Mindy looked stunned. "What's this all about then? No such thing as a history tour?"

Susan looked angrily at Lynn. "Stop it, Lynn!" She turned to Mindy. "She's just saying that because she's not interested in history like I am, and her parents made her come; she didn't want to."

"Stop with the lies, Suz...really...this is just going to end badly and we both know it! Plus, it's wrong, wrong, wrong!"

"Well, before you start lecturing me, why don't you tell me what you've been up to with Ian? I heard he was missing today when the boys were supposed to go to an audition. Well?"

Lynn blushed.

"Ah, ha! I know what that blush means! You got here last night, right? You haven't been doing something like a 'tumble in the sheets' as they say here, have you?"

Lynn's face turned even pinker. "Now, Suz...I couldn't find you... and the, um, opportunity just presented itself..." Her voice faded.

Susan smiled, triumphantly. "So, then...Here *you* are, probably having sex every five minutes too...and you're lecturing me?!"

"But I'm not in love! I'm just...well..."

Mindy was looking back and forth between them, not understanding fully what they were talking about.

The song ended and Susan saw James take off his guitar. She leaped up and ran over to him.

"Can we leave now, please? I told your dad we'd be back for dinner and I'd help him."

"Dinner? We're having dinner with my dad?"

"Yes; it's supposed to be a surprise for you."

He looked at her and smiled. "That's nice of you. I think my dad is becoming very fond of you."

She turned around and saw Lynn talking to Mindy, waving her arms around in the air. She saw her take her iPhone out of her purse and show it to Mindy. Mindy had a puzzled look on her face. Susan had a sinking feeling in the pit of her stomach.

"Can we leave now, please?" she asked. "Right now, please? I can talk to Lynn more tonight."

He looked at her oddly, then said, "Sure, if that's what you want." He wondered what had made her so agitated.

When they were both in his car, he turned to her and again asked her what was wrong. She assured him she was fine, just a little anxious over the dinner and wanting to make sure it was perfect for him.

"Well, that's as it should be..." he thought. "Making things perfect for me..."

Susan would have been annoyed if she'd known what he was thinking. Male chauvinist...

Chapter 13

The Perfect Dinner

Susan was still agitated and seemed nervous when they arrived at James's house. James asked her again if something was wrong, but she told him not to be silly. She was just anxious about dinner was all.

Mel had put the beef roast in the oven as Susan had directed him and the potatoes were on the boil. Susan immediately went into the kitchen, popped the bread in the oven and started on the Creme Brulee.

"You don't happen to have a blow torch, do you?" she asked looking at Mel, eyebrows raised.

"A blow torch? And what would you need a blow torch for?"

"To caramelize the sugar on top of the custard when it's done," she replied, as if it were the simplest thing in the world.

"Well, yes, I do have a small blow torch I use to repair the plumbing from time to time. You want to use it on the custard then?"

"If you don't mind," she said, whipping the eggs and cream together then adding the vanilla to the cream mixture.

James watched and listened, a bemused expression on his face.

"You're in the way," she said, looking at him. "Go play the piano or something."

He gave her a quirky smile. "Certainly, m'lady," he said with a small bow.

Mel looked amused. "Have him wrapped around your little finger, don't you?"

"I wouldn't say that."

"Well, certainly looks like it to me. I find it quite amusing. A different side of Jimmie, that's for sure."

She threw her head back and laughed, forgetting about Lynn and what she might be saying to Mindy. She certainly wouldn't be able to tell her the truth. Mindy would never believe it.

The iPhone was the problem, however. What would Mindy think of the iPhone? Would Lynn show Derek and Ian? What had been going on between Lynn and Ian anyway? She'd caught the unmistakable way Ian had looked lustfully at Lynn, knowing they must have been together intimately, especially with Lynn's blushes.

She dashed the thought from her mind and concentrated on putting the custard into glass cups she'd found in a cabinet and placing them in a water bath before putting in the oven with the roast and bread. She heaved a great sigh.

"Something troubling you, dear?" asked Mel, who'd been observing her while setting the kitchen table for dinner. She could hear James at the piano, playing another Scott Joplin tune.

"No...no...nothing at all...just worried about getting everything right. I'm a bit of a perfectionist..." she said, taking the salad out of the refrigerator, tossing it with the vinaigrette then dividing it onto three salad plates.

"I'm thinking you might be too good for him, you know."

"Oh! How can you say such a thing?" she asked, now hearing James dabbling at the piano, the notes of *"All My Kisses"* reaching her ears. She did her best to act normal even though her heart was pounding and she felt rather faint.

"You just seem so much wiser for your years. You know so many things...gardening, cooking, music, taking care of household things... and you talk so sophisticated-like...we're just simple people..."

"I'm nothing special, Mel. I was just raised by my grandparents. They're from the old school. Women need to know a lot of things early...the domesticated things...my grandfather is insisting that I go to college, but I've really been raised just to get married and have babies."

"Is that what you want to do?" he asked, brightening.

"No, not at all. I have too rebellious of a spirit. I couldn't be under any man's thumb. That's why I thought it was so funny when you said I had James wrapped around my finger. I don't think he's the type to let a woman rule him. I always have to have my way, and so does he. That could be a problem."

Mel was thoughtful. "You're probably right." He thought to himself, "If those two end up together, there will certainly be a lot of fireworks between them...But, fireworks will often calm down to burning embers..."

Susan opened the oven and took out the roast, removing it to a platter to let the juices settle, then set the roasting pan on a stove burner and lit the gas to make gravy. She stirred some cold water into flour, adding some salt, then added it to the drippings in the pan. She stirred and added water until it was the right consistency then turned the stove burner down to low. She checked the green beans. They were perfectly tender. She turned off the burner and removed the pan from the stove. She took the bread out of the oven.

"Can you please slice the bread?" she asked Mel as she set the salad plates on the table. "I'll go get James."

She walked out of the kitchen and came up behind him at the piano, wrapping her arms around him as he started into her favorite song again.

"Close your eyes while I touch you... You know how I love you... Remember me while you're away... And then while you are gone... I will try to go on... And send all my kisses your way..."

He stopped. "So, what do you think," he asked. "Will you remember me every day when you're on your tour?"

She wanted to cry. It was like a knife pierced her heart as the reality of leaving hit her full force.

"Stop!" she screamed at herself silently. "Don't even think about leaving! Don't think about it...not now...not now...!"

"Dinner's ready, Sir James," she said softly into his ear, avoiding his question.

When they went into the kitchen, Mel was slicing the roast and Susan went to mash the potatoes, adding a generous amount of butter and the bit of whipping cream she'd saved from the Creme Brulee. She checked the clock. Another forty minutes on the custard.

Everything was on the table and they sat down to eat. James and Mel looked at each other, contemplating the extravagant feast before them. They'd never seen the likes of it.

"Well, dig in!" Susan said, looking at them both a bit shyly, wondering if they'd like her cooking.

"Fabulous!" said Mel. James just smiled, nodding in agreement.

As the meal came to an end, Susan jumped up to check on the custard. It was done. She removed the tray with the glass cups from the oven and set it on the counter to cool a bit, then she went to gather the dishes.

"Mel, can you please get the blow torch now, then why don't you guys go in the other room and play something else for me on the piano? Scott Joplin would be nice. I'll take care of cleaning up the kitchen then we can have dessert."

"I don't know if I can handle dessert as stuffed full as I am," said Mel, walking outside to the potting shed, where he kept the blow torch and a box of other tools. He was back a minute later and showed Susan how to use the torch. "You sure you don't want me to do this for you?"

"Positive. I've done this a lot before. You and James just go and relax."

She put the leftovers in the fridge, washed the dishes, dried them then put everything away. She wiped down the kitchen table and counters, swept the floor then fired up the blow torch and held it over the sugar she'd sprinkled on top of the custard. When everything was done, she went into the other room where James and his dad were companionably playing the piano together. She smiled at the picture they presented. This was actually quite wonderful.

"Okay, I'm sure you have a bit of room for Creme Brulee," she said smiling. "It's one of my specialties."

After enjoying dessert, James realized it was almost time to leave for the club. He raced upstairs, put on a clean white shirt and tie and donned a jacket, thinking Ryan might show up at the club to listen.

"Can we please stop by the hotel first so I can change out of this dress I've worn for two days now?" she asked.

James looked at her like it really wasn't important.

"Really," she said, "I need to get out of this dress." She turned red as she realized what she'd said, thinking of other things.

James smirked and Mel stifled a cough.

"You young people be off then," he said.

Susan picked up her purse, then winked at Mel as she and James went out the door.

Chapter 14

Another Night at the Dusky

Susan inserted her key into the hotel room door and opened it. The first thing to assail her nostrils was the smell of cigarette smoke. She looked over to the bed and saw an ashtray on the night table filled to the brim with cigarette butts.

"Oh, gross!" she said, pinching her nose. "Lynn and Ian must be staying here. I sure hope my clothes don't stink!"

She pulled her suitcase out of the closet and began taking her clothes off the hangers then out of drawers until everything but her bathroom items were packed. She kept the green dress on, wanting to get out of the smelly room as soon as possible. No big deal about spending another few hours in it after all.

"I think I should get all my stuff out of here," she said looking at James. "Can we put my suitcase in the trunk of your car?"

"Sure, but hurry, okay. I don't want to be late in case Ryan stops by the club. He said he wanted to listen to more of our songs."

"Just give me a few minutes, okay?" she said as she headed into the bathroom. She closed the door then used the loo. On the counter, was her bag of cosmetics. She eyed it then looked at herself in the mirror. "I look pretty plain," she thought as she opened the bag and took out some eye shadow. "I think I'll do some beautification here real quick. Ah yes, here's some green shadow; it'll match the dress nicely..."

When she came out of the bathroom five minutes later, James had her suitcase in hand and was ready to walk out the door.

Until he looked at her. He stopped dead in his tracks.

"What's that stuff all over your face?" he asked.

"Make-up," she said. "I thought I'd make myself beautiful for you."

"You look cheap and tawdry. Go wash it off...and hurry...I told you I don't want to be late."

Her mouth dropped open and she froze.

"Wash it off? Wash it off!!!" she said indignantly, stung by his words.

"I believe I spoke in English," he replied. "Yes, wash it off. You look better without it. I think you're just fine the way you are."

"Well, you might think so, but maybe I don't. Maybe other people would think I look nice with makeup. Maybe I want to feel pretty... Maybe..." Her voice rose an octave with each word.

"I don't care what other people think. Go wash it off!"

Her stubborn streak kicked into high gear. "Make me," she challenged him in a pouty, little girl voice. As she'd told Mel earlier, no man was ever going to tell her what to do. She defiantly crossed her arms over her chest, her feet planted on the floor.

He set down her suitcase and came up to her, saying softly, "I washed the stuff out of my hair for you, didn't I? I expect it's not too much to ask that you wash that mess off your face for me?"

If she hadn't been so flustered, she would have seen the warning signals in his eyes.

Mess?! He was calling her a mess! She fumed.

"You either go back into the bathroom and wash it off yourself, or I'll go get a washing cloth and do it for you," he said quietly.

"Why you arrogant asshole! How dare you order me around!! You're being an A-number one shithead about this!"

He grabbed her arm above the elbow. "What did you call me?"

"You heard me loud and clear, I think. Do you want me to repeat it?"

"I think you owe me an apology," he said coldly, squeezing her arm tighter. "And your swearing has *got* to stop!"

"Ow! You're hurting me!" she said.

He immediately released her arm, looking at her with eyes blazing. "I said you owe me an apology. And I mean it; quit the damn swearing!!"

She thought back to the incident at the practice where he'd insulted her with the *"I'll Have You"* song and how she'd told *him* to apologize.

"Fine then!" she said as sarcastically as possible. "Fine, fine, fine! I apologize."

He grabbed her arm again, this time gently but enough to keep her from pulling away.

"Say it like you mean it," he said firmly, his eyes boring into hers.

She shook herself loose and turned her back to him. She was shaking and suddenly very confused. Was she being really stupid here? He didn't like the make-up and told her to take it off. What was the big deal? It wasn't like she had to look at herself. If he liked her looking plain, why was she being so stubborn? And, he had a point; he'd washed the greasy stuff out of his hair for her...

"Because I don't like being bossed around!!" she said to herself. "Nobody bosses me around!"

"Well?" he said softly behind her. "I'm waiting."

Suddenly, she wanted to cry. She just couldn't make her mouth say the words, "I'm sorry." "What the hell is wrong with me?" she said to herself.

"You want me to leave you here then?" he asked, sounding wounded and disappointed, the anger fading from him as quickly as it had come.

Tears welled up in her eyes and her shoulders started moving up and down as a sob burst from her. The tears poured down her cheeks along with some of the eye shadow and mascara, stinging her eyes.

He moved forward, took her by the shoulders and turned her around. "Is it so hard for you to say you're sorry?" he asked. "Why? It's not that difficult you know."

She reached up to rub her burning eyes.

"Come here," he said pulling her into the bathroom. "Let me take care of that."

He took a wash cloth off a shelf, ran cold water over it and started gently wiping her face and eyes. She stood still, arms hanging limply at her sides. When he was done, he leaned in and kissed her softly on the tip of her nose.

She sniffed. "Thank you," she whispered.

But she didn't say she was sorry. He didn't seem to notice.

〜◌

Lynn and Mindy were already sitting at their regular table near the front of the club against the wall when Susan arrived. It looked like a couple of girls from the other side of the room had come over to join them. One of them was Sara. There was no sign of Hilary anywhere. They all smiled at Susan as she came up to the table. Her eyes were red from crying, but no one seemed to notice due to the dim atmosphere of the club and the dingy cloud of smoke hanging over the stage area and tables.

Susan suddenly thought to herself that James hadn't smoked since the first night she'd met him when he put out the cigarette. She wondered how he was handling it. The withdrawal from smoking was supposed to be really, really hard. Maybe she'd distracted him enough, but she figured it must still be hard. Maybe that's what had made him so angry at her over the makeup. Maybe he was having withdrawal symptoms. And there she was, being a total bitch over some stupid makeup. She felt contrite. Then, she looked up as the boys came onto the stage area and put on their guitars. Derek stepped up to microphone and started to sing. The two new girls at their table as well as the girls on the other side of the room, started screaming.

"Oh, oh, oh... You've been sweet to me...I've been so glad...Instead of blue... And forever more, I want to be...In love with you...What I really want...Is to love you girl, love you girl...Oh, oh, oh..."

So...this was the beginning then...screaming, frantic girls...

Susan wanted to start crying all over again.

Lynn had her iPhone in her hand and was very obviously trying to get Susan's attention to draw her off for a private chat, but Susan was being very good at avoiding her. Mindy looked at her oddly, her eyes contemplative.

"She must know," Susan thought, despairingly. She didn't know what Lynn had said to her, but it was obvious Mindy knew she probably wasn't really a history student and her whole being here was a lie.

158

She just prayed that Derek and Ian wouldn't say anything to James if they'd been told of her deception. Little did she know that, in fact, the only thing Mindy had told them was that Susan wouldn't be coming back after the history tour. They hadn't said anything to James. They didn't think he'd take it very well and it would lead to an argument or worse. They didn't want to risk it after the audition and the possibility of making a record.

"Yeah now, that's so good, mama...That's so good of you...That's so good mama, wow, those crazy things you do...Yeah now, that's so good, that's so good....That's so good now mama, those lovin' things you do..."

James stepped up to the microphone. "This is for my girl," he said.

"I saw stars in the sky but I never saw them shining...no, I didn't see them before...not before you..."

It was the same song they had sung together at the practice that very afternoon.

"And there was sunshine...and beautiful sweet peas...that sent out a fragrance reminding of you..."

As Susan listened to the words, she wanted to cry all over again. She felt like a watering pot. Her emotions were at a breaking point. Maybe Lynn was right and she should get out of here right now before things got even worse than they already were.

Some inkling in the back of her mind was also telling her that James might not be the paragon she'd always thought he was. She could see definite signs of a very over-bearing nature, and she knew it would be hard, if not impossible, to submit to it without blowing up at him. She took a few deep breaths as her eyes connected with James's and the song ended.

"There were birds all around...but I never heard their chirping...no, I didn't hear them before...not before you...not before you..."

All the girls in the room were looking at her. She felt like they were closing in on her. The room was suddenly very hot and her head was spinning. Her skin felt clammy.

She fainted dead away, crumpling onto the floor. James ripped off his guitar as he saw her go down and ran off the stage area to where she was laying. He yelled for some water and cradled her in his arms.

"Susan," he said, "Susan...are you okay?" He dipped his hand in the glass of water Sandra had run over with and sprinkled it on Susan's forehead. Her eyes fluttered open and she looked up at him.

"I'm getting you out of here," he said as he scooped her up in his arms, walked carefully back through the club, up the stairs and out the front. He carried her down the alley and into the practice room where he gently placed her in a large stuffed chair that was sitting on the side of the room.

He heard Derek, Ian and Blue continue to play, knowing they could carry off the night without him if they had to. He briefly thought about Ryan, but chased the thought from his mind as he looked at Susan's pale face. "I'm taking you back home," he whispered to her.

She rubbed her eyes and sat up straight, then tried to stand up.

"Just stay there a minute, while I tell Derek something," he said, urging her to sit back down.

A short time later, he was back and they both went out to his car and drove home. Susan was relieved she didn't have to talk to Lynn. By the time James pulled up to the house, she was feeling much better.

Mel was surprised to see them. When James explained that Susan had fainted, he was concerned.

"Are you okay, luv?" he asked.

She nodded. "I think maybe I just overdid it today," she said. "And it was so hot and smoky in the club, I didn't feel like I could even breathe."

"Well, why don't you go upstairs and lay down then? I'll take you up to James's room," he said motioning her to go upstairs. James followed them.

"If you want to go back to the club, go on," said Mel. "I'll make sure she gets tucked in all right and tight. I'll leave a blanket and pillow downstairs for you on the couch," he added pointedly.

"You okay with my going back to the club?" James asked Susan as she laid her head down on the pillow of his bed.

"Of course I am," she smiled up at him. "Just don't go home with any of those other girls, okay?"

He leaned down and kissed her tenderly. "Never in a million years," he said, turning off the light and going downstairs.

She snuggled into his pillow, wrapping both arms around it tightly and breathing in the scent of him. She was asleep before he went back out the door.

Chapter 15

Back to the Cottage

James and Susan were sound asleep on the couch, pressed tightly together due to the small space when Mel came down the stairs the next morning. A blanket covered them and James's leg was on the edge almost ready to fall off. Mel shook his head. Here he thought James would be the one sneaking back up to his bedroom to join Susan in his bed, but instead it appeared that Susan had come downstairs to join James on the couch. Mel sighed. They both looked so innocent... and so young...and so in love. He went into the kitchen to make some coffee.

Both of them woke up at the smell of the coffee, realizing they'd fallen asleep before Susan thought to go back upstairs to James's room. James kissed her softly, whispering, "I think we've been caught."

"Is he going to be angry?" she whispered back.

"Nah, not Dad. He told me just yesterday he knew what it was like to be young and in love. He understands...and, he likes you a lot. Plus, we've got all our clothes on, you know."

James slipped off the couch then stood up and stretched. "You can sleep some more if you want," he said. "I'm going upstairs to take a shower and shave."

"No, I'll get up." She stood up and did her best to straighten the dress she'd been wearing since forever it seemed. "You chicken...making me face your dad alone."

"I said you could stay here and sleep some more."

"Yeah, as if I could do that now. He's probably heard us talking."

James winked at her and headed up the stairs.

"Didn't mean to wake you up," said Mel, as Susan went into the kitchen.

"Good Morning, Mel." Susan was blushing. "James's up taking a shower and shaving."

Mel didn't seem to notice her pink face.

"I've got some eggs and kippers here ready to go for breakfast and some toast," he responded.

"Kippers?" Susan thought to herself. "Wasn't that some kind of fish?" It didn't sound appetizing.

"I'll have it all ready in a few," he added, "in time for when Jimmie comes on down."

He busied himself at the stove for a minute, then turned the gas down and turned to face Susan.

She looked over at him.

"Have a seat," he said, pouring two cups of coffee and sitting down across from her.

He looked down at his cup for a minute, then back up at her.

"Can I ask you a few questions?" he said, then paused. "And will you answer them truthfully?"

"What do you mean?" she asked, looking down at her hands in her lap. "Do you think I've been untruthful with you?"

"No, no...I don't think you've been untruthful..."

"What then?"

"Just evasive..."

"Oh." She looked up at him for a minute, then back down at her hands.

"When you were here yesterday, it seemed you tried to turn the subject on me when I started talking about some things."

"Some things?"

"Yes. When I asked you if you two loved each other, you said 'yes, *but...*' and something about things not working out, then you changed the subject. And when I asked you why you were leaving for your history tour on

Friday at midnight and what was going on with the other students, which I thought was pretty odd, you changed the subject again."

She looked up at him. He was being very serious and she was feeling very trapped.

"So, can I ask you a few questions then?"

She nodded, dreading them.

"And will you be honest in your answers?"

She nodded again, and whispered a small, "yes."

"So then...I don't have any questions about you and James loving each other. I understand whirlwind love and know it can happen sometimes...but I want to know about this history tour of yours...mainly if you plan on coming back after it's over."

She turned away from him and took a deep breath.

"Exactly how long is this history tour supposed to last?" he asked.

She shook her head, but no words would come out.

"Are you coming back at all then after you leave on Friday?"

Susan looked at him square in the face and met his concerned eyes.

"I can't," she whispered, the pain clearly reflected in her eyes. "It's not possible."

Mel sat back, staring at her intently. "And why is that? You don't want to come back?"

"Please...please, Mel," she pleaded. "Please don't ask me anymore. It has nothing to do with me *wanting* to come back; it just won't be *possible* for me to come back. I never should have come here in the first place!"

"But why can't you come back?" he persisted.

"Don't make me beg you to stop asking, please," she said again. "I just won't be able to come back..." She started to sob. Tears overflowed her eyes and ran down her cheeks. "It won't be possible. Please don't ask, please..."

Mel stood up and came over to her chair. She stood up and he wrapped his arms around her, patting her on the back.

"It's okay, luv. I won't ask any more...but will you be telling James then?"

She shook her head, sobbing some more. "No, no...I can't...I just can't...Please don't tell him, please..."

Mel gently pushed her away from him so he could look into her face.

"Why?" he asked.

She saw pain and concern in his eyes and knew it wasn't just for his son, but for her as well.

"Because I want us to have just a few more days of happiness...and because when I'm gone, I'll be just a dim memory to him...I don't expect you to understand..."

James walked into the kitchen at that moment and stopped dead at the sight of Susan being held in his dad's arms.

"So, what's all this?" he asked. "You making my girl cry, Dad?"

"She was just telling me how much she loves you, and it brought tears to her eyes, right luv?" he said looking down at Susan and releasing her from his arms.

She ran to James, wrapped her arms around him and gave him a quick kiss. "That's it exactly!" she said, wiping the tears from her cheeks. "Go sit down. Your dad has breakfast about ready."

James sat down at the table while Susan went and poured him some coffee.

"So, how did the audition go?" Mel asked, looking at James.

"Great!" said James. "We'll find out by next Monday if we're to make a record. Ryan made a couple of hours of tapes of our songs and took them with him. We're keeping our fingers crossed he'll want to record all of them."

"Pretty ambitious, aren't you?"

"Oh, James, I just know he'll want to record them all! You're going to be world famous some day!" exclaimed Susan.

"You think so?" said James, smiling. "I'm sure you're right! I've always thought I'd be rich and famous someday!"

"Now Jimmie, there you go with your pipe dreaming again; always thinking how fabulous you are..."

"Oh, but he is!" Susan exclaimed before she could stop herself. "Their band is going to be known as 'the Fab Four'!"

Both James and Mel looked at her.

"Looks like Susan here shares your pipe dreaming," said Mel.

"Well, maybe she's right, you know. She has intuition."

They all smiled. Susan jumped up to help with the toast as Mel finished the eggs and kippers and set them on the table. He then got out three plates and forks. Susan finished buttering the toast and sat it on the table with some jam.

"My own jam," said Mel proudly. "Made from the blackberries that grow out by Annabelle's cottage."

"Speaking of the cottage, Dad, I thought Susan and I would head back out to Little Dippington after breakfast. We want to do more sketching and maybe take a dip in the pond."

Mel looked at James and said, "I was figuring you might be wanting to go back out there. It's a romantic spot, isn't it?"

Susan could feel the heat coming into her face again. She sure spent heck of a lot of time blushing! It was embarrassing!

They all chatted a bit more as they ate breakfast...Susan politely refused the kippers...and then she got up and carried the dishes to the sink.

"You two stay right there," she said as Mel started to stand up to help her. "I can take care of the dishes while you two chat."

She picked up the rest of the dishes, re-filled their coffee cups and started filling the sink with hot, soapy water. When the sink was filled, she excused herself for a minute to go to the bathroom.

Mel looked at James over the rim of his coffee cup as he heard Susan head up the stairs. "So, now that you've taken her innocence away, what are your intentions regarding her?" he asked pointedly. "I know the crowd you hang around with is flighty, but Susan doesn't fit in with that sort of thing. I told you before I wouldn't have you hurting her. So then...What are your intentions? Have you talked to her about giving up this history tour thing?"

James sat up straight in his chair. "Why, my intentions are honorable, of course, Dad. I'd never hurt her. I don't plan on letting her leave on the history tour! I'll convince her to stay, I will!"

"Not leave, eh? Perhaps you wouldn't hurt her intentional-like, but the way you run around now with all the girls, that would hurt her deeply."

"Dad, I said I'd never hurt her," said James.

Mel shook his head, a worried expression on his face. "I certainly hope not. She's a good girl, that she is. But, I'm rather worried about this history tour..."

Susan came back into the kitchen right then, and Mel and James quit talking.

"Talking about me, are you?" she asked, hoping that Mel wasn't saying anything to James about her coming back after the history tour.

They both smiled.

"Just remarking how beautiful you are," said James.

She went to the sink and starting washing the dishes. Mel stood up, went over next to her and started to dry.

"Well then," said Mel. "Seeing as you're going back out to the cottage, you might as well take more provisions. Country air makes a person hungry, you know."

"We can stop in Little Dippington and get some stuff if we have to," said James. "We need to replace a few things of Auntie's that we've used up."

"And I need to do some washing and cleaning," Susan added. "Always the polite thing to do when you stay for a while at someone's house."

"And I want to finish up the song I've been working on for Susan," James said.

Susan froze for a moment, wondering if the song was *"All My Kisses."* She thought it probably was.

The dishes were finished. Susan went upstairs to tidy up James's bed even though she'd only been in it for a couple of hours the night before.

While she was upstairs, Mel took James aside again. He pulled a handful of bills out of his pocket and held it out to James. "Give this back to Susan," he said. "Yesterday, she insisted she pay for the dinner things, including the beef roast, and gave this to me. I think she should have it back."

James stood stock still, an odd expression on his face. "She gave this to you?"

"Insisted she wanted to pay for a nice dinner for us both. Very generous girl, but I think she should have it back."

"So, you paid for everything yourself then?"

"Yes, of course."

James was silent for a moment, wondering why he hadn't questioned the extravagance of the dinner or where the expensive beef roast and cream for the dessert had come from. He must not have been paying attention, too wrapped up in his love for Susan and his amazement at her cooking skills. He also hadn't seen his dad so happy as he was when Susan was around, so that likely had distracted him as well.

"And just how much did it all add up to, Dad? You're on a small pension and your part-time job doesn't pay much, which is why Chad and I try to help out as much as we can. How much did she have you spend?"

"I'd rather not say. It's not important."

"A beef roast costs a lot of money! And all that other stuff is priced pretty dear. Why didn't you just tell her no?"

"Didn't have the heart to. As I said, she wanted to do something really nice for you."

"I don't care about a nice dinner...she shouldn't have done it! I made it perfectly clear she wasn't to be spending her money. I'll see ya straight, Dad, I will...not sure when or how...but, I'll see ya straight." He shoved the bills in his pocket.

"No need...really, James...I'm fine...I don't need much, as you know, and I'll be going out a few days early to King's Head tomorrow morning to go stay with Annabelle before I bring her back on Sunday. The pension check comes in next week, so I'll be fine."

James was suddenly very silent and appeared to be brooding. His face was flushed and there were sparks in his eyes. He clenched and unclenched his fists at his sides.

Mel patted him on the back. "Expensive tastes your young lady has," he said. "Hope you're both right about you and the boys becoming rich and famous. You'll be needing it." He was teasing now, sensing James's changed mood. Maybe he shouldn't have said anything about Susan giving him money.

James was getting angrier by the minute. He thought his dad was probably going out to King's Head early because he was now totally broke until the pension check came in and at least he'd get free meals for a few days out at his other sister's house.

Susan came tripping down the stairs. "Ready to go?" she asked cheerfully.

James said nothing, but Mel went up to her and took both of her hands in his. "Delightful seeing you again, my girl. Have James bring you by again any time at all."

Impetuously, she wrapped her arms around his neck and planted a smacking kiss on his cheek. "You're the best, Mel!" she said. "I think I might like you better than James!"

Mel and Susan laughed at the joke, but James remained silent.

"Are you coming then?" he asked coldly, opening the front door.

Susan didn't notice his mood and skipped out the door and down the steps to the car. Her suitcase was still in the boot from the day before. She thought she'd sort everything out and do some washing when they got back out to Annabelle's.

James opened the car door for her and she got in, giving a last wave to Mel, who stood in the doorway. James got in the other side, started up the car and they drove away.

"I'd offer to drive, but having the steering wheel on the wrong side of the car would be a problem," she said jokingly. "Plus, driving on the wrong side of the road."

"And what makes you think *we* drive on the wrong side of the road and you don't?" he snapped at her. "Besides, I'd never let a girl drive while I was in the car. Girls shouldn't be allowed to drive at all!"

She turned to look at him. "Is something wrong?"

He didn't respond.

She bit her lip. Something was definitely wrong. She tried to think. Had she said or done something?

For the next half hour, Susan made several unsuccessful attempts at conversation and tried to wrack her brain to figure out what she had said or done wrong. She couldn't think of anything.

James appeared to be fine and cheerful at breakfast and they'd spent a happy and cozy night together on the couch. What could it be? She thought maybe he was worried or distracted about what had happened at the audition, but then again, he didn't seem worried. She sensed he was angry or upset about something. He appeared to be pouting, but why would he be pouting?

She wasn't only puzzled, but she was beginning to feel hurt that he wouldn't even talk to her or tell her what was wrong. She discovered that she didn't like this side of him; she didn't like it at all! The least he could do was tell her what was wrong. The silent treatment was torture. And it was rude.

She wondered how often he got into these moods, if it was something he did regularly or just now and then. Even now and then would be too much. It was very uncomfortable. She quit trying to make conversation and scowled at the scenery out the window.

When they came to Little Dippington, James drove straight through, not stopping for any provisions as she thought they'd planned to do.

"Aren't we stopping then?" she asked, breaking the dead silence in the car yet again.

"No," was all he said.

He was holding a tight rein on his temper, if she only knew it, but he didn't know how much longer he could keep it in check. He'd made it very clear that she was *not* to spend her own money on anything that was needed, and she'd blatantly disobeyed him, tricked him even by giving money to his dad! She'd humiliated him.

He was livid just thinking of her extravagance and the money his dad had spent on a dinner he never even asked for. His dad should have refused to take the money and they could have made do with whatever was on hand for dinner. Eating wasn't important to him.

But, his dad was a pushover when it came to her; he knew that. And, he really didn't have any idea at the moment as to how he'd pay him back. After buying the bread and cheese at the shop on the way out to Annabelle's on Sunday, a new cup to replace the broken one, plus the shockingly expensive dress Susan had to have, he was near broke. The band wouldn't get paid for another two weeks and he still had to buy petrol for the car. These trips to the countryside were expensive.

He wondered how he could put some sense into her, make her understand that what she'd done was wrong and that he wouldn't again tolerate her flagrant disregard to what he asked of her.

There were so many things he didn't understand about her. The fact that she was an American could account for some differences, but there were other things that were puzzling. For example, how was it that, at age seventeen, she could cook so well or could speak so well on such a large range of topics, sing, paint, dance, and most mysteriously of all, make love with such aggressiveness and wild abandon.

First of all, however, he was going to have to deal with what she'd just done, and if he had to be harsh, so be it. He didn't recall ever being so angry in his life, and the more he dwelled on her outrageously independent nature and extravagant tastes, the angrier he became. She would have to be brought to heel and taught a lesson. Especially if they were to make a go of it.

Susan was feeling a cross between anger, resentment at being given the silent treatment for some unknown sin, and disappointment at discovering another not so pleasant side of James's personality. Thinking back to the future, she'd heard stories of his moodiness and controlling nature, but hearing about it and experiencing it were two different things. She didn't like it one bit. It made her stomach hurt and she wanted to lash back at him in some way, so he'd understand how bad he was making her feel.

Chapter 16

James's Cruel Outburst

When they got to the cottage, Susan started to, automatically from habit, open her car door to get out. James leaned over and painfully grasped her wrist. "You wait for me to open the door," he growled, looking straight into her eyes. "Remember?"

She released the car door handle as he let go of her wrist and took a deep breath as he got out and came around to the other side. He opened the door and she stepped out.

"I'll get your suitcase later," he said, striding up to the front door of the cottage and taking out the key from his pocket. "I have something to say to you."

"Here it comes," she thought.

He stalked into the cottage and paced into the kitchen, stopping in the middle of the floor and abruptly turned around to face her.

Susan softly closed the door behind her and took her time walking into the kitchen to stand in front of him. Her heart was beating frantically and she felt a little afraid for some reason, but didn't know why other than this was a side of James she wasn't expecting to see...and she didn't know how to deal with it.

He reached into his pocket and pulled out the handful of bills Mel had given him and waved them in front of her face. "Are these yours?" he asked menacingly.

She stared at them, speechless, then took a deep breath. So, Mel had given the money back to James...

"Well, are they?" he repeated.

When she didn't answer, he grabbed her hand and shoved the bills into it, closing her fingers around the money. He continued to glare at her, squeezing her fingers. She felt as if she could see fire sparking out of his eyes.

"My dad's on a pension and his job doesn't pay much," he said. "He gave this back to me this morning. You evidently thought it was okay to pay for your extravagant dinner last night, but as I made clear before, you *weren't* to be buying things with your money. Dad paid for all that stuff nobody asked for or needed, and now I've got to figure a way to pay him back. Did you think of that?! *Did you?!!"* His voice reverberated throughout the room.

She took a step backward, away from him, her eyes open wide in dismay. He was yelling at her!

She didn't know what to think or say or do. She knew he was far too angry to be appeased by any words, but at the same time she could feel her own temper rising along with resentment at the way he'd treated her on the drive.

As if he still had something pent up inside, he continued. "Do you know how selfish and extravagant you are? Like that expensive green dress you had to have? Ever think about it? Always having to have your own way and not thinking or caring about anyone else but yourself!!"

He'd gone too far. The whole reason for the dinner was because she cared so much and wanted to do something special and nice. And, she had tried to pay for the dress with her own money; she'd even offered to return it. Flames burned in her eyes as she tossed the money onto the floor, swung her arm backward then forward again as hard as she could, slapping him full on the face. The impact turned his head and his cheek was left with a red palm print on it.

She gasped as he grabbed her shoulders and it appeared as if he was about to shake her, but instead, he brought his face close to hers.

"And while we're talking about you, why don't you satisfy my curiosity on another point. How is it that you know how to do so many things, specifically all those things you do in the bedroom? You're just a whore like the rest of the girls at the club, aren't you!? With all your

174

sweet words and tricks...like the virgin thing...how did you manage that one?"

She pushed as hard as she could against his chest and broke free of his grasp, but he wasn't finished.

"Oh, you're thinking," he mimicked her. "...'*But, you know I was a virgin; I proved it to you.*' Well, you proved nothing to me! That can all be faked, can't it? It's been done by girls since the dawn of time! So then, how did you manage to fake it so well? Who was it that taught you all your whore's tricks?!"

She was speechless at his cruel and hurtful words. She didn't recall a time in her entire life, past, present or future, where someone had said something that hurt so badly. She felt as if she would burst into tears, but she was even too pained to do that. She backed away from him, their eyes still locked.

Suddenly his hands and arms went slack and dropped to his sides as the impact of what he'd just said made itself felt. He was breathing heavily and he looked like an angry bull. He quickly turned away from her, strode to the door, opened it then slammed it shut behind him so hard that the tea cups in the cabinet rattled. She saw him pass the window and head up the hill to the big tree where they'd had their picnic and sat drawing.

She was shaking. Tears welled in her eyes. She put both hands up to her face and started sobbing. Her heart was breaking...She wanted to go home. She didn't belong with James...not now...not ever...

Lynn was upset and concerned. She watched Susan faint and, even if no one else had noticed, she'd seen her tear-stained face when she'd come into the club. Susan looked pained and exhausted. She thought it might be the after effects of the near attack in the alley, but she knew better. She knew Susan was in way over her head and she was worried about her.

When she and Ian got back to the hotel room, she wasn't in the mood for frolicking in the bed.

"Worried about your friend?" Ian asked.

"Yeah," said Lynn. "I wish she'd never decided to come here. It was a huge mistake. I can already see that she's regretting it."

"Doesn't look like she's regretting it to me."

"Well, you don't know her and I do. We've been best friends for fifty years. We can almost read each other's minds."

Ian sat back at her remark. "Fifty years?"

"Yes, that's what I said. Fifty years."

"You're funning me, of course."

"No, I'm not." She sat down on the bed and patted the space beside her. She pulled her iPhone out of her purse and turned it on. "Come look at this and then you'll believe me," was all she said.

An hour later, Ian felt stunned.

"Don't worry. I can't change history or anything. Once we're gone, you won't even remember us. We'll just be a vague memory."

"So what do you want to do now?" he asked.

"Find Susan and James," she said. "I've got to convince her to go back *now!*"

Susan felt numb and confused. How had such a small thing escalated into such a giant and hurtful exchange of words? Why had she lost control and slapped him? Was James right about her being selfish and extravagant? She could almost agree with extravagant, but she didn't consider making a nice dinner to be in any way selfish. She knew what he'd said was all said in anger, but that was no excuse. And then his other cruel words, implying she was a whore and had faked being a virgin. That was going too far, way too far.

She suddenly realized, however, that she'd been dreadfully wrong in regard to the dinner, not because she'd been "disobedient," which wasn't a word that was even in her vocabulary, but because she hadn't even considered the financial circumstances in which James and his dad currently lived. It didn't really matter that he would be a millionaire someday. This was still 1962 and James lived frugally. She'd not only embarrassed and humiliated him by making him appear poor, but she'd rubbed it in his face that she had money and he didn't. She tried to justify all this as a reason for his over-the-top anger and the hideous words he'd spewed out at her. He'd simply lost control and was probably regretting what he said at this very moment.

And, she told herself, "You slapped him and left a big red mark on his face. You were the first to lose it."

She took a deep breath and hung her head. She owed him a real "I'm sorry" apology, but she needed to wait until he cooled down some to be able to accept it.

She went out the back door and sat on the stoop leading into the garden and contemplated matters more. She knew she could gather up the wherewithal to be able to make a sincere apology, and she knew that if she waited long enough to do it, he would forgive her.

Buttons came up and rubbed against her arm. She gathered the cat in her arms and put her face in the soft fur. Buttons turned on her purr motor.

"Oh, Buttons, tell me what I should do now..." she murmured. Buttons just kept on purring.

Her mind wandered. What kind of relationship was this anyway? Nothing more than a whirlwind of lust and passion brought on by a wager, her out-of-control hormones and her taunting him with innocence and virginity. They had first come together physically without fully knowing each other emotionally. Her physical attraction to him was toxic. Where in the hell had her sixty-two-year-old brain gone off to?! It certainly wasn't anywhere around here!

Well...maybe just a tiny piece of it was here...

And, although James was incredibly talented, artistically and musically, far surpassing anything most people could ever remotely aspire to, there were so many things she enjoyed talking about that were of no interest to him at this young stage of his life. He might be intelligent, but she didn't think she could ever hold a stimulating conversation with him related to the economy, politics, science, history, religion or another hundred topics she found interesting or exciting. And, it was an obvious fact he was overbearing, chauvinistic, expecting to have his way in everything, demanding obedience. Didn't that make *him* selfish? The only way she would ever be obedient is if it were beaten into her. And she would certainly never tolerate that!

Thoughts of her real life in the future flooded over her. She was never treated like James was doing now, not even when she was impulsive or unreasonable, which she knew she often had been over the years. Yes, her future mate was just as moody in many ways, and he yelled sometimes when she frustrated him, but he would never say such awful things to her, and he would never grab her or hurt her physically. He was much more intelligent than James, bordering on genius in fact. And, he loved her deeply and unconditionally. Why had she ever even imagined that James would somehow be better?

She thought back to James, remembering how he'd grasped her arm at the first practice session and dragged her outside, and how he'd squeezed her arm so tight that it hurt just the day before when they went to the hotel to get her things. Then she thought of just today. He'd grabbed her arm again when she started to open the car door for herself, and she was certain he was about to shake her just a short time ago. What would life be like with someone who had such a short fuse on his temper? Her own fuse was short enough. What would he do next if she made him angry, and it was very obvious that, with her rebellious nature, she would often make him angry. Would he slap her or push her? Would she slap him back? It was something she didn't even want to think about.

It was still an era in time where men ruled and women obeyed. Not a place where she'd fit in very easily. She and James would likely end up destroying each other. Returning to the future was looking better and better.

More than a half hour had passed since James left. Susan knew that if there was any chance of them making up, it would have to be her going to him and apologizing, maybe even begging forgiveness, and it wasn't in her nature to do it. It never had been. In situations like this, she typically just waited for things to cool down, and then just pretended all the hurt or bad feelings would go away. Time seemed to be a cure of its own. If you waited long enough, everything got better again all by itself.

Didn't it?

But, she knew that wasn't going to work with James. He was as stubborn as she was, possibly more. She would have to make the first move, beg for forgiveness and hope she wouldn't have to grovel too much. She steeled herself for the task, sighed heavily and stood up as Buttons jumped off her lap.

"Well, here goes," she said to the cat. "This might be one of those learning experiences Mika was hinting at. Maybe I'll learn something valuable here that I can take back with me to the future...like maybe how to apologize or say 'I'm sorry.'

"Mrow," said Buttons.

She sighed again, went back into the cottage, and out to the car to get her suitcase out of the boot. She washed her face and changed into a clean dress that buttoned down the front. She omitted the bra. The dress had a ruffled collar and a v-neck, revealing only a modest amount of cleavage like the green dress. It was fit to her waist and flared out at the bottom. It was shorter than most of the dresses she'd worn, stopping a few inches above the knee. She looked at herself in the mirror and let her hair down from the pony tail she'd tied it up in that morning, then brushed it out. She pinched her cheeks to put some color in them. Then she pulled off the clean pair of panties she'd just put on. If all else failed, she could try her womanly ways on him either with tears, her body or both.

Feeling she was now up to the task of apologizing, she went out the front door and headed up the hill to try and find James.

He was sitting at the base of the big tree, knees drawn up, arms crossed on top with his chin resting on his arms.

His anger was fading, but not as quickly as it usually did. He knew he had a hot temper when someone crossed him, but he typically was able to keep it in check.

But not with her. He was totally out of control when it came to her.

He was contemplating why. Was it because he loved her? Did he, in fact, really love her? Yes! Of course he did! He was obsessed with her.

And when you really love someone, your feelings about everything are more intense, both the good ones and the bad ones.

She had just wanted to do something special and nice for him. She didn't think about the money aspect because she'd never experienced the lack of it. Why should he be so angry with her for trying to please him? Casting aside the thought of the expense, she'd worked very hard to make everything perfect...and it had been perfect.

And... She wasn't like other girls. In addition to being beautiful, she was musically and artistically talented. She could draw, sing, dance and play the piano. So what if it was a mystery as to how she had acquired all these abilities.

He envisioned future hours spent together drawing and maybe even painting. They could make music together like his mum and dad used to do. He pictured her in the kitchen, cooking his favorite meals and keeping everything tidy. What other girl had he ever met that did any of that stuff? No one. He knew he could also talk to her about anything and that she would listen and understand. He could just see her knitting baby booties by the fireside, Sunday mornings driving through the countryside, puttering in the garden together, even though he wasn't overly fond of getting his hands dirty; how could he ask for more?

And, as icing on a cake, she had a passion for lovemaking that far surpassed anything he'd ever experienced before. She seemed to know instinctively how and where to touch him to give him the most pleasure and she made love with wild abandon, crying out shamelessly as she reached her climax. Just the thought of it made him harden with desire.

He deeply regretted the painful words he'd said to her about being a whore and faking being a virgin. He knew she hadn't faked it. And, while he didn't still comprehend how or where she had acquired her passionate nature, he was in the process of convincing himself that it must be due to her reaction to him. Although young, he was experienced when it came to the bedroom, and she most likely was simply responding to his extraordinary talents and own passion.

Certainly that must be it!

On the down side, he had discovered she was impulsive, head-strong and fiercely independent, but that could all be changed. She was young enough to be molded into whatever he wanted, and he intended to start working on it soon. She would learn to be submissive, especially now that he'd taken her virginity and felt he would have to do the "right thing" by her. Yes, if they were to make a go of it, she would have to change and understand who had the upper hand.

A shadow fell across the grass in front of him and he looked up to see her standing there. She was barefoot and her tawny blond hair was streaming down across her shoulders and arms. She was wearing a short dress, revealing her long, tan legs and he could see the outline of her breasts where they pushed against the bodice of the dress. Her face was bleak and her expression subdued. Had she come to beg his forgiveness then?

After Lynn told Ian the truth about herself and Susan, incredible as it was, Ian had a different perspective of her. The mystery was solved as to how she knew so much about sex and how to satisfy a man in bed… She'd had years and years of experience! At first, the thought of her being sixty-three-years old in the body of an eighteen year old, was a bit of a turn off, but memories of their pleasure the night before, negated all the "weirdness" of the situation and he was actually feeling quite anxious to see what else she might be able to teach him.

"Why don't we ring up James's dad and see if they're at his house or if he knows where they went off to?" he asked Lynn.

"Great idea!" Lynn exclaimed, reaching in her purse for her iPhone.

"I don't think that will work here, you know," said Ian.

"Oh! Of course not! I knew that!"

Ian reached for the phone on the night stand and dialed James's number. Mel answered.

"Hey Mel. Ian here. Can I talk to James?"

"Not here at the moment," said Mel.

"Oh, and do you know where he's off to then?"

Mel hesitated, knowing James and Susan only had another couple days before she had to leave on her tour, and hoping they would take the time to firm things up for the future. He really liked Susan and was hoping they could make things work out between them on a permanent basis. He didn't actually believe her when she said she wouldn't be able to come back after the history tour. And, he had hopes that maybe James could talk her out of going at all.

"Not sure," said Mel. "They left a few hours ago, but didn't say where they were off to or when they were coming back."

"Oh, so they're coming back there then?"

"Most likely," Mel lied.

"Ta, then, Mel. I'll check in a bit later."

Ian hung up and turned to Lynn. "They appear to be missing at the moment." He looked at her with hooded eyes. "Might you want me to get a little frisky with you while we wait for them to come back? Might as well enjoy ourselves a bit, don't you think?"

He reached for her and tumbled her back on the bed, reaching up the skirt of her June Cleaver dress.

She giggled. "You can get as frisky as you like," she said, pulling him close.

Chapter 17

The Apology

As Susan looked down at James, she became tongue-tied. She thought she'd found the words to say to tell him how sorry she was, but they were stuck in her throat. Why was this so hard? She loved him, didn't she? If you loved someone, it shouldn't be so hard to say you were sorry.

He looked up at her expectedly and then patted the grass next to him, indicating that she should sit down. She lowered her eyes as she sank down on her knees and lowered herself back onto her calves. She looked him full in the face and took a deep breath.

"I'm sorry, James...I'm so, very sorry...I'm extravagant and spoiled... and I wasn't thinking..."

This was a lot harder than she thought it would be. It bordered on humiliating.

He said nothing, waiting for her to say more.

"I wanted to do something special, not just for you, but for your dad. I like him a lot..." Her voice trailed off and she looked away.

James still didn't say anything. He was making this more difficult for her and she was beginning to feel bitter about it. She turned back toward him and met his eyes. She was going to have to beg, damn it!

"Please...please, will you forgive me?" she pleaded, squeezing a few tears from her eyes.

He couldn't stand her tears, and it suddenly made him angry and resentful as he thought she was just using them to make him weaken against her. A typical womanly ploy. He tried to calm himself. He reached forward, gathered her in his arms and kissed her hair, but he still said nothing. He tilted her face up to his, looking at her forced tears, before forcefully pressing his mouth to hers in a demanding and punishing kiss.

As his tongue shot possessively into her mouth, he knew what he was going to do. He was going to take her right here on the grass. It would be her penance. He didn't fully understand why, but if she thought her tears and a few sweet little words were supposed to make everything right, this time she was mistaken. She had a lesson to learn.

Looking at her bare legs and seeing her breasts outlined so clearly in the dress, had aroused him to a hardness that needed immediate satisfaction. His pent up anger continued to grow, thinking that she was just toying with him, taunting him with her body, that she wasn't really sorry about anything at all.

Before she could protest, he pushed her roughly down on her back, ripped open the front of her dress, pulling her breasts out and brought his mouth down on her nipples, nipping at them hurtfully. She moaned beneath him and he knew it wouldn't take much to make her ready for him, but he wasn't going to take the time. He just wanted her now, at this very moment, and he was going to have her now, ready or not.

Anger, lust, love and desire all melded together, one emotion pushing against the other in a battle of wills.

As she realized what he was about to do, she tried to push up against him, uttering a small, feeble protest, but he forced her back down. She squirmed beneath him, trying to get up and away, but her efforts were futile. He was stronger than her.

"Please...no..." she murmured trying to push him away again.

He pulled up the skirt of her dress, noticing she wore nothing underneath, and opened his trousers. His throbbing manhood sprung out and, without any consideration for her pleasure or readiness, he pressed her knees open with his and plunged deeply into her. He began heatedly thrusting in and out, taking total possession of her.

She struggled against him for only a moment before wrapping her legs around him as he rode her, trying to find pleasure in what he was doing. He shortly reached his release, collapsing on top of her, panting, then pushed up on his elbows to look down at her. There had been no pleasure for her. Their eyes met.

"Well, madam?" he asked, his chest slightly heaving from the exertion. "Have you learned your lesson not to cross me then?"

She stared back at him, waiting for some kind of apology for his cruel remarks and from what he'd just forcefully done to her, but it didn't come. It was as if he didn't even remember saying the cruel words or didn't want to admit saying them.

"Well, have you?" he asked, pinning her wrists painfully to the ground and boring his eyes into hers.

Tears burned behind her eyes and she fought to hold them back. "You're hurting me!"

"Then answer me, damn you!"

He was scaring her. She didn't know what to say. Her heart was beating wildly and her breathing was fast and shallow. When the pain in her wrists became unbearable, she capitulated.

"Yes...yes, I've learned my lesson."

She was shaking. Something was very, very wrong about this!

He rolled off her onto his back, and tucked her head into the area just below his shoulder. His arm came around her and pulled her close.

"Good...as you should have. Keep it in mind for the future."

She could feel him relax against her and his breathing become slower. He trailed his fingers up and down her arm then ran them softly through her hair, kissing the top of her head. She felt frozen and confused, even shocked.

"I do love you," he whispered, continuing to touch her gently until he sensed she had relaxed.

But she wasn't relaxed. Her eyes were squeezed shut, but felt as if they were wide open. Open to some indescribable feeling that was playing havoc in the pit of her stomach. She tried to gather her thoughts and make sense of what had just happened, what he had just done and said to her, but for some reason, it just wouldn't register.

Every other time they had argued about something or James had been angry with her, she'd found a reason to justify his words and actions. Any excuse to keep him the paragon that he'd always been to her in her mind. Why? She was a strong and worldly woman of sixty-two years, not in body, but certainly in mind. Why was she so accepting? It wasn't in her nature. Or, was it? Had she deserved what he had just said and done to her? Or was she just trying to conjure up another excuse for him, a reason to still love him no matter what he said or did to her? It was a sobering thought.

She sighed deeply then flung one leg across him and wrapped her arm around his chest. They both became drowsy as their heartbeats slowed back to a steady rhythm and they fell asleep.

But, she hadn't said, "I love you too." She really didn't think she loved him after all…she was very torn and confused…

Ian and Lynn spent the rest of the morning and most of the early afternoon frolicking in bed, smoking their way through another pack of cigarettes and taking cat naps. It was almost two in the afternoon before they tried to call James's dad again, and when they did, no one answered.

"Want to take a ride out to the countryside?" asked Ian. "I've got a motorbike that'll fit us both."

Lynn sat up and said excitedly, "Oh yes! I'd love to!"

"Let's get dressed and be off then."

He hopped out of bed and pulled on his boxers and pants, then slipped his arms into the shirt that had been laying crumpled on the floor.

Lynn got up and went into the bathroom, pulling a pair of jeans out of her suitcase, mentally thanking Marta and Mika for thinking to include them with the *"Leave it to Beaver"* wear.

They were soon on their way, speeding through the streets of Brighton then out of the town onto a two-lane road bordered on both sides by trees. The road opened out into the countryside as they sped along, the wind whipping their hair behind them.

"This is fabulous!" Lynn thought.

It was several hours before James and Susan woke up, feeling languid and lazy. James's arm had fallen asleep and Susan had a crink in her neck.

During their long nap, Susan's mind did its usual work to erase all the bad and uncomfortable things that had just happened between her and James. She just wanted to forget the most recent, horrible incident between them.

She had convinced herself that she was the one at fault. He'd made it clear she wasn't to be spending her money. She'd forced Mel into a situation to pay for her selfish extravagance.

Yes, she really was selfish, just as James had accused her of being. Sure, she wanted to do something special by making a great dinner, but cooking and making nice dinners was one of her favorite things to do.

She had done it for herself more than them. She deserved his anger and what he had done to her. Didn't she?

"Let's go take a dip in the pond," suggested James, shaking his arm awake then standing up and holding out his hand to pull Susan up.

"But I don't think I brought my bathing suit," she said, not knowing if Marta and Mika had included one in her suitcase full of clothes.

"Don't need a bathing suit," he said, looking at her half nakedness.

Instinctively, she reached for the top of her dress and pulled it together to cover her breasts. He reached over and playfully slapped her hands away.

"Leave it," he said, quirking a smile. He grabbed her hand and they ran down the path together, her bare breasts bouncing, the necklace between them. They were laughing and, for all intents and purposes, back in perfect harmony again, the recent storm all but forgotten.

When they reached the pond, James stripped off his clothes and dove out into the middle. Susan quickly followed. They both surfaced together and embraced, their feet barely touching bottom. As Susan pressed her bare breasts against his chest, she could feel James's manhood spring into life again against her thigh. She smiled at him wickedly, wrapping her legs around his waist and lowering herself onto him. He threw his head back and moaned, then grabbed her bottom and moved her up and down on top of him.

"You are truly shameless, madam," he said, crushing his lips down on hers. Small waves rippled around them.

"You make me that way," she whispered huskily into his ear.

"Ah, just as I thought," he said to himself. "It's me that makes her this way..."

It was about a half hour later that Ian and Lynn rode into Little Dippington. Ian stopped the motorbike and turned his head over his shoulder and said, "Want to stop here or want to keep going? James's Auntie Annabelle lives just a few minutes down the road. We could stop and say hello. James and your friend might even be there. I got the feeling James's dad wasn't being totally honest as to where they were."

"Let's go on to Auntie Annabelle's then," she said.

A short time later, they were turning off the road onto the lane leading up to the cottage. Ian spotted James's car in front.

"Looks like we found them!" he said.

"Thank God!" said Lynn, getting off the back of the motorbike.

They walked up to the front door together and knocked. There was no answer. Ian tried the handle to the door. It was unlocked. They both went inside, Lynn calling out Susan's name.

There was no one in the kitchen or living room. The door to the bedroom was open and the bed was made up neatly. A fluffy black and white cat was sleeping on the foot of the bed.

"Checkers!?" exclaimed Lynn. The cat looked exactly like Susan's cat she had in the future.

The cat looked up at her.

"No, that's Buttons. She's Auntie Annabelle's cat," said Ian.

"Mrow," said Buttons.

Ian went upstairs. There was no one there either.

"They must have gone on a walk or something," said Ian. "Let's go look up by the big tree. James said he used to spend a lot of time here when he was young, sitting up under the tree."

She slipped her hand in his and they went out of the cottage up the path to the big tree. There was no one there either.

"I think James mentioned a pond or something down that part of the path," Ian said, pointing. They began walking in the direction of the pond, but halfway down the path they both stopped and looked at each other, a bemused expression on both of their faces.

"I think we've found them," said Ian with a smirk on his face.

"Oh my!" exclaimed Lynn, her face turning bright pink as she heard the obvious sounds of an erotic encounter coming from where the pond must be. She turned around and headed back up the path, Ian close behind her.

"Hmmmm...what now?" she asked when they were back under the big tree.

"I think we leave them to their privacy," said Ian. "Let's go back to Little Dippington and grab something to eat. I'm starved."

They ran back down the path to the cottage, not wanting James or Susan to know they'd been there...even though it was doubtful they ever would...hopped back on Ian's motorbike and sped back to Little Dippington.

Chapter 18

James's Intentions

Susan was out in back of the cottage looking around the garden and contemplating what she should make for dinner. They'd had some rolls and cheese earlier when they came back from the pond, but it was now close to six o'clock and she figured James would be hungry again.

He was at the piano, dabbling with the *"All My Kisses"* song when she came in the back door with a large zucchini and some onions in her arms. Every time she heard the opening notes, she gave a start, as if hit with an electrical shock. The song had always affected her that way. Hearing it being written was certainly a novel experience, but she still felt the electrical shock every time he started the song over.

"Close your eyes while I touch you
You know how I love you
Remember me while you're away
And then while you are gone
I will try to go on
And send all my kisses your way."

She gave a winsome sigh as she looked at him. He was adorable. Maybe not the right thing to say about a guy. Most girls went for "rugged" or "handsome." But James was cute and adorable, like a puppy dog or baby kitten that you just wanted to cuddle up with and hug. And those eyes…Oh my God! Those eyes!

As she stared, she suddenly was overcome with sadness. She only had two more nights with him before she had to leave. Should she tell him the truth? Would he even believe the truth? She had her iPod, so could show him so many things about his future. Once she was gone, he'd forget it all. She winced. Once she was gone, she would only be a dim memory to him. But, what would he be to her, she wondered. Would all that had happened back here in the past be a dim memory to her too?

She reached up to finger the ballerina shoes hanging on her necklace. She didn't understand why she felt the way she did. One moment she felt so good being with him, and the next she wanted to run as fast as she could back to the future.

He stopped playing and looked over at her. "A penny for your thoughts," he said, knowing that she'd been standing silently looking at him.

"I love that song," she said.

"I wrote it for you, you know."

She smiled sadly. "I was hoping you'd say that. It'll be a good memory for me after I'm gone."

"And for when you come back after your tour," he added.

Her eyes looked away from his. He stood up and came over to her. "You are coming back, you know...after the tour and all...you'll come back here to be with me..."

"But you'll probably be in London by then making records..."

"Then we can meet in London, right? You *are* coming back to me... you have to...you know you have to..."

She refused to look at him. She felt tears starting in her eyes yet again. He gently took her chin in his hand and turned her face towards his. "Promise me you'll be back. Promise me."

Her eyes met his.

"I promise," she lied.

Ian and Lynn motored back to Brighton and to the hotel room, where they both took showers before heading out for a night at the clubs. They went down to the wharf and hopped from one club to another, drinking beer and joining in the boisterous singing.

Then they went back to the hotel room, where they frolicked some more in the moonlight shining through the window, smoked a few more cigarettes and fell into a deep, satisfying sleep.

Susan was in the kitchen shredding zucchini and chopping onions. James was back to poking out tunes on the piano. They'd managed to use up virtually all of the food they'd brought on the day of the picnic, and hadn't stopped in Little Dippington on the way back out to the cottage to get anything else. But, that didn't stop Susan from concocting something for dinner.

With the garden bursting to the seams with vegetables and Auntie Annabelle's well-stocked kitchen, it was only a small challenge to figure something out. She was going to make a salad and zucchini pancakes, a nice vegetarian meal. Give him a taste of the future, even though he didn't know about it yet.

In the seventies, James would become a vegetarian at the urging of his wife, also named Susan. In the real future, over forty five years later, he would still be a staunch vegetarian, actively promoting the lifestyle along with his son, Robert, a world-famous vegetarian chef.

She hummed to the music as she worked until it trailed off and stopped.

She looked over at James, who was staring intently at her.

"What?" she asked.

"I was just watching you, is all."

"And what are you watching?"

"Nothing in particular. The way you're standing there."

He got up and came over to her. "Put those things down for a minute," he said, taking the knife from her hand and laying it down on the counter. He took her other hand in his and led her over to the couch.

"Oh, no you don't!" she said, trying to pull away. "At least let me finish making dinner."

"I'm not going to ravish you or anything. I just want to talk to you. We can do more ravishing later." He smiled as he pulled her down beside him and turned to face her.

She felt an alarm go off inside her. "What was this all about?" she asked herself.

He looked down for a moment, then back up, meeting her eyes. He was still holding one of her hands.

"My dad asked me this morning what my intentions toward you were," he started.

The alarm inside her went off again, this time loud and clear.

"He likes you a lot, you know."

"And I like him..." she said.

"So, I've been thinking that I should do the right thing by you." He lifted her hand to his lips and kissed it.

She jerked her hand away, stood up abruptly and turned her back to him.

"What's wrong?" he asked, jumping up to stand behind her. He put his hands on her shoulders and turned her around.

"I don't want to talk about this...about your intentions..."

"But..."

"Please, James...please no... Don't say what I think you're planning to say... please don't." She looked down at her hands that were clasped together in front of her.

A hurt and puzzled expression came over his face. "You don't love me?" he asked in a small voice.

"It's not that...it's not that at all..."

"Then what is it?"

She sat back down and looked up at him standing over her. "Everything's happened too fast...I feel like my head is spinning...we don't really even know each other..."

"All we have to know is that we love each other!"

"You're wrong...you're so, so wrong," she thought to herself.

He was so young, only twenty years old. What did he really know at twenty years old? He was on the brink of being world-famous. A fantastic and incredible future lay before him. One that couldn't and wouldn't include her.

And, as she'd come to realize this morning, they would never be suitable together. That's what Mika wanted her to learn from all of this, most likely. All her dreams of him over the years were only dreams. She'd made him into a paragon of perfection in her mind, when in reality, he was far from perfect. If she had anything close to perfection, it was what she already had back in the future.

This interlude between them had been doomed from the start. It was nothing more than physical attraction and infatuation at its finest.

They were both head-strong and stubborn. They were both controlling and had to have their own way. He couldn't keep his temper in check and she'd turned into a watering pot, crying all the time. And did she really love him? The words were easy to say, since she'd thought about loving him her whole life...and they were easy to feel when he held her in his arms and made love to her, but it wasn't enough. It was far from enough. And she knew she had to make herself realize that.

Susan was back in the kitchen, finishing dinner. James was in the living room, sitting on the couch, thinking and brooding over her abrupt refusal to talk about his intentions toward her. It upset him and he could feel tinges of anger beginning to stir inside him. He knew, however, that getting angry would only make matters worse.

Why didn't she want to hear him out? What girl wouldn't want to hear the words he was about to say? Did she really love him?

Yes, it was true they'd only known each other for a few days, but if you met the person who was right for you, what did it really matter if you knew that person for days or weeks or months? She'd cast a spell on him somehow, and there was no breaking it.

Then it dawned on him that he'd probably scared her by speaking too soon. Maybe he should wait until she came back from her history tour. That would give her enough time to think...and to miss him horribly.

He pictured her in his mind, running into his arms when she returned from her tour, her love for him clear on her face, tears on her cheeks that he would kiss away. He imagined her telling him how awful it had been to be away from him. The longer he thought about it, the more convinced he became that she would come back worshiping him and never wanting to leave him again.

But then another thought hit him. It was so simple, it almost stunned him. What if he just didn't let her leave? What if they didn't go back to Brighton but stayed here? What if she missed her bus? He pushed the possibility into the back of his mind. For now, at least.

He got up and went into the kitchen when she said dinner was ready. He sat down at the table and looked at what she'd put on his plate.

"And, so, what's this?" he asked, holding up a forkful of green stuff.

"It's a zucchini pancake," she replied. "Try it; you'll like it."

He sniffed. "Doesn't look all that appetizing."

"Just taste it."

He put it in his mouth and began to chew. She looked over at him. "Well?"

"Not so bad," he said, taking another forkful. "But this is just a vegetable. Where's the meat?"

"There is no meat...or chicken...this is it. We're eating vegetarian tonight."

"Vegetarian? Isn't that what Hindus or strange people who don't eat meat do?"

"Yes, and it's good for you. I'm making you healthy."

He looked at her over the top of his glass of orange soda as he took a sip. "Nice of you to keep me healthy."

"If you only knew..." she thought to herself.

James and Susan sat at the kitchen table and ended up talking until midnight. Susan was curious to know his views on politics and some random world events, but soon realized he had no interest in either of those topics at this time in his life. She asked him about any books he'd read and what his favorite book was. He responded that he wasn't interested in books or reading; he thought it was a waste of time. Then she asked him about gardening, knowing that both his dad and aunt had wonderful gardens, but his only comment was that he didn't like puttering around in dirt all that much. This would all change later, she knew, but for now, his all consuming passion was his music. Another reason, she thought, they would never be suitable together. Although she loved music, other than her dancing, in reality she couldn't sing or play any kind of musical instrument. Mika had only given her those talents for this journey into the past.

When they got in bed, James reached out for her with a lustful look in his eyes, but instead of encouraging him, she just laid her head on his shoulder.

"Want to sleep for a while then?" he asked kissing the top of her head.

"Umm...mmmm," was her response, closing her eyes.

"That's all right then. I'll just wake you up later..."

He fell into a deep and satisfying sleep, visions of their future together floating through his mind.

She, on the other hand, was restless. As soon as she knew he was sound asleep, she slipped out of bed, tip-toed out of the room and quietly closed the door behind her. She reached for her purse sitting next to the couch and pulled out her iPod. She scrolled through the songs, smiling as she passed by her favorite song, the one that James had just finished writing, tempted to play it. She knew she couldn't.

When she got to the "M's," she stopped at the Jim McCrow/Beth Gill song, getting goose bumps all over as she recalled the words to the song. Then she got an idea. She reached for her sketch pad that was laying on the coffee table and grabbed a pencil. She put in her ear buds and hit "play" to listen to the song. As it played, she wrote down the words. She had to listen to the song five times to get it right. She read back the first verse of the song to herself.

"Darlin' I've been dreaming all day... Thinking of nothing but you all day... Of touching you...kissing you...Here's just what I need to do...Lay down with

you...Pull you close to me...As close as we can be...Making love...All through the night...Feeling you hold me so tight...Drain my strength away...Don't let me go...I want you now to feel what you know...Until the night is gone...Until we see the sun...Making love..."

She tore the sheets of paper off the pad then put them in the piano bench. Tomorrow would be their last night together. She envisioned them at the piano, her playing the tune and both of them singing... and then...She was going to make it a night he'd never forget...despite what Mika had said about her only being a dim memory once she was gone. He'd most certainly remember the blond-haired, green-eyed wanton who had graced his bed; she didn't even doubt it. She smiled to herself wickedly.

Buttons had been sitting on the top of the couch watching her and licking her paws after eating Mel's can of potted meat that Susan had put out for her.

"So, what do you think of my plan, kitty?" she asked Buttons.

"Mrow," Buttons responded.

They awoke just as the sun was starting to come up, casting pale threads of light through the open curtains onto the carpeted floor and up the wall. Susan smiled as she reached down under the covers to find James was erect.

"My, my, what's this?" she asked coyly.

"Something special, just for you," he said sleepily, nuzzling her neck.

She pulled him on top of her. "I like special things," she said softly, taking him into her warmth and closing her eyes as he began moving inside her.

Later, in the kitchen while they were drinking coffee, James suggested they go back into Little Dippington and see if they could beg some pastels off Simon then head back up the hill under the big tree and do more sketching. They ate some toast, joined hands and headed down the lane towards the village.

Simon was more than pleased to see them again and to provide them each with a box of pastels.

"Enjoy!" he said, as they headed out of the studio.

As they passed Emily's shop, Susan noticed her Granny sitting on a stool just outside the door. She was staring so intently at Susan that a shiver went down her spine. Granny smiled a near toothless grin and began nodding her head. Susan linked her arm with James's, then looked away, quickened their pace out of Little Dippington and walked back to the cottage. It was close to noon.

Before heading up the hill to the big tree, Susan took a couple of left-over zucchini pancakes out of the refrigerator and handed one to James.

"They're good cold, too," she said.

"But they're green-looking," he said.

"Just eat it." She took a bite of hers. "Mmmmm."

They grabbed their sketchpads and pastels and headed out the door.

For a half hour, they worked with their pastels, Susan concentrating on James's profile again, and James working on a picture of the cottage down the hill below.

James was in a pensive mood. Susan wondered what he was thinking, but before she could ask, he said, "So, I think you need to reconsider going on this history tour of yours." He wasn't looking at her, just concentrating on his sketchpad. He tried to sound nonchalant.

Pastel still in hand, she looked over at him.

"What did you say?"

He put down his pastel to rub his thumb across the paper to blend some of the color. He still didn't look over at her.

"I said you should reconsider going on the history tour. I don't want you to go."

She placed her pastel back in the box at her side and set down her sketch pad. She turned to face him.

"That's not possible," she said. "You know that's what I came to England for."

"It doesn't matter what you came here for. It's all different now, you know...with us and everything."

"That might be, but it doesn't change the fact that I'm leaving tomorrow for the tour."

"At midnight, too...right?"

"Who told you that?"

"My dad." He continued to work on his picture. "Odd time to leave...but he said it was a turnaround to London."

"Yes, it is. What's so odd about that? Buses come and go twenty-four hours a day all the time."

"Just odd because it's in the middle of our gig at the club and I've never heard of any bus leaving Brighton at midnight before."

"Well, I didn't know you when the tour arrangements were made... And I don't run the bus company..."

"Not important, then. I just don't want you to go on the tour."

"I know you don't want me to go. You think I want to go?"

"Then stay here and don't go."

"I told you that's not possible."

"But it is, you know. You just have to make the decision to stay."

He set down his sketchpad and turned to look at her. "Tell me you'll stay," he pleaded reaching out for her.

"This is ridiculous!" she yelled at him, grabbing her sketchpad and box of pastels, then abruptly standing up. She looked down at him. "You have to stop this!"

She ran down the hill and into the cottage. When she reached the kitchen, she tossed the sketchpad and box of pastels on the kitchen table. The box went over the edge and opened, spilling all the pastels out onto the floor. She didn't care, and raced out the back door into the garden where she stood, arms crossed, with her back to the door. She was shaking.

She heard James come out the back door. He came to stand behind her and ran his hands up and down the sides of her upper arms. Slowly, he pulled her back into him and leaned around the side of her neck to softly nibble her ear, then trailed kisses up and down the side of her neck. She could feel his erectness pressing urgently into her bottom.

She was certain he'd be angry; they couldn't seem to go a day without arguing about something, but he wasn't. All her defenses crumbled, and a shiver of pleasure went through her as he cupped her breasts in his hands and rubbed her nipples through the fabric of her dress. What in the hell did he think he was doing? She wouldn't... she couldn't...change her mind about leaving tomorrow. She had no choice, and even if she'd had the choice, she now didn't think she would make the decision to stay anyway.

She didn't belong with him. He'd have another Susan at another place and time; the right time in his life for him and for her. And she had someone in the future that she suddenly realized she didn't appreciate enough and missed terribly.

Staying here would be a disaster. He'd feel obligated to "do the right thing" by her. She'd end up having a baby and living with his dad while his career blossomed and he enjoyed a bevy of beautiful girls and groupies. He'd divorce her, just like Derek would divorce Mindy, and where would she be then? She, Mel and a James junior hustled off to some remote place to live anonymously.

She blanched at the thought. No! It was unthinkable!

One of his hands reached down in front of her dress and inched the skirt part up to her waist, then he reached down her panties and began rubbing her most intimate and sensitive part. She squirmed against the pleasure he was bringing her. He held her close and quietly for a moment before saying softy into her ear, "I'm not going to let you go, you know. I've been thinking what's best for us, and especially for you. I'm not taking you back to Brighton until Saturday morning, after I'm sure your bus has already left. You won't be on it."

She stiffened. Her blood turned to ice in her veins. She was stunned and not even sure if she'd heard him right. She squirmed again as he inserted a finger into her wetness.

He was kidnapping her? He was going to keep her here against her will? Is that what he was really saying?

While her seventeen-year-old body and happy hormones responded to his caresses, her sixty-two-year-old brain kicked into gear at his incredible statement. Throwing a fit or tantrum now would get her nowhere. Would he tie her up? How would he stop her from just walking out the door, going into Little Dippington and taking a bus to

Brighton? She assumed buses came out this way. It wasn't all that far from the city.

No, he would never physically restrain her; she was sure of that. She could just tell him right now that it was over, that she didn't really love him, that this was all a big mistake and he would let her go. She could even, if she dared, try to tell him the truth, show him her iPod, get confirmation from Lynn, who had probably told Ian and Mindy anyway.

But, she didn't want to hurt him. And, she did love him. She did! She did! Despite everything, she did love him. Just for this one week, for this brief space in time, she did love him with all of her being. And, at this point in her life in her true past, she'd only dated Donald, who was to become her future mate, once. She wasn't in love with him yet; she barely knew him. So, this was all okay, right? Loving James like this was okay, wasn't it?

Her thoughts became muddled and confused as James began to stroke her toward a climax. He stopped and turned her around to face him. For a moment, she thought she saw tears in his eyes, but then he lowered his head to hers and kissed her teasingly and gently, savoring the taste of her. He took his time with the kiss, probing her mouth with his tongue, exploring and tantalizing all of her senses until she became weak in the knees. Her arms twined around his neck in an attempt to pull him closer into her, and her breath became soft sighs, her eyes fluttering open then closed again.

He scooped her up in his arms and carried her back into the cottage and into the bedroom, where he gently laid her on the bed. Their eyes were locked together. She reached up her arms and pulled him down on top of her in surrender. Buttons was on the bottom of the bed and stayed there.

Chapter 19

Susan Escapes

James had been insatiable, loving her over and over, as if trying to prove to her that leaving him would be impossible for her. They were both exhausted. James fell into a deep sleep, but although her body felt like rubber and her eyes yearned to close, she knew that this was her opportunity to escape quietly without causing a scene of crying and recriminations.

She slipped out of bed without making a sound, and looked at James as he slept, his long eye lashes sweeping down across his cheeks, his hair tousled on the pillow, his lips slightly parted. She wanted to reach out and touch his cheek one last time, slide her fingers through his hair, have him wake up and make love to her one more time.

But, she couldn't think of that. She retrieved her clothes from the floor next to the bed and went out into the main room, where she quickly slipped them on, scooted her feet into her sandals and slung her purse strap over her shoulder. Buttons padded out to the kitchen and rubbed against her legs. She reached down and picked up the cat, cradling it in her arms.

"Oh, Buttons, I'm going to miss you," she crooned into the cat's ear. Buttons turned on her purr motor again, louder than ever.

"I'll tell you what," she said to the cat. "You come back to me in the future, and I'll name you Checkers, how would that be?"

"Mrow, mrow," responded Buttons.

Susan put another saucer of milk down for her on the kitchen floor.

As a last thought, she picked up her sketchpad off the kitchen table, but didn't take the time to pick up the pastels that were scattered all across the kitchen floor. She wasn't worried about taking her suitcase or any of its contents.

She'd decided she was going to walk to Little Dippington and see when the next bus to Brighton left. She hoped it would be soon, and that she'd be on it before James even woke up. As soon as she got to Brighton, she planned on going to the hotel, where she knew Lynn was, and they could use Lynn's iPhone to transport them back to the future.

It was close to 5:30 as she ran down the lane away from the cottage to the road leading into Little Dippington. She walked quickly and determinedly to the village and arrived just before 6:00. There was no sign of any bus station or bus stop. The village was small, with just one main street, and it looked like all the shops were getting ready to close for the day.

Then she noticed Emily's Granny standing in the doorway of Emily's shop, her eyes intent on Susan. A shiver passed down her spine. There was something about her that seemed so familiar, but she just couldn't put her finger on it...then suddenly, something came into her head and she shook it. No. It couldn't be. Could it? She looked at Granny again, and Granny smiled, beckoning her over with a gnarled finger.

Could Granny be connected to Mika somehow? Had she been watching over her?

Slowly she walked over to the shop and went in. Granny followed her and closed the door behind them.

"So, she's come then?" asked Emily from the back of the shop, startling Susan.

"Yay, as I said her would," replied Granny.

Surprise was written all over Susan's face. "How did you know I was coming here?"

"We were waiting for you. Granny told me some things about you. She has the sight, you know."

"And exactly what did she say about me?" asked Susan, setting her purse on the counter and looking back over her shoulder at the shop door, as if she expected James to burst in at any minute.

"Ye learned what ye needed to know," muttered Granny.

Emily ignored her.

"She just said she saw trouble between you and James, and that you'd be coming here. She said you're from a different place and time and that you'll break James's heart terribly and horribly if you stay here. I'm not really sure what to think about it," said Emily.

"Well, what I need to do is get back to Brighton and back to my friend, Lynn. We're supposed to leave tomorrow night for our history tour, but I'm thinking maybe we should leave earlier..."

"What happened between you and James then? Never seen two love birds more intent on each other, that's for sure. And I don't understand why Granny thinks you'd break his heart."

"It's a long story."

"Plenty of time to tell me, dearie. The last bus for Brighton left a few minutes ago. You just missed it. Next one's not until 6:00 tomorrow morning."

"Oh, my God! What am I going to do until 6:00 tomorrow morning?! Can I rent a car or something?"

"No cars to rent here, plus not sure you're licensed to drive one, are you?"

"Well, in America I am, but not here, no."

"Doesn't matter, dearie, you can stay here with us. We live upstairs and I have a spare cot I can bring out."

Susan's mind was in a whirl again.

"I can help ye get back now, ye know," said Granny.

Susan turned to her. "Oh! But, I can't! Lynn would never forgive me. She would worry. I need to get back to Brighton first, then she can use her iPhone to send us back. We're supposed to go back together."

Emily looked confused. "I what?"

"Never mind," said Susan. "I think Granny knows what I'm talking about."

Granny nodded her head.

"Can we please go upstairs then?" asked Susan, glancing out the shop window again.

"Of course," said Emily. "Then we can have a nice chat, and you can tell me all about things. By the way, what does Annabelle say about all this?

"Annabelle? ...oh, James's auntie? ...actually...I've never met her... that is to say...she went to visit her sister in King's Head last Friday..."

"Och! So that's how it is then..." Emily said.

Susan blushed.

"Don't worry, dearie. I don't make judgments on people, especially innocent-looking, young girls..."

"Well, that's exactly what I was when James brought me out here on a picnic last Sunday..." Her voice trailed off.

"Up we go," then," said Emily, turning off the shop lights, locking the door, and leading Susan through the back of the shop and up a narrow set of stairs into a cozy parlor. Granny followed.

∽◯

James didn't wake up until the sun was about to set. When he looked over at the other side of the bed and saw it empty, he assumed Susan was out in the kitchen making some kind of dinner with whatever she could scrounge up from the refrigerator, cabinets or garden. He wondered what it was going to be tonight. The zucchini pancakes were very good, but he didn't think they'd ever be a favorite.

He sniffed the air. Nothing cooking yet. He got up and slipped on his trousers then went out into the main room. No sign of Susan. Around the corner, in the kitchen, no sign of Susan, and the pastels were still scattered all over the floor. That wasn't like her. She was a person always tidying things up. A finger of alarm went through him.

He ran to open the back door, expecting to see her in the garden. No Susan. He ran upstairs, calling her name. No Susan. Maybe she'd gone back up under the big tree?

He ran out the front door and up the path to the big tree. No sign of her. The pond? No sign of her there either. He ran back to the cottage, out of breath by this time, alarm bells going off in his head. He saw her purse was missing from the end table in the main room. Her sandals were gone off the floor by the couch. Where had she gone? Did she run away? Why would she run away?

Then, he remembered his words to her in the garden just before he'd carried her into the bedroom.

He was certain she'd run away. But where?

Emily made a pot of tea for herself, Susan and Granny, then settled herself in a rocking chair by the window. Susan sat in a comfortable over-stuffed chair across from her, and Granny sat on a stool. Susan figured that was her normal place, even though it didn't look very comfortable.

Susan looked down at her hands in her lap, not knowing what to say or where to start.

"So, when did you get to England then?" asked Emily, giving her an opportunity to start somewhere.

"Friday night. Midnight."

"She come from ta future..." Granny mumbled.

Emily and Susan both looked at her. Susan bit her lip. She just didn't want to go into that unless she absolutely had to, even though it appeared Granny might have told Emily something about it.

She hedged a response. "America is a lot different from here," Susan said. "It seems very futuristic compared to here, that's true."

Granny just smiled her near-toothless grin and shook her head. Before she could say anything else, Susan began, "I came here to join a group of other students to go on a history tour of England. We're studying the important shipping ports and their histories. We were supposed to start in Brighton, which is why I'm here, but then the other students were delayed, and now they're in London. I'm to join them tomorrow. Another student, a good friend of mine, Lynn, also came to Brighton. She got here on Monday, so both of us will be going to London together."

"How did you meet up with James then?" Emily asked.

"Well, after I checked into my hotel on Friday, I thought I'd just go for a walk to see what was around, and a couple of blocks away, I heard music. The sign outside said it was The Dusky Club, so I went in and thought I'd listen to some music. I found a table near the front, right by the wall, and sat down. James looked over at me during one of the songs, then he came over to my table and offered me a cigarette during a break."

"Noticed you right off, did he?"

"For sure...twas meant to be..." Granny muttered. Emily and Susan ignored her.

"Well, yes, it seemed like he did. There were some girls on the other side of the club who didn't look happy about it. One of the waitresses, Sandra, who'd brought me a drink, said they were mad. I hadn't done anything. I was just sitting there."

"I've seen some of the girls James and his mates hang out with, dearie, and they're all pretty tawdry. You likely looked like a breath of fresh air to him."

She thought about how she must have looked wearing the June Cleaver dress. Breath of fresh air? More like breath of fresh ridiculous.

"Well, I don't know about that...but he came and talked to me again during another break, and asked me out for coffee after they were done. I should have said, 'no,' but I didn't. I guess I was taken in by his looks and the polite way he talked to me. But, it was pretty stupid to go out with somebody like that without knowing anything about him."

"James has always been a good boy," said Emily. "Never got in any trouble or anything, according to Annabelle."

"Well, yes, I guess I thought he was okay, so we went out for coffee and talked about a lot of things, mostly about our background and our families. I felt I got to know him pretty well actually, but I'm sure that sounds pretty dumb."

"Not dumb at all; that's how things start off between two people."

"Okay, so he walked me back to my hotel, and asked to walk me up to my room, but I wouldn't let him. He even wanted to kiss me, which

I thought was pretty presumptuous just knowing him for a few hours... but I let him kiss my hand."

Emily chuckled. "Kissed your hand, eh? I'll bet that threw him a bit; I'll wager it did."

"Well, that's it right there," Susan said. "I didn't know it, but he'd made a bet with the other boys in the band that he was going to...I mean that I would...rather than we'd..."

"Wagered on your virtue, now, did he?"

"Exactly! How tacky is that?! That's just horrible! That's just... ooooo...it makes me mad thinking about it again."

"So how did you find out about the wager?"

"Sandra told me the next day. We went shopping. She showed me around, and we went to lunch. I was really, really mad about it. And, I'd already agreed to go to James's practice session later that afternoon. I was so mad, I told Sandra about the hand kissing, and she thought it was hilarious and served him right. But then, Sandra told some other people, so by the time I got to the practice, the other boys were making fun of James and he was all mad at me."

"Go on."

"Well, he started singing this song with the words, 'I'll have you,' and that really, really made me even madder than him. I started yelling and told them all off for being so disgusting, betting like that, but when I tried to leave, James stopped me and ended up apologizing. He seemed so sincere that I said it was okay, so we kind of made up."

"Fireworks from the start, I see."

"So I went back to the club that night and James asked me out again. After it was over, he had to stop by his dad's house to drop off his gear, he said. When we got there, he went upstairs to change and I ended up meeting his dad."

"So, you met Mel then? What did you think of him?"

"Oh, I just love Mel!" Susan exclaimed, a big smile spreading across her face. "He's the best!"

Emily started rocking in her chair, her face pensive.

"So," Susan continued. "We went down by the wharf and listened to some music then went back to my hotel. James walked me up to my room, even though I tried to stop him, but he didn't get past my door, I can tell you that! I know he wanted to come in, but I knew it would be wrong. I'm not that kind of girl."

"As I thought," murmured Emily.

"What?" asked Susan.

"Nothing."

"Well, here's where I made my mistake. James asked me to go on a picnic in the countryside with him on Sunday, and I thought it sounded nice, so I said, 'yes.' He said he was taking me out to his Auntie Annabelle's cottage. I assumed his Auntie Annabelle would be there, making it all proper and safe enough. I have to admit that being around him was making me kind of weak in the knees, if you know what I mean..."

Emily nodded.

"I mean...we'd talked about so many things, and the way he looked at me, and he held my hand...and then I let him kiss me at my hotel room door...left that out, didn't I? Well, that, I think was the beginning of the end for me. I should have put a stop to everything then, but I didn't...So, we got to Annabelle's cottage, and when I found out she wasn't there and wasn't going to be there, I felt warning bells go off in my head. I should have asked James to take me back to Brighton, but I didn't. It was like there was electricity between us. I could feel it, and I had all these butterflies in my stomach. It was very disconcerting, I can tell you."

Granny cackled. Susan heard her, and tried her best to ignore her.

"Well, then we had our picnic under this big tree on a hill overlooking the cottage, a really, really nice spot. We each had a glass of wine, which is another thing I shouldn't have done...and then he took me down another path to show me the pond where he and his brother used to swim. I took my shoes off to test the water and almost fell in. He caught me just in time...and then..." Her voice trailed off as she blushed again and stared down at her hands with a deep, brooding sigh.

Emily's rocking stopped. "So, he seduced you then?"

"Well, not exactly," whispered Susan. "I kind of encouraged him..." She closed her eyes in embarrassment.

"Hmmmmm..." was all Emily said.

Susan looked up. "I'm no better than those other girls the boys hang out with, am I?" she said contritely, remembering she'd asked Mel the same question.

"I would never say that at all, dear. I don't think you stood a chance against his winning ways. Maybe it was fate, as Granny seems to think."

"Mel said just about the same thing."

"Well, after that, I assume it only took a minute or two to fall in love. I could see the way you looked at each other when you came in to buy the teacup."

"Yes. It didn't take very much to fall in love..." Susan's eyes were moist as she thought back to Sunday and Monday, and after telling her story, she suddenly missed James so much, she felt like sobbing her eyes out. She missed his mischievous smile, his dreamy eyes, his soft hair, the way he laughed, the way he held her, sang to her, kissed her, made love to her. Oh, what had made her run away?

Emily broke into her thoughts. "So, what brought you here tonight then?" she asked.

Susan sighed. "He told me he didn't want me to leave or go on the history tour. He started talking about doing the 'right thing' by me. Then, he said he wasn't going to take me back to Brighton until he was sure I missed the bus to join the other students in London, so I wouldn't be able to go on the history tour."

Emily became serious. "He had no right to do that," she said.

"That's what I thought...so when I knew he was asleep after we...I mean, when I was sure he was asleep, I ran away...and here I am."

Emily reached over to pat her hand. "As I said, there's a bus for Brighton at 6:00 tomorrow morning. I'll make sure you're on it. In the meantime, would you like a bite to eat, dearie? You must be hungry. Me and Granny ate earlier, but I can heat something up for you."

Susan shook her head. "I don't think I could stomach anything right now," she said. "But, thank you anyway. Would you mind showing me where the cot is? I think I'd just like to lay down. I don't feel very well."

Granny looked as if she were about to say something, but didn't. Emily brought out the cot and placed it under the window with a blanket and a pillow. "Here you go, lovey. Try to get some rest then."

Susan thanked her and laid down on the cot. She didn't think she'd be able to rest, but was soon fast asleep, dreaming of James holding her.

⤬

James felt sick to his stomach, thinking of Susan gone somewhere, who knows where, all alone, lost, and probably frightened. It was almost dark outside. He didn't know what to do or where to look for her. He could only assume she'd walked into Little Dippington and caught a bus to Brighton. She was a very sensible girl in many ways, certainly not dumb like some other girls he'd been out with. In fact, she was very resourceful. He was quite certain she'd gone back to Brighton.

He drove into Little Dippington, thinking to stop and ask Emily or Simon if either of them had seen her, but both Emily's shop and Simon's studio were closed for the night, so he drove on. It was close to 9:00.

When he got to Brighton, the first place he went was Susan's hotel. Ian answered the door. James had woken him up, but Lynn was sound asleep. Susan wasn't there. Then, he checked in at the club, where he was waylaid for a while by some acquaintances. After that, he went to Derek's.

Derek was annoyed at being woken up, as it was now past 1:00 and it wasn't a night they played at the club. James checked the pubs down by the docks and the coffee shop where they'd gone the first night he'd met Susan. Finally, he went to his house, thinking maybe she'd gone there, but there was no one sitting on the porch steps, where he'd envisioned seeing her, and no one out back in the garden. It was close to dawn and James was exhausted.

Mel had left that morning for King's Head to visit Annabelle and his other sister, Ginny, and wasn't home. James let himself in and sat on the couch in the dark, trying decide what he should do next.

He couldn't think of anything. He wanted to scream. He wanted to cry. He wanted to put his fist through the wall or break something. He went limp, fear for Susan overcoming all else. He put his face in his hands as sobs erupted from him. "Oh please," he pleaded, looking up at the ceiling. "Please, let her be okay!"

Chapter 20

Reunited

Susan was on the 6:00 bus to Brighton, but the bus didn't leave until close to 6:30 because the driver was busy shooting the breeze with an old friend from a small cafe that served breakfast. By the time Susan got to Brighton, with the bus stopping numerous times, it was almost 8:00.

During the trip, she opened her sketchpad, pulled a pen out of her purse and started writing a goodbye letter to Mel. She couldn't think of what she could possibly write to James. Her eyes blurred a few times as she wrote, thinking of the wonderful man Mel was and how it was hurting her as much to leave him as it was his son. When she was done, she folded it and put it in her purse, not knowing how she was going to get it to him.

As the bus pulled into Brighton proper, she impulsively gave the bus driver the name of James's street and asked if he knew where it was. She thought maybe she could give her letter to Mel in person before going to her hotel to wake up Lynn. She felt she owed it to him; he'd been so kind to her. She didn't really know what she would say to him after he read her letter, but she wanted one more hug from him.

As it turned out, James's and Mel's house was only five blocks from where the bus driver let her off. Quickly she walked in the direction the bus driver had given her.

She wondered where James was right now, hoping it wouldn't be at his house in Brighton. She didn't know if she could bear to see him again.

After an hour of sleep the previous night, she'd woken up and not been able sleep again, thinking of him and their whirlwind love affair. It was getting so close to leaving him forever, and she forgot about their arguments and disagreements. She forgot about his quick temper and dictatorial personality. She forgot about his arrogance and stubbornness. She only remembered the things she loved about him. Even though she realized they would never be suitable together, she wanted to leave with love in her heart for him, not regret.

As she turned the corner onto his street, she froze when she saw him halfway down, sitting on the stoop in front of the door. She thought of turning and running, but she was rooted to the spot and couldn't move. As if he sensed her closeness, he looked down the street and saw her. He leaped up and ran towards her. Likewise, she ran towards him, her hair streaming behind her.

They met halfway and embraced each other so tightly they could hardly breathe. James kissed her cheeks, her nose, her eyes, her hair, her neck. She was crying, and all she could say was, "I'm sorry," over and over and over. He tilted up her chin to look her full in the eyes, shaking his head at her and mouthing the words, "Why?" She just kept saying she was sorry, with tears running down her cheeks.

He took her hand and they walked down the street to his house and went inside. They sat on the couch, facing each other, holding both hands. Neither of them spoke for several minutes, just looking at each other, trying to read the other's mind.

James was the first to speak. "You know I wouldn't have kept you out at the cottage, captive or anything if you really told me you wanted to go."

"But, I wasn't sure," she said, her voice quivering.

He hugged her tightly to him. "You don't know how worried and scared I was when I discovered that you were gone. I didn't know what to think...where to look. I've never felt so lost or scared in my life...

Susan, I love you so much...I know you have to go...but, please, promise me again you'll come back." He looked searchingly at her.

"I'll be gone two months," she lied, employing her 'avoiding the question' tactics. "That's only eight weeks. It won't seem that long. You'll be in London yourself, making records. You won't have time for me anyway."

To herself, she thought, "Besides, once I'm gone I'll just be a dim memory to you; you won't even remember me..."

"I'll always have time for you. When you get back, I won't let you leave my side."

She looked into his eyes. "But, you're going to be rich and famous, you know. I won't be so important then."

"Don't say that! I know I'm going to be rich and famous; I've always known it, even though my dad always says I'm daft. So, when I'm rich and famous, we'll travel the world together; how would you like that? I can show you some of Germany, and we can go visit your grandparents and explore any place we want."

There was sadness in her eyes. He didn't notice.

"That sounds wonderful," she said, then thought to herself, "And that's exactly what you'll do, but just not with this Susan..."

It was 3:30 and still James hadn't shown up for the afternoon practice. Derek was upset and angry. Lynn was worried and scared.

"Where in the hell is he!?" Derek asked no one in particular for the fifth or sixth time. "That damn American girl has him all bamboozled and messed up! Here he shows up at my house in the middle of the fookin' night and gives me this new tune he wanted us to rehearse today and he's not even here, damn him!"

"What new tune?" asked Ian, sounding interested.

Derek reached in his shirt pocket and pulled out a few sheets of folded paper. He shoved them in Ian's hands. "This goddamn song!" he said.

Ian unfolded the papers and looked through them. "I heard him picking through this tune on Tuesday," he said. "Looks like he finished it then. Why don't we try it out?"

"Why should we?"

"Well, it looks like a good song, that's why," said Ian, picking out the opening notes on his guitar.

Lynn froze. "Does the song have a name?" she asked, knowing already what it would be.

"Sure does," Ian said. *"All My Kisses"*...Looks like a good tune."

"James's supposed to sing the first part, then I'm supposed to join in for the second part. You can join in, Ian. I don't want to," remarked Derek sourly.

"Be a sport, Derek," said Mindy. "James's just in love, you know. He'll settle down after Susan leaves on her history tour."

"Forgot about that," said Derek. "She probably decided not to leave, which is why he isn't here."

"What?!" exclaimed Lynn in alarm. "Oh no! She has to leave! We have no choice!"

"That's right," added Mindy. She hadn't told Derek about any of the bizarre or strange stuff Lynn had told her or shown her. It was too far-fetched. "They'll be leaving for sure, and James will come back to earth, you'll see."

"Yeah, she's got to leave at midnight tonight," said Ian. Lynn had also told and shown him all the stuff about the future and how she and Susan had come to be here for a week. He thought it was too fantastic of a story to tell anyone else, but he suddenly realized that Mindy had been told much of the same. He looked at her and she nodded.

"Right, then, let's see how it sounds." Derek picked up his guitar, took the sheets of paper back from Ian and pinned them to an old music stand he'd pulled out from the corner of the room.

Lynn just shook her head, thinking, "Oh, this is going to tear them both up at the end. She should have come back with me on Tuesday..."

Chapter 21

The Necklace

"James," Susan said, reaching her hands up around the back of her neck. "Take this to remember me by...please?" She lifted the silver necklace she always wore from around her neck and up over her head. The tiny pair of ballerina toe shoes dangled on the end of the silver chain. She held it out to him.

He took it and cupped it in his hand, looking down at it for a moment. "I'll look at this and cherish it every moment you're gone."

"Which will be a very long time," she thought to herself. "I wonder if you'll even remember how you got it after I'm gone...I wonder if it can even stay here with you in the past..."

He bent his head and slipped the necklace over it tucking it under his shirt, then looked back up at her and gently touched her face. "Thank you," he said softly. "And what would you like of mine to remember me?"

She smiled a wicked grin, got up from the couch and reached for his hand to pull him up. She led him to the stairs then up to his bedroom. "Some memories..." she said softly, pushing him back onto the small, single bed. "Some really, really good memories..."

James and Susan made love and slept the rest of the morning and through the afternoon. Both had little, if any, sleep the night before, and the only place they wanted to be was in each other's arms.

When they got up, it was past dinner time. Susan looked in Mel's refrigerator to see what she might use to make dinner. It then occurred to her that this would be the best place to leave her letter to Mel. She figured James wouldn't be looking in the refrigerator for anything, but Mel certainly would.

While James was taking a shower, she retrieved the letter and the pictures she'd drawn of James from her purse and slipped them in under what looked like a plate of cheeses. Then, she spied some of the leftover chicken and tomatoes that she'd made Monday night and re-heated it, making some new pasta and a salad to go with it. They ate dinner in silence, both thinking their own thoughts about the short length of time they had left before Susan had to go.

After Susan cleaned up the dishes, she went upstairs to take a shower and wash her hair. James dabbled at the piano. When she came back down and saw him at the piano bench, she noticed he wasn't wearing his dingy shirt or leather jacket, but instead had on a long-sleeved white shirt, vest and tie. His hair was clean and brushed down over his forehead. The sight of him was intoxicating. She sat down next to him on the bench.

"Play something else for me?" she asked.

"How about you play something for me?" he said.

She thought for a moment, then played a brief tune, singing along.

"I give him my whole heart...that's what I do...we'll never be apart...if just he knew...oh, how I love him...He tells me everything...and lovingly...the thrill my sweetheart gives...he gives to me...oh, how I love him...Bright is the moon that shines...dark is the night...I know this love of ours...is just so right...oh, how I love him..."

She looked over at him. "How was that?"

"It was beautiful. Can you play it again?"

"No. I think that said it all, don't you?" She leaned over and kissed him.

He looked at the clock. "I missed practice. Derek's probably mad as hell. It's time to leave if I want to be on time."

"Already?" She sounded panicky.

"Yeah, already." He stood up.

"Wait!" she said impulsively, pulling him towards her, opening his trousers and taking him into her mouth.

He tossed back his head and moaned. "Susan! What are you doing to me?"

He immediately sprung to life. She stood up and pulled him over to the couch, took off her underwear, and eased herself on top of him. "Just one more time...so you remember me..." she said as she began moving on top of him. Might as well use up the last of the seventeen-year-old raging hormones...

"Oh, yes!" said her hormones. "We're all for that!"

James and Susan arrived at the club shortly before the boys scheduled start time. It was Friday night, and the club was starting to get crowded. Mindy and Lynn were at their regular table and waved at Susan when they saw her come in.

Lynn noticed that Susan's face was glowing, most likely due to her and James being alone together for the last few days, but the glow didn't carry to her eyes. There was a sadness there that was hard to look at. As Susan sat down next to her, Lynn put a hand on her arm.

"You okay?" she asked.

Susan turned to her and silently shook her head. Her eyes were sparkling with unshed tears.

"Oh no...oh no...this is very bad," thought Lynn. "She got herself in way too deep. They both did..."

She looked at James. He had the same bright glow and sadness in his eyes. Looking back and forth between them both, Lynn started to feel sad herself. Again she thought, "She should never have come here."

Ian stepped up to the microphone and started singing.

"I found it all out...What love is really and truly all about...And every day, in every way...It sure lets it come out...I see my sweet baby...I get wobbly in my knees...There ain't nothing movin'...But the breeze in the those trees..."

Lynn reached down and held one of Susan's hands, then looked over at her. "Where's your necklace?" she asked, noticing it was missing from around Susan's neck. Susan always wore her ballerina necklace.

She'd been wearing it since she was twelve years old. It had been a birthday present from her grandfather.

"I gave it to James to remember me by," she replied.

"You can't do that! You can't leave something here in the past!"

"Why not?"

"I don't know, but I'm sure you can't."

"Well, he's wearing it under his shirt..."

James started singing:

"You're tellin' me you're gonna leave me...that you really need to go...You said you'll be dreamin' about me...But how am I to know...One day when we're far apart...Knowin' you have stole my heart...At that time I'll remember...What we had today..."

"Oh, Lynn!" Susan moaned. "I don't want to go! I don't want to leave him now! I can't! I just can't! And I don't even know why I feel this way!"

Lynn wanted to shake her. "You knew the rules before you came. You knew you'd only be here for seven days. You knew you'd have to leave. Don't make it harder on yourself. You can't change history. You don't belong here!"

Derek moved into the next song.

"Way, way down in Mississippi...Not far from New Orleans... Way back up in the mountains...Well, you know where I mean...There stands a country fallin' down shack...Made of old stones and wood... Where hides a young, tough country boy...Name of Ricky D. Good... Run, Ricky run...Run, Ricky run...Run, Ricky run...Yeah, Ricky D. Good..."

Susan was inconsolable. "It doesn't matter...it doesn't. I can't leave him now. Maybe if I could have just one more week..."

"Well, you can't, so get over it. You have to face reality, Suz. Get a grip on yourself!"

Lynn was starting to panic as she looked at her watch and realized it was almost time to leave.

"Susan, don't do anything stupid, like run up and hold onto him or something," she thought to herself.

Ian started singing then.

"Hey there...Do you want to know what I know...Will you promise not to say...oh, oh, oh, oh...nearer...let me say it in your ear...say just what you want to hear, girl...I want you to be mine...I want you to be mine...Mine all of the time...oh, oh, oh, oh..."

The club had become packed to overflowing. Every table was full and there were girls crammed up against each other, talking excitedly, some of them even starting to scream as the evening progressed. The frenzy that would sweep the world in a very short period of time was well underway. The boys broke into the next song, James smiling all the while at Susan as he sang.

Lynn noticed that the boys shook their heads, saying "Ooooooooo" in the middle of some of their songs. Their hair was clean, and when they tossed their heads, it went flying around in what would be their signature look that would drive girls crazy.

It was five minutes before midnight when James started singing.

"I'm sending you a letter...to promise my love to you...You'll know that I will always...be so true to you..."

He was looking at Susan as if there was no one else in room. She looked back at him. Their eyes were locked together. She took a deep breath, trying her best to compose herself, knowing that there was nothing she could do to prevent what was about to happen soon. She tried to smile, then winked, as if teasing him to remember their last intimate moments together. He smiled and winked back, thinking of how he was going to kiss her, hold her, touch her right before she got on the bus to leave. Maybe she would still change her mind. He kept singing.

"Love deserts you when we're not together...keep me in your heart forever... You know I love you...yes you, only you... When you come back again to me love...and I know that you will, love...You know, I love you...you, only you..."

It was almost two minutes before midnight when James motioned to the boys to play the new song he'd written for Susan. Then, they were going to take a break so James could walk Susan the two blocks down to her hotel to meet the bus. He started.

"Close your eyes while I touch you... You know how I love you...Remember me while you're away...And then while you are gone...I will try to go on...And send all my kisses your way..."

Susan began to cry. Lynn squeezed her hand, holding on tight, just in case she tried to break away or run up onto the stage area. Lynn looked at Ian and he winked at her. She smiled back.

"I'll remember your sweetness...Our moments of sheer bliss...And know that you'll come back to me...And I'll also remember your tender surrender...So sure that we always will be...All my kisses I will send to you...All my kisses... Only meant for you..."

As the song wound down into the final lines, Lynn looked down at her and Susan's hands and saw them start to glow and become transparent. Susan didn't notice; her focus was glued on James.

"Close your eyes while I touch you...You know how I love you..."

Susan closed her eyes, almost feeling as if James were touching and kissing her one last time.

"Remember me while you're away..."

She turned for a brief moment and looked at Lynn, seeing that her entire body was starting to glow faintly, almost pulsing with the music. Then she looked down at herself and saw that the same thing was happening to her. A silent scream tore up from her belly into her throat, but no sound came out of her mouth.

"And then while you are gone...I will try to go on...And send all my kisses your way..."

Susan stood up so quickly that the bar stool she was sitting on fell backwards and clattered to the floor. Mindy looked over and gasped. Susan reached out her arms to James and screamed his name, but it wasn't loud enough to be heard over the music.

"All my kisses I will send to you...All my kisses...only meant for you..."

James couldn't quite see her through the haze of smoke, but he could see what appeared to be the outline of Susan and Lynn's bodies glowing against the stone wall. He didn't understand what he was seeing.

Derek heard Mindy scream, this time at the top of her lungs. Everyone in the club turned towards their table as James tried to figure out what was happening. But, he kept singing the final words to the song he wrote for Susan.

"All my kisses...all my kisses...all my kisses...only meant for you..."

Susan finally found her voice and screamed *"No!!!"* her arms still out-stretched towards James, then both she and Lynn exploded into a million sparkling fragments, just like confetti, which floated upward, outward and away.

The club exploded into raucous shouts and screams. No one could comprehend what had happened. James pulled his guitar strap up and over his head in one swift movement, then ran toward Mindy and the empty table, yelling "NO!!!!!" and dropping to his knees in disbelief and confusion, but Susan was gone.

The necklace, however, was still around his neck. He grasped the silver ballerina shoes in his hand, tilted back his head, closed his eyes and moaned Susan's name over and over again, tears pouring down his cheeks...

Chapter 22

Back to the Present

Lynn came back quicker than Susan, materializing on one of the beds in Mika and Marta's cabin right at the stroke of midnight. She felt a little dizzy, but Marta was sitting on the bed next to her, helped her to sit up and gave her a glass of wine.

"Here, drink this," she said. "Mika's added some herbs to help you come all back together."

"Where's Susan?" Lynn asked, looking over at the other bed that was still empty.

Marta looked at Mika with a worried look on her face, then back at Lynn. "She's fighting it," was all she said.

"What do you mean fighting it?"

"She doesn't want to come back yet."

"But, she has to come back, doesn't she?"

"Yes."

There was silence in the cabin as Mika lit some candles and started burning some herbs, then she started chanting in a low tone.

"What's going on?" asked Lynn.

"She's bringing her back by force. Don't worry; she'll be okay."

As Lynn looked at the other bed, she could see the faint outline of a body, almost like a shadow that slowly began to brighten. The minutes dragged on, but finally Lynn was able to recognize the body as that of Susan, but for some reason, it wouldn't solidify.

"She's almost back now. Don't worry," said Marta taking Lynn's hand and squeezing it.

"Is her heart going to be broken when she gets back?"

"Wait and see. She made her own decision to go back and she made her own choices while she was there. She could bring back a lot of pain for herself from what she learned. It might be something she really didn't want to know or didn't want to accept. That's the way it is for those who fight coming back."

"Oh, I hope she doesn't bring back what I think she might," moaned Lynn. "It was bad enough before."

Marta responded, "As I said, she may also bring back what she learned, which is why she really wanted to go in the first place, even though she may have not realized it at the time. She wanted to know the truth about this person she so wished to meet…And, I believe she may have found it out."

Finally, the shape on the bed materialized into a complete and solid Susan. She was writhing and moaning as if in agony, and screaming, "No! No! James! James!"

Marta was ready with the glass of wine and herbs. Mika went to the other side of her. Both of them helped her to sit up, then forced the wine down her throat. She choked a little, but they were able to get the whole glass down. She was panting and her eyes were squeezed closed. No one said anything, and after a few minutes, her breathing slowed down and she opened her eyes. They were glazed over as if in a trance, then slowly cleared.

"Suz?" said Lynn, getting up from the bed she was on and going over to her. "Suz, are you okay?" She clasped Susan's hands in her own.

Susan's eyes were clouded over and tears began pouring down her face. Marta motioned to Lynn not to say anything but to wait a few minutes.

Susan's shoulders shook uncontrollably as she continued to sob. She covered her face with her hands, taking deep breaths and hiccupping every now and then. After a moment, her breathing started to slow more and the crying stopped. She removed her hands from her face and instinctively reached for her necklace.

It wasn't there.

Lynn looked at her, hoping she wasn't going to remember what she'd done with it. Mika looked surprised, as if leaving a physical object behind wasn't supposed to happen. Perhaps the necklace symbolically represented something that had to be left behind, a part of Susan that must never again be part of the present.

"Suz," Lynn asked again. "Are you okay?"

Susan shook her head, "yes," and took a deep breath. "Yes, I'm fine...I'll be okay...I don't understand why, but I just didn't want to leave..."

"But you knew you had to..."

"Yes." She looked down at her hands, her eyes focusing on her wedding rings, and she sighed heavily. "It would never have worked out between us, would it? He wasn't what I thought he would be..."

Lynn reached over and took her hand. "I've been telling you for years that what you have here has always been better."

Susan looked up at her. "You have, haven't you? I thought he'd be different...I even thought that maybe I could change him somehow... but it never would have happened, would it? I thought maybe if I could stay a little longer...I'd find out more good things about him than bad things..." Her voice faded to a whisper.

Lynn shook her head and continued to listen.

Tears came back into Susan's eyes. "It was all just beginning for them, wasn't it? They were on the brink of it all...the adoration...all the girls...being famous...he would have cheated on me, left me...He was so young..."

"And immature," Lynn added. "And unpredictable and moody..."

"And he kept expecting me to be submissive..."

"As if that would have ever happened!"

That got a shadow of a smile out of Susan. "Yeah...it would have been a cold day in hell before that ever happened..."

"And he didn't like cats! That's enough right there to know you wouldn't have gotten along."

"That's true...And...he didn't like to read, wasn't interested in science or politics or history; he didn't care for gardening. I wouldn't have had anything to talk to him about."

227

"Well, he was only twenty-years-old…So, you've listed all the reasons he wouldn't have suited you, right? Why would you have wanted to stay? What good would it have done?"

"Nothing. We would never have suited." She was silent for a full minute, twisting the rings on her left hand. She started to cry again. "Oh Lynn, how could I have been so foolish to think he could even hold a candle to what I have now? I've been so wrong to even think it would be possible!"

"But you had to find out, didn't you? You had to know for sure. It was the only way to end your obsession, don't you think?"

"But why then didn't I want to come back? It makes no sense to me."

"Maybe because it was a part of you for so long, you just didn't want to let go."

Mika nodded her head in the shadows, then stepped forward.

"And now I will tell you the truth of what you have learned. Your husband in this present time *is* this James person you thought you would find when you went back. You have just been blind to it. Look at what you experienced and you will see it to be true. The James you *wanted* to meet does not exist and never has. The James you've always wanted is what you have now. It was what you asked for, remember? And that is what you needed and wanted to learn, is it not?"

All Susan could do was nod her head, enlightenment beginning to flicker in her eyes.

Mika continued. "Your husband came to you at a time in your life when you weren't quite ready to accept who and what he was. But that is the way of the Universe. The Universe sent him to you because it knew what you wanted. You drew him to you by the force of attraction that rainy day in your art class.

You have fought against the truth for so many years, thinking this James person was who you wanted. It is now time for you to realize the true happiness that lies within you. It is the happiness of what you have now. This James you so wished to meet pales in comparison, does he not, especially now that you have been with him in person? From the moment you met your husband, this James person ceased to exist. Because your dream did come true when he asked you to marry him. And that is why you are still married. You were destined for each other. He was and is your Dream Prince. Do you understand now?"

Susan's eyes filled with tears again. She suddenly really did understand. It was as if a veil had been removed from her eyes. "All this time...all these years," she whispered. "And I've been so blind. I've been so wrong..."

"Your husband loves you with all his heart and always has. He has loved only you, and now it is time for you to love only him. Do you understand?"

Susan looked up and sighed heavily. "Yes...yes, I do."

"Then go home and give all of yourself to him. You can do it now. You are free."

A giant smile spread across Susan's face, and she laughed. "Oh...I most certainly will!!!"

Then she reached for her necklace, noticing it was gone, and smiled again. It had been her link to James. And now it was gone, just like he was.

Epilogue

It had been a week since James and Susan had been in Annabelle's cottage outside of the village of Little Dippington. Annabelle had just made her and Emily a pot of tea and poured each of them a cup, Annabelle using the new hummingbird teacup James and Susan had bought at Emily's shop. She took her cup over to the piano and set it on top to cool, asking Emily if she'd like to hear a tune she'd been practicing before she had gone to King's Head. Emily, who was sitting at the kitchen table, said she'd love to hear it. Annabelle shooed Buttons off the piano bench to retrieve a music book from inside the bench. There were three sheaves of what looked like drawing paper on top with handwriting on them. She picked up the first piece of paper and started to read the words.

"Oh my...oh my!" she exclaimed, her face turning a rosy shade of pink.

"What is it?" asked Emily.

"Oh my...! Just look at this! I wonder if James wrote this for that American girl you said he had out here!"

"Wrote a song, you mean?"

"Yes...here, take a look at it." Annabelle handed Emily the pieces of paper.

"Oh, my!" Emily exclaimed, her cheeks tingeing pink and remembering her conversation with Susan the night she had run away from James.

It was the words to the Jim McCrow/Beth Gill song that Susan had put in the bench, intending for her and James to sing together on their last night at the cottage before retiring to the bedroom. The name of the song was, *"Making Love."*

"Making love...All through the night...Feeling you hold me tight...Take my strength away...Don't let me go...I want you now to feel you know...Until the night is gone...Making love..."

Annabelle and Emily looked at each other and both began to laugh.

"Those are quite interesting lyrics, aren't they?!" Emily exclaimed. "Maybe you could put a tune to it, Annabelle!"

"Oh yes! Let's collaborate, shall we?"

"Yes, indeed, Annabelle!"

Mel found Susan's letter in the refrigerator when he got back from picking up Annabelle in King's Head and driving her back to her cottage.

"Now what's this?" he said as he picked up the plate of cheeses. It looked like art paper, folded twice into a square. Inside was a small pile of money. It looked the same as what Susan had given him to pay for the dinner feast and that he'd given back to James. There were also two pictures of James, one drawn in pencil and the other in pastels. He spread all of the papers open on the kitchen table and looked at them. Then, he began to read.

Dearest Mel,

By the time you get this, I will be far, far away, both in time and place. I know you don't understand what that means, but as I told you, I won't be able to come back. Thank you for not pressuring me to tell you why; the reason is too incomprehensible. Let's just leave it at that, okay?

I wish there had been the opportunity for me to give you one last kiss and hug. Even though I was only with you a few times, you came to mean a lot to me. James is lucky to have a dad as wonderful as you.

I really enjoyed playing the piano with you, working in the garden and talking, but most of all cooking our "feast" for James. I got in big, awful trouble over the beef roast, but that's neither here or there. I just enjoyed being with you so much.

I also want to thank you for your kindness to me, especially making me feel special and different from the girls James usually hangs out with, and for not judging me as a bad girl when James and I came back from your sister's cottage. As I told you, I feel what happened there was as much my fault as his. I appreciate your understanding.

I'm sorry if my leaving has hurt James, but I don't think it will be very long before he is swept away into the fame and fortune that he believes is his future. It really will be his future. Never mind how I know that; I just do.

Lastly, please know how much I came to love your son. My own heart broke at having to leave; it's too painful for me to even describe. Just know that, although I loved him, a life with him would have been full of too many fireworks, if you know what I mean. We're too much alike. That, and his career would have taken him away from me anyway.

I love you, Mel!

Susan

⁓◯

It was a Sunday night in February, 1964, and Susan's grandparents, mother and brother were all in the living room in front of the television. The Ted Flannagan show was about to come on. Her grandparents and mother watched it every week.

The phone rang in the kitchen and Susan ran to answer it. It was Lynn.

"I've been trying to call you for over an hour!" Lynn said. "The stupid people on the party line were hogging it up."

"Yeah, well, they do that a lot. You could have just walked to my house, you know."

"Yeah, I know, but I wanted to make sure you're going to watch the Ted Flannagan show. They're going to be on! I'm so excited!!!"

"I know, I know. I'm going to watch it, but it just seems like a lot of fuss for four guys from England."

"You saw their pictures in the magazine I brought over a couple of weeks ago. They're all so cute. I think I like Ian best."

"So who do you think I should like best?"

"Just go watch and pick one, but you can't pick Ian; he's mine. They're about to come on any minute now. Then, I'll come down to your house and you can tell me what you think and who you picked to be your favorite."

"I don't think I'm going to have a favorite."

"Just watch, okay? I want to know what you think of Ian. He's so dreamy..."

"Dreamy? Geez! Okay, okay, I'll go watch. See you later."

Susan hung up the phone, went into the living room and sat on the floor, her elbow on the coffee table and a bored look on her face.

Ted Flannagan was talking about four "young gentlemen" from England. He flung his hand to the side and the camera focused on the band. They were dressed in matching suits and had long hair that almost touched their collars.

Susan's grandfather made a "hrumphhh" sound.

"Beatniks!" her mother said.

Susan ignored them. She watched as three young men slipped guitar straps over their shoulders. Another went to the drums. The girls in the audience were screaming frantically, some of them crying as the camera panned over them.

The one with the guitar pointed to the left stepped up to the microphone.

"One, two, three, four, five!...Close your eyes while I touch you...You know how I love you...Remember me while you're away...And then while you are gone...I will try to go on...And send all my kisses your way..."

Susan sat up straighter and scooted closer to the t.v. Her mother yelled at her to move back before she hurt her eyes. There was something interesting about the guy on the left, the one with his guitar pointed in what looked like the wrong direction. Her eyes became glued to the t.v. Which one was he? As much as she hated to admit it, he was kinda cute. When the camera closed in on his face, she was suddenly captivated by his eyes and long eyelashes. She fingered the ballerina slippers hanging on the silver necklace she'd just got for her twelfth birthday the month before. Then she thought, "Well, since I have to pick one, I think I'll pick him... I think his name is James..."

Preview for The Necklace II – Back to Brighton

Chapter 1

The Link Remains

It was November of the same year that Lynn and Susan had taken their girl's cruise where Susan had traveled back into the past to the year 1962 to the Dusky Club in Brighton, England. Lynn had followed her when she realized things were getting out of hand, but it had been too late to stop the torrid love affair between Susan and James, the person Susan had gone back to meet, a person she had been obsessed with since she was twelve years old. The cruise had been in June and five months had passed since their adventure.

Although she had come back from her time travel experience with a new outlook on her present life, Susan couldn't let go of the memories of being with James or forget all that had happened between them. She didn't understand why she felt so unsettled or anxious, or why she kept seeing his face when she closed her eyes at night to go to sleep. She didn't want to see his face! It was unnerving.

When she tried to explain her feelings to Lynn, Lynn became annoyed and scolding.

"You've just got to stop this, Suz!" she urged. "It's over. You learned what you needed to learn, and that's the end of it! James was not for you; you even admitted that you two would never have gotten along.

Be happy with what you have! You have the best thing in the world and you know it!"

While Susan agreed with her very best friend outwardly, knowing she was right, her mind just wouldn't let go of James. He was like a cancer, eating away at her peace. When she started to have more and more flashbacks to the seven days she'd spent in the past, she called her other best friend, John, for advice, who she had relayed her time travel adventure to shortly after she and Lynn had returned last June.

John and Susan had been good friends since high school, where they'd eaten lunch together just about every day, and had maintained contact through all the years since. John often came to her house for dinner with her and Susan's husband. They talked frequently on the phone, and John knew just about as much about her as Lynn did.

"John, something is wrong with me," she wailed. "I should be over this, but it keeps coming back. I just don't know why. I *know* I have everything wonderful. I *know* we would never have suited, but I just can't stop myself from thinking about James. It's like I have no control! I feel like I'm trapped in a spider web or something!"

Instinctively, as she'd been doing for the past five months, she reached up to pull on her necklace, but it wasn't there. She dropped her hand back into her lap and sighed. "What should I do John? Why do you think I feel this way?"

John contemplated her comments and question for a minute then said, "Maybe you need to try and find that Mika lady from Haiti who sent you back. Maybe she could tell you. Maybe something went wrong when you came back or she forgot to do something."

"She told me I would be just a dim memory to *him*. But, she didn't say what *I* would remember. I thought she said he'd be a dim memory to me too, but I just can't stop thinking about him and everything that happened. And, the really horrible thing is that I don't remember the bad stuff, just the good stuff. It's unnerving!"

"Then I think you need to track her down and ask what's up. If anyone would know, it would be her."

"Yeah, I guess you're right. Her granddaughter, Marta, gave me her e-mail address in Haiti. I guess I should e-mail her. Geez! I just hate this! I thought going back would cure me of this 'James thing,' but I don't think it did."

"Well, e-mail Marta and ask. Let me know what she says. If you need me to help in any way, just let me know."

"That's so nice of you, John. Lynn doesn't understand and I don't blame her. I was a basket case at that concert last year, when we went to see James, and then she had to come and try rescue me when I went back to the past in June. I don't have anyone else to talk to about this. I'll let you know right away what Mika or Marta says."

Susan sent the e-mail to Marta as soon as she hung up the phone after talking with John. She was grateful for his advice. She should have thought of contacting Marta on her own, but sometimes it just took someone else for you to see what was right in front of your face.

It was eight days before she got a response from Marta. It said:

"I explained to Grandmere about your problem, and she is concerned for you. You should not be having this reaction! What happened to you in the past should have made you put this James person out of your mind and your life forever. She remembers that you left a necklace back in the past and wants to know where you left it. Did you, by chance, leave it on the person of this James? She thinks you did. If so, that is the problem. In fact, if that is what you did and he is still wearing it, you will not be a dim memory to him or others connected to him until he removes it. She thinks he has not yet removed it and that's why the past is vibrating into your present."

Susan gasped as she read the e-mail for the second time. "He's still wearing my necklace!" she exclaimed to herself. "I wouldn't have thought... I mean, I figured I'd become the dim memory like Marta said I would, and that he'd forget all about me and the necklace."

She immediately wrote back to Marta asking what she should do. It was nice that Marta had responded with a possible explanation, but she'd offered no advice as to what to do. If it was five months later back in the past, the boys' were now becoming well-known and on the brink of being world-famous. They would be recording their second record any minute now. The thought sent shivers through her.

Then she started wondering... What was James doing? Did he get back together with Hilary? Were he and the boys still making wagers, or did they just have to nod their head at any girl and instantly have her fall at their feet? A pang of jealousy tore through her and she had to shake it off. What the hell did she care anyway?

She closed her eyes and took a deep breath, again reaching up to her chest where the necklace had been since she was twelve years old.

And then she thought, "I want it back. I should never have left it with him. If I get it back, this link, or whatever it is, will be broken. Won't it?"

She didn't even recall the reason she'd so impulsively taken it off her neck and given it to him. She thought it must have been an impetuous moment triggered by her hormone-inflamed body. She blushed at the thought. She'd certainly been a wanton during those seven days. Well, at least for most of them. It hadn't taken much at all for her to surrender. A shiver coursed through her, and she blushed even more. Damn him for affecting her that way!

It was another eight days before she heard back from Marta again. As she read the e-mail, she began to tremble and shake her head. Oh no! Oh no!

What Marta wrote confirmed Susan's own thoughts:

"By leaving your necklace in the past, you created a bond that cannot be broken. The only way to sever it is to return to the past and retrieve the necklace. While he wears it, he cannot forget you or what you mean to him. If he removes it, you will become a dim memory to him, but if you do not bring your necklace back into the present, YOU will never be released from the hold he has on you. Grandmere thinks she needs to send you back to retrieve your necklace."

Susan sank back in the chair and covered her face with her hands. She didn't really care about James right now. He'd end up taking the necklace off sooner or later and probably discarding it somewhere, like in the bottom of a drawer or something. But as long as it remained in the past, she was doomed to the same yearning and desire she believed she had obliterated by her trip into the past. And while he wore it around his neck, he would be suffering from her memory as well. It might even be affecting his relationship with the boys and their rise to fame.

What to do...what to do...

She picked up the phone and called John. He was both stunned and disturbed to hear what Marta had told her.

"So what are you going to do?" he asked.

"I don't know. What do you think I should do?" she responded, sighing heavily.

He paused before he spoke again. "Well, are you going to go and try to get it back?"

"Oh, John! How can I? What would I say to him after being gone for five months? What would he think? What kind of story could I make up?"

"Well, if he's still wearing the necklace, he's just as doomed as you are, at least for the time being. And, he doesn't even know it."

"But what would I say? How could I get it back without, well... you know... getting involved again? Oh geez! I don't think I could handle getting involved with him again..."

"Well, I'm sure you could think up enough stuff to explain why you're back or what happened when you vanished last time. You do have a crazy imagination, you know."

"Okay, so I'll take that as a compliment. I'm just not sure I could pull it off. I'd have to go back in the same seventeen-year old body... and you know what kind of trouble I can get into with that." She could feel the heat flood her face. She felt as if the seventeen-year old hormones were laughing at her and her inability to control them. She frowned.

John laughed. "Well, I won't speculate on that then."

"Wait!" Susan said suddenly. "I have a brilliant idea!"

"All your ideas are brilliant. They're also crazy and insane, but don't let that stop you. What do you have in mind?"

"Simple... You go with me."

"I what?"

"You heard me... You go with me. I'll say you're my brother. I told him I had a brother, so you can be my brother."

"Just like I said, you're crazy and insane. What good would it do for me to pose as your brother?"

"Well... you could protect me, you know. Stop me from being wild and wanton. Like Lynn might have done if she'd gone back with me the last time."

"You know, I'd really like to help you out, but I don't know about this traveling in the past stuff. It's just too weird. And I have no clue how to stop you from being wild and wanton when it comes to that guy."

"It is not weird! You don't even feel a thing. You just 'poof,' and there you are in the past, and then, 'poof,' and you're back. It's as simple as pie. Plus, just think, you could be eighteen again. I never told him how old my brother was, so he'd never know."

"I don't feel good about this for some reason… And you're not saying what I could do to stop you from being wild and wanton."

"Oh, come on… Have I ever led you astray? With you there, I could nab the necklace and we could poof right back without me even getting to anything wild or wanton. Piece of cake!"

Her seventeen-year old hormones giggled. "Wanna bet?" they whispered.

John paused on the other end of the phone. "I think this whole idea is a mistake. I think you should ask Marta if there's another way to break this vibration or connection or whatever it is."

"Oh, please, John, please? Pretty please? We won't be gone long. And besides, I'm going to be alone all next week when Donald is going on his annual ski trip with his dad. He just won his last case in Federal court last week and is taking a break. It would be the perfect time, and I might not have another chance for a year. Please? I couldn't stand to feel this way for another whole year!"

She could hear him breathing through the phone, then he said, "I can't be gone too long, you know."

"I told you, I could make it quick. I just have to think of how I'd get it off him or convince him to take it off and give it back to me. I could cry maybe…"

"Lynn told me that's all you did the last time you were with him, and he hated it when you cried."

"That's just the point. I could cry and beg him to give it back to me. Explain how I'd had it since I was twelve years old and that it was sentimental."

"But you gave it to him as a token of your love. What would he think if you just asked to have it back?"

"I'll think of something."

"You always think of something… and that's the problem. You get yourself into too much trouble by thinking too much."

"Which is why I need you to come with me… to keep me out of trouble. Besides, don't you want to meet 'the boys?' Hear them sing? Go to a practice session? It's really awesome."

"And then when James slips you off somewhere and I can't find you?"

"That won't happen. I'll be real careful. I still have my old and aged brain, you know."

"I just don't know if I can trust you when it comes to him…Lynn told me all about the last time."

"Oh, come on. Of course you can. I'm not the innocent weakling I was on the last trip."

Her hormones giggled again. She ignored them.

"Let me pray about it first, okay? I don't feel right doing this."

"Okay, I understand. Pray all you want. But get back to me by tomorrow. I'd really like you to go… but if you don't, I'll go by myself. I was going to ask Lynn, but she'd just get all pissy with me. You know how she feels about my 'James thing.' She thinks I can just set it aside, like putting a book back on the shelf. But, I can't."

"You'd really go by yourself?"

"Yes… yes, I would!"

"What if you got stuck back there? And, have you thought about this? What if you go back and find out you're five months pregnant because of what you did the last time?"

"Oh, geez! I didn't think about that! I don't think that could have happened. I did come back to the present for five months, you know…"

"Well, it might be something you'd want to check with those Haiti ladies."

"Yeah, okay, maybe I'll do that. So then, go and pray on it. I understand that's what you need to do; I understand what your faith means to you. Then let me know tomorrow if you'll go with me or not. I want to get back in touch with Marta as soon as I can. I have to figure out the logistics of this. I wonder if we can do this through Skype. I hope so.

There's no way I can fly back to Haiti or meet them somewhere. Talk to you tomorrow then?"

"Okay, I guess so. Have a happy night and I'll call you, probably tomorrow night."

"Thanks, John. You're a great friend, you know that?"

"Yeah, uh huh. Bye then."

"Bye, bye."

As she pushed the "End" button on her phone, she smiled. John really was a great friend. She was sure his prayers would guide him to go with her, especially if he could keep her out of trouble.

But would he be able to? She shrugged her shoulders.

Maybe…maybe not…It didn't really matter. She was going back anyway…

Made in the USA
Middletown, DE
21 December 2020